I0633057

RULE NUMBER FOUR

RULE BREAKERS SERIES
BOOK 4

NICKY SHANKS

LIMITLESS PUBLISHING, LLC

Rule Number Four

First Print Edition: November 2018

Limitless Publishing, LLC

Kailua, HI 96734

www.limitlesspublishing.com

Formatting: Limitless Publishing

ISBN-13: 978-1-64034-451-8

ISBN-10: 1-64034-451-9

ONE
OLIVER

RULES.

What are rules good for, anyway?

Not a damn thing, that's what.

Rules don't keep you safe; they don't shield you from yourself and whatever you can possibly do to sabotage your own life. They don't care who you are or what you deserve—they only care about the ways they can hurt you and how quickly your life can fall apart.

Rules are supposed to keep your world balanced and help keep you from wrecking everything good in your life. But rules are only as good as you make them, and mine destroyed everything I've ever believed in. Not that breaking the rules *wasn't* worth it...or sometimes, fun. It's just really hard to enjoy life when you're looking over your shoulder, wondering what bad thing is going to happen next.

I've done this shit to myself.

I'm Oliver Jackson, Grade-A asshole.

Always and forever.

1

Rule number one didn't stand a chance. I let my guard down and let Julie into my life...despite it being the best damn decision I've ever made. Little did I know she would end up being the little girl I met years ago when I was coming out of my worst period—and she was just going into hers.

Rule number two literally almost fucking killed me. I took *everything*—including the love of my life—for granted, and before it was too late I tried to fix it...but ended up nearly slipping away from her altogether. The pain I caused her by ignoring my second rule doesn't even compare to the dark mark that's been stained on my heart from it. I'll never stop trying to make it up to her...as long as I live and breathe and she's by my side.

By the time the first two rules were broken, it only made sense to start backing away from them for the sake of my sanity and my love for Julie. Not that anything any of us ever do makes any damn sense.

Rule number three had *everyone* keeping secrets— mine were *especially* fucked up, and I still haven't told Julie about Lucy in my apartment yet—and now look where we are. I'm sitting across from the woman who gave me life and then tried to take it away, and all I can think about is the damn rules.

Why? I don't even know.

...Wait. Yes, I *do* know.

Julie.

My Julie.

She's everything to me. She's always *been* everything to me. I can't imagine a day where I can't see her or talk to her. I don't want to think about a world where she isn't in it, and I damn sure don't want to wake up one day without her. A different me would've been shy to admit that she's literally the only reason I care to breathe. Maybe in a different lifetime I could admit that to someone out loud, but for now, it's my own little oasis inside my head. I keep memories of her there that I don't want anyone else to share: little things, like the way the sunlight hits her honey-colored hair just right and forms a glow around her. It's so fucking magical it electrifies my entire body sometimes. She's the one I've been looking for before even realizing it.

And she's mine.

All fucking mine.

I'll do anything for her.

Even if it means sitting across from my wretched mother as she deteriorates in a ratty, orange jail jumpsuit. Her stringy, badly bleached hair mats to her face as she sweats from the anticipation of speaking to me this closely. She'd received treatment for the gunshot wound in her shoulder that Mary, the crazy bitch, gave her in the woods. She's lucky it missed anything vital, but I know it's gotta still hurt like a bitch.

I see myself in her tired eyes; they match mine and it's like looking into a spooky mirror. She doesn't deserve to look like me, and she damn sure doesn't deserve to call herself a mother.

I can't say that I'm surprised that we're here after everything she's done; I *can* say that I'm surprised it's taken her this *long* to get here.

She taps her jagged fingernail on the table in front of me. "Did you hear me, kid?"

No, I'm fantasizing about Julie.

I nod. "Yeah, you want me to drop the charges

against you. And, like always, you're delusional and you're not getting what you want. You're an accessory to kidnapping—think about it."

I recap everything in my mind like a bad movie about why my mother is even in jail.

She wanted money.

I said no.

She kidnapped Julie and hurt her.

If she hadn't already been dead to me, she fucking would be now.

My teeth grind together and I can hardly look at her. I know that some of this is my fault for being so stubborn and acting on my "mommy issues"—to be fair, I *was* right about her all along. "I can't drop the charges. You can rot in here for all I fucking care. It might be the best thing for you *if* we're being honest."

Her tone changes instantly from what it was before. She's sweeter now, or maybe she's just too tired to put on a show—either way, it's like another personality staring back at me now.

"I didn't expect that you'd try to drop the charges, Ollie Bear. I just wanted to see you one last time before they send me to Brownsville."

My veins crawl with ice; it makes me shiver and take a deep breath. "Why there? Isn't that a place for murderers?"

"I committed a felony, kid, and it's not my first offense. I don't think they discriminate against who goes there or not. I'll be in there until I get sentenced and then, who knows."

Who knows.

I feel bad, but I know I shouldn't. Her being *in* here

isn't my fault—this is her own damn fault. Still, no matter how much she hasn't been, she's still somewhat my mother, and that means something...I think. I wouldn't know, honestly, since I've never had a real mother, but I know what Julie would want me to do in this situation. She would want me to think about someone else besides myself.

"I'll talk to Julie, but I'm sure she'll want to make sure you don't end up at Brownsville."

She shakes her head. "No, you go and you live your life with that girl. You love her like there's no tomorrow and you treat her like she's the only one in the entire world you care about."

"She *is* the only one in the world I care about."

I notice Randy on the other side of the glass on the door. He taps his watch and makes a swirling motion with his finger to hurry me up. I know this is going to be my only chance to ask questions that I've had locked away in my mind for years.

"Our time's almost up." The sadness in her eyes draws me in, kneading at the soft spot Julie's created inside my rock-hard heart.

I bite my inner cheek. "I have questions and I want answers."

Her tongue wets her lips and she looks thirsty, so I push the small cup of water in front of me toward her. She smiles at my kindness and sips the water like it's going to poison her instead of nourish her. She has trouble tipping the glass to her lips because of her hands being cuffed together, but she somehow manages. I'm not sure what the fuck I'm even looking at—she's changed so much from the last time I saw her that I don't even feel that weak connection we once had anymore.

"Ask away, we don't have much time."

Now, I'm speechless.

What do I ask first?

Fifteen million snippets of questions zip around my brain and it's starting to give me a fucking headache. I can't be a disaster about this. I have to ask something.

"Why did you leave me on the floor when I was five?"

She sighs—deeply. "I know you think I have these elaborate answers for everything, kid. I wish I had an excuse for everything, I really do. I'm sorry that the answers are going to be nothing like what you think they'll be."

"Stop stalling. I see right fucking through you."

"I left because I loved Mac and drugs more than you." Her tongue clicks against her teeth. "Is that what you want to hear? I was weak and scared. Colin—your father—he wanted me so badly that it *suffocated* me…do you know what that's like? It's scary, kid. Really scary."

I scoff. "I love Julie with every fiber of my fucking body; you're not telling me anything I don't know. The difference is, I'd never leave her. I'd never choose anything over her. Not a damn thing."

"For what it's worth, she's a good match for you."

The anger fills my head so quickly that I nearly explode all over the table. "Don't speak about shit you know nothing about. You don't know her, and you sure as fuck don't know me. Kidnapping her and holding her for ransom doesn't get you a free pass to talk to me like a mother about my fiancée."

She nods. "I understand. I crossed a line. Anything else you want me to answer? Any more dreams you want me to crush?"

You're fucking kidding me.

"If you loved drugs and Mac more than me, why did you come back for me and try to take me from Mrs. Atchley's house?" I notice Randy again and wave him off.

She shakes her head, her thin fingers tapping lightly on the cool metal table. "Just because I felt that way doesn't mean I *kept* feeling that way. I missed you— you're my son. I got clean for three months and the night you looked at me like a stranger…" A tear forms in the corner of her eye. "That was the night I relapsed and never looked back. I'd lost you for good, and that hurt."

I growl and slam my hands on the table. "Stop trying to make me feel sorry for you."

"You're not going to like any answer I give you, but I'm telling you the truth."

My hands slam down again. "*Enough!* None of that shit matters now; you're going where you belong. I don't ever want to see your face around Julie again, you hear me? You're not going to be locked up forever. I'll see what I can do about getting you out of this mess, and when you get out, I'm giving you twenty grand and you better fucking leave and never, *ever* come back."

Her shoulders slump down in defeat. "Okay, kid. I promise you'll never see me again."

I feel so damn guilty.

I sigh and cross my arms over my chest. "Julie

would've liked you if you hadn't done what you did, just know that. If you would've gone about this in a different way, maybe I would've eventually forgiven you. I'm not perfect, but this shit is unforgiveable."

Her smile is actually warm and inviting. "I'm glad you have her, kid."

The door opens and someone comes in. Veronica's face grows grim and she holds her arms up to be taken. Randy, Julie's brother and a detective for Rockford PD, comes around into my view and narrows his eyes down at me like he knows I'm starting to cave into her once again. They don't let her speak to me before they usher her from the room and the door slams behind them. Randy remains.

"What the hell was that about?" He lowers down into the seat where Veronica had sat seconds ago. "Did she threaten you? What did she say to you?"

I run my tongue across my teeth in annoyance. "That's none of your fucking business."

He sighs. "Look, I'm just trying to help you out, okay? Where's Julie?"

"She's with Staci."

He breathes in deeply and holds it for a few seconds; his eyes glaze over and I know what he's thinking. I've seen that look before plenty of times, especially when I'd catch Casey—my former best friend —making those eyes at Julie. "What's that face you're making?"

Randy isn't one for making a scene, but the atmosphere between us is so strange that it's hard to ignore. "What face? That's just my face."

"No." I narrow my eyes at him. *"What?* Do you have a thing for Staci, or something?"

He clears his throat. "This really isn't the place—"

My laugh overpowers his voice. "Isn't the *place*? Have you *met* me? Weirder shit than this has happened no more than an hour ago."

"I'm not talking about this with you."

I cross my arms over my chest. Randy is a stoic sort of person, but that doesn't change the fact that I can see right through him. I know what it looks like to like someone and try to put her out of your mind. Hell, sometimes I feel like I've *created* that look that's on his face right now.

"If you don't talk to me about it, you know Julie will find out and grill you."

He groans. "Fine. I've asked her out."

I snicker and press my lips together so nothing regrettable falls out. "I see. When did this happen?"

"A few weeks ago, when you were in that accident. She came over to the house to update me on everything and we sort of…hit it off. I realize it may be a little weird for everyone to get used to, and I'd like to be the one to tell Julie if you don't mind."

I scoff. "Fine by me. You know she'll want to know about this, though. She's not going to be happy that this was kept from her by either of you."

"I know." He taps his fingers against each other. His eyes shift back and forth nervously, making the air in the small room stagnant and awkward. "Hey, can I ask you something?"

"Uh…sure." I wipe a smirk off my lips. "Ask away."

"Well, it's been a long time since my wife—*ex-wife*—

Marianna left, and I haven't *exactly* been on a proper date since then—"

Well, this is unexpected.

"And you want help with planning a date?"

He clears his throat and unfastens the top button of his shirt. The redness of his face amuses me; Randy isn't exactly an emotional man, and planning a date probably isn't even in his mental wheelhouse.

I furrow my eyebrows and his cheeks turn red. "Wait, you said, *'exactly.'*"

"What?" The scratchiness in his voice bounces off the walls and smacks me in the face. "What do you mean by that?"

The laugh catches in my throat; it's going to be fucking hard to keep this one in. "You said *'exactly.'* You haven't *exactly* been on a date since she left. What does *that* mean?"

The horror on his face is so amusing that a snort escapes from my locked-up laugh. "I'm not *exactly* sure of what you're getting at."

I can't hold it in anymore. "You've had sex since then, right? Didn't she leave when Clyde was like five?" The pit of my stomach is sour when I realize Clyde and I have something in common—being abandoned by a mother at such a young age. "Tell me you've had sex in the last eight years."

He clears his throat and looks around the room. When he finds his words, they're hardly over a harsh whisper, but the annoyance wrapped up inside is enough to scare me a little. "Of course I have, you idiot. I'm just not public about it like you are."

I snort. "I have no issues having sex in public."

"This is awkward enough being where we are and asking this, but can you at least *pretend* that you're *not* amused by this? Julie trusts you for some reason, and I'd like to think that since we're going to be in-laws soon, you'd respect me enough to help me without making a scene."

He's right. We'll be in-laws soon, but Julie and I haven't talked about that lately, and now that there's the problem with her pseudo marriage to Brandon looming over our heads...who knows when the subject will come back up. I'm not exactly thrilled about the idea of talking about it anyway, and I'm going to stall for as long as I fucking can.

"Okay, look..." I rub my chin and think of something to say that will actually help him. "Staci likes the finer things in life, right? She's spoiled without showing it. So, take her to a dimly lit fancy restaurant, order the most expensive bottle of wine you can afford, and afterwards...take her on a swan boat ride on that lake in the park."

"Swan boats?" His voice cracks. "What's a swan boat?"

"Oh, Jesus." I shake my head and tell myself that there's no way he can be this oblivious. "You're a cop in this city and you don't know about the swan boats? They're those pedal boats that people rent to go out on the lake and make out in. It's like a classic first date move."

He nods. "Okay, yeah...that's good. Any suggestions on the restaurant?"

I shake my head. "Maybe Dilaggio's or something

fancy like that. Plus, I know Julie loves the chocolate cake there, so it's safe to assume Staci does, too."

He accepts all of my suggestions and makes a sour face. "Okay, thanks for the help. I know it's not the best place or time, but I didn't know when else to ask, really. I assume that you'll be seeing Julie sooner than I will, so maybe you should mention this to her."

My eyes narrow. "I thought *you* wanted to be the one to tell her?"

"I do. I just never see her anymore, so maybe you should tell her."

I snicker and place my palms on the cold table, lifting my body up to stand. He doesn't bother joining me because he already knows I'm saying no. "*You're* the one dating her friend—you're the one who gets to tell her. What are you so afraid of? It's not like she's going to care."

Randy groans. "She may care that I'm considerably older than her friend."

I walk around the table, put my hand on the door-knob, and twist it. Before I leave him alone in a room full of his own wicked thoughts…I stop and think about what kind of man Julie would want me to be in this situation. After all, she's the expert on creating a better version of me.

"If you think Julie will be upset about something like that, you don't know her at all. She's going to embrace the fact that you and Staci are happy and *she'll* be happy. I still think you should be the one to tell her, but don't wait too long. She'll kill me for keeping this from her."

"Hey," he calls me back before I walk through the

now open door, "you're good for her. I know I haven't always shown you the respect you deserve, but now I see it. You really love her."

I nod. "She's everything to me. No questions asked, no explanations needed."

He smiles, but I leave him behind before he can say something that will make us both more uncomfortable. The truth is, I don't mind Randy that much. He's protective over his sister and that's admirable, because I'm also protective of her. Maybe a little bit more, if I'm being honest.

I have to protect her.

My Julie.

TWO
OLIVER

I'D LIKE to say that I went home and had the best sleep of my life—that I picked Julie up the next day and we shared our hearts and our secrets, breaking all the rules and vowing that we'd never make another rule again in our lives. I'd like to say everything around us was like silk in the wind and the scent of her strawberry shampoo kind of amazing...that we ran off into the moment and never lost sight of anything ever again.

Well, maybe a week ago I would've said all of that.

Now...it's the day before Halloween and I miss her more than I've ever missed her before.

She's not far away—she's been staying with Randy, trying to mend their relationship. She's been keeping in touch with me; she calls me at least five times a day and tells me she's coming home soon. She promises me that nothing's changed and she just needs time with her family. So, now as far as I know she's been going to her classes and pretending like nothing ever happened.

Even me.

I've barely heard from her these past few days, though. I've let her have her space, but this is too fucking much. *What about me?* I need her just as much as she needs the space, and it's hard not to be selfish.

But…I want her back now.

It's raining so hard that I can barely see the road in front of me when I pull the car out of the parking garage of my apartment. All I've thought about for the past nine days is when Julie is coming back; I haven't been worried about finding a replacement Jeep for the one I've totaled at all. I want that to be something Julie and I do together; I want to give her everything I can, and she needs a car of her own. Julie is independent and strong now—she deserves to have her own things.

"Fuck," I mutter and turn on the wiper blades as far up as they'll go. I make sure my seat belt is on just in case Julie gets into the car. She'll give me that hard look she gets when I do something she doesn't approve of.

I'd give anything for that look right now.

My heart races the entire drive to Randy's house. I make sure to drive as carefully as I can so I make it there this time in one piece; I don't need anything else putting stress on her. I already lost control in the rain once and nearly died…I'm not acting a fool and ending up like that again.

When I park outside the house, something keeps me in the car. It takes a few minutes to clear my head and focus on a single thought, but the one I come up with is so fucking genius that it even surprises me.

I know what to do.

The rain hurts my skin as I bolt from the car and jog up the pathway to the front door. I'm already soaked when I reach the entrance and hit the bell three times frantically, followed by several loud booming knocks on the door itself. It doesn't take long for the lights to come on, and then I'm blinded by the overhead front door light.

Clyde's wild red hair comes into view first. It's only been a little over six months since I've seen him last and he's grown at least four inches taller. His snide smirk, however, hasn't changed.

"What do *you* want?" he snarls.

The smile that spreads across my face annoys him even more. I think hard about how our conversation went the first time we met—when I picked up Julie for the first time and everything changed. I want it to go back to that so desperately, I think that I can recreate the moment and recharge all of it.

"I'm here for Julie?"

He shakes his head, confused. "Uh, okay?"

He's not getting it, but that's okay. Julie will understand what I'm trying to do. I'm trying to reenact the first time I picked her up from this house and Clyde answered the door. I thought it was a perfect plan until the frown on his face puts it into a whole new perspective.

"Can you just get Julie?" My voice shakes.

The door slams in my face.

Okay, that didn't go like I planned it in my head.

The door opens again and Randy stands in the doorway. "She's in the pool house." He nods and smiles at me. "Packing her things."

"Where's she going?" I hear the panic in my voice

over the steady rain still falling around me. "Tell me she's coming home."

He shrugs his shoulders. "You're welcome to come through the house...you're soaked and need to get dry and warm—"

"—I don't give a shit, I want to see her."

He sighs and looks up at the sky; the rain pings on his glasses and he wipes the fat drops away with his fingers. "Oliver, it's cold and raining. Come inside and dry off."

I run down the stairs, and even though my pants and sweater are drenched and I'm freezing cold, I make it to the pool house door and try the handle. It's locked, so I start banging my fists on the cold surface as hard as I can before I start to lose my breath.

Her lights turn on and my heart nearly beats from my chest.

Fuck the rules.

All except for rule number four: I'm not going to destroy my own happiness.

Wait. I changed that rule.

Rule Number Four: There *are* no more rules.

All is fair in love and...whatever else there is that doesn't matter.

Now I'm going to do whatever it takes to keep her.

Nothing's going to get in my way ever again.

"Oliver?" She says my name before she opens the door. I can barely hear her over the rain, but it's there... and it's all for me. The rain soaks my body and I gasp for air as she opens the door and I put my hands on the doorframe. "What's wrong?"

I say nothing and reach for her, pulling her quickly

17

against my wet body. My cold, rain-soaked sweater instantly freezes the both of us as I press her against me as flush as I can.

I fucking miss her.

"Come inside," she says into my chest as I hold her. "You need to get out of those clothes."

"I don't want to come in; I want to go home."

She gently tugs on my arm and pulls me into the warm pool house, shutting the door behind us. I tower over her—which sends shockwaves straight to my dick already—but I've never seen her this intense and sexy. My eyes lock on the bright blue fireballs of her eyes and I don't notice the dozens of small moving boxes littering the room for a few seconds.

She blushes when she notices the break in my gaze. "I started gathering my things so I can bring them home with you."

I instantly sweep her into my arms and the wetness of my sweater seeps into hers even more. My lips are cold and dripping wet, but that doesn't stop me from pressing them against hers. Our lips stick together for what seems like hours before my fingers find the bottom of my sweater and I pull it off, throwing it on the floor next to us. She sucks her bottom lip into her mouth as her eyes trail down my chest and stomach. Her gaze lands on my side, where a light scar lives after I had my stitches removed.

"I'm all better now," I say in a low, raspy voice. "Don't worry about me."

Her finger runs over the scar and I tremble when her touch leaves my skin. The tips of my fingers find her hair and they take down the long braid running down her back, letting the tresses run free for me to glide through. When my lips reach her neck—the most sensitive place on her body—she tenses her muscles and her body vibrates underneath my weight.

"I want our lives back on track," I whisper as my fingers find the bottom of her soft, pink sweater. "Let's go back to the cabin before we move into the new house." She struggles finding her voice underneath my spell. "You have finals coming up, right?"

She licks her lips. "Monday."

I moan into her neck and look down into her eyes. "That gives us three days to shut ourselves into the apartment. We can eat chocolate chip ice cream all day long in bed."

"What about Halloween? It's tomorrow." She giggles as my fingers play with the small area of exposed skin on her stomach.

"We can hand out candy at the new house if you want." I feel the wickedness of the grin that pops onto my mouth. "We have some christening to do in that place anyway."

She blushes. "Just how much are you thinking? A few rooms?"

I run my hands up her sides and lift the sweater from her body, making damn sure my thumbs rub against the sides of her tits as they pass them. A heat wave rushes through my body once I realize that she's not wearing a bra, and it's like opening the best gift I could ever fucking ask for.

She's vulnerable and perfect and she's all for me.

Her fingers search for the metal clasp of my jeans; she swiftly unbuttons them and tugs both sides of the open jeans closer to her. I watch her lips open and close and it's making me so hard that it starts to hurt from how fucking badly I want her.

"Doesn't your leg still hurt?" She frowns and kisses the wet fabric of my jeans at my kneecap. "It hasn't been the full six weeks yet; are you healed enough to be not going to physical therapy?"

I snort. "I've never been to physical therapy, why start now? I'm fine, baby, don't worry about me."

Her body travels back up against mine. "I have class tomorrow," she whispers against my lips. "I think we should just stay here—in the pool house—tonight, don't you?"

I can't fucking think about anything except the wet thickness of her lips and how badly I want them around my dick right now.

Jesus. Get a grip, Oliver. Focus on her words, not her perfectly round, C-cup tits staring you in the eye and wondering why your lips aren't on them.

I can't fucking focus.

What's wrong with me? I can't stop thinking about her… like, at all.

She presses her lips onto mine and starts lightly sucking them together. I kick my jeans off with little effort since she's already stretched them out as she teased me. My boxer briefs come down with my jeans and my hard-on presses against her leggings; the soft material drives me wild.

With one swoop, I gently pick her up and place her on the sofa in a sitting position; I lean down in front of her, completely unfazed by being totally naked. My hands run up her legs and I find the waistline of her leggings, gently tugging them toward her feet. She giggles and wiggles her toes in the air as I kiss the bare flesh of her thighs and get closer to the soft flesh of her sweet spot. I feel her legs tense and then tremble and I smile into her flesh, amused that I'm making her squirm more than she can handle.

"You do know I was coming back, right?" she asks as I nibble on her inner thigh. "I wasn't going to stay here forever."

I nod. "I know, I just don't like being away from you for that long."

In my defense, she *was* recently kidnapped by my mother and her disgusting, drug-fueled boyfriend and held for ransom. I grunt and pull off her black lace panties, throwing them to the side. "It's my job to keep you safe."

"Even from you?" She winks and giggles as I sit on the sofa and pull her on top of me, her clear blue eyes trying to find mine. My eyes are glued on her collar-bone—my favorite thing to press my lips against on her entire body—and I let out a satisfied sigh.

"Even from me." I smile, letting it creep fully across my lips. "Who's going to protect me from *you*, though?"

She acts offended and I grip the flesh of the sides above her ass and squeeze. "Protect you from *me*? I'm not sure I know what you're talking about."

I groan. "Oh, but I'm sure you do."

"What do you need protection from?"

"How much you completely fucking *slay* me." The laugh that escapes her mouth fuels the fire in my body. No matter how much I tried to fight it at first, I'm the luckiest man in the entire damn world. The woman sitting naked in my lap is the best thing any man could ever dream of.

Being with her is just so…simple.

She doesn't care about the materialistic things in life, which attracts me to her more. I don't care if her nails are done each week or if her hair is perfectly shaped around her face. That's how I know love truly lives within us; I look at her and see past what isn't there to get to the part of her I really crave.

Her heart.

My hard-on thickens underneath her weight, so she shifts a little to give me some breathing room. The grip her legs have on my thighs tightens. My eyes narrow and the air is so still it's hard to catch my breath from the thoughts running around my mind.

"I know a lot of people don't understand what we have…" Some of my fingers find her face and rub against her jawline. "…and sometimes even *we* don't understand it, either. I just know that I'll never love anyone like I love you. You were made for me, and I belong to you. I don't care what you do to me—I'll always be yours."

I don't give her time to say anything; I pick her up and lower her onto my pulsating dick. I slide into her warm flesh with ease and for once she doesn't mention anything about condoms or protection because we both know it's too easy to see our future together to even care about those things.

I know she's my future.

The rules aren't part of our future.

We've thrown those out of the window.

All is fair in love and war now.

THREE
JULIE

MY THIGHS TIGHTEN around Oliver's legs as he moans and throws his head back in pleasure. His hands slide up my back and then back down, gripping my ass so he can hold me into place while he thrusts harder into me. Somehow, my fingers get twisted in his hair and I tug a little to make him moan louder.

"I fucking love you, Julie," he whispers as he pulls me closer to him. The space between us disappears and our bodies are flush tightly against each other. "I never want to live without you."

I pull his face upward so our eyes can meet. The sadness that consumes him makes it hard for me to breathe. He slows his thrusts and we drink each other in without caring that we were just going at it like animals. My lips find his and I lock them together as tightly as I can. His arms slide around my back and lock me into a bear hug and he buries his face into my hair.

"I want you, Oliver. Only you," I whisper, feeling his lips find my collarbone and his hips start bucking me softly up and down again. "There's no one in this world that compares to you. No one I'd want more... you're my best friend."

A fire lights in his eyes and he pushes harder into me, tipping my head back so he can glide his lips over my breasts. They suction around my left nipple first and I keep my head tilted so I can moan into the air without startling him. He palms both breasts and his breath is ragged and hot against my skin.

I don't even realize he's lifted both of us up until I feel the soft mattress of my bed underneath me. He gently lays me down and locks our lips together, never pulling out from inside of me for a second. Our lips are raw and red when we part and he bucks into me with such force that I have to grip the comforter to keep myself on the bed.

Explosions.

The last moan that escapes my throat is primal and so loud that I don't hear someone knocking on the door of the pool house. Oliver quickly kisses my lips and smiles down at me, looking at the door and alerting me that someone's out there, wanting in.

"Don't get dressed." He laughs as I try to focus on reality. "I'm not done with you yet, baby."

I blush and cover myself with the comforter the best I can. I'm suddenly *very* aware of how completely naked I am and how much of me he can see. "Who is it?" I gulp as he peeks out of the window next to the door.

He glares back at me, shaking his head. "It's Staci. Were you meeting her?"

I shake my head. "No, she must've just wanted to stop by. She knows I've been staying here."

We both hurriedly tug back on our clothes and there's a sour look on his face. At first, I think it's because his clothes are still soaking wet. But he knows something, and he's keeping another secret from me. Since Staci is standing outside in the rain I don't have time to prod him for information, so I let it go to the back of my mind where I can retrieve it later and clobber him with questions.

Oliver takes a quick glance at his body to make sure he's fully clothed, smiles at me to show me that he's trying hard to be nice, and opens the door for her. Staci's smile fades when she sees him, but he moves to the side so she can step in out of the rain and get warm.

"Staci." He nods at her.

She scoffs and closes her neon green umbrella. "Oliver."

When she fully enters the pool house, she hugs me and puts her large, baby pink tote bag on the sofa so she can place both of her hands on her hips. Her index finger wiggles in between me and Oliver, wagging at us like we've done something wrong. "So, you two are back together then?"

Oliver growls. "We never broke up."

She snorts. "Well, whatever you call it...you're back?"

He looks at me for help but I don't know what I can do that I haven't already done. I've asked her to be nice, I've asked him to be respectful and so far...he's the only one delivering. I'm not going to talk to her in front of him and embarrass her, so I paste a fake smile on my face and try to ignore her distaste for the love of my life.

"Is there something you want, Staci? Are you here to share some information, perhaps?" Oliver glares at her and something in her demeanor changes when she has time to think about what he's said. Now I *know* they're both hiding something from me, and I don't like it.

"Are *you* sharing any information?" She glares at him and scoffs.

"Okay…" I clap my hands together and shake my head. "I don't like secrets—you both *know* I don't like secrets, so what's going on?"

Staci looks shocked. "I just came to see if you wanted to go to dinner." She puts her hands in the air in defeat. "I don't know what you're talking about."

Oliver groans. "She deserves the truth."

Her eyes grow wide, but she doesn't make eye contact with him. "I can't be here with him." She snorts and picks up her bag. "People in glass houses shouldn't throw stones."

He starts to cough and moves to the kitchenette to find something to quench the tickle in his throat. What he's doing doesn't matter as much to me as what she's hiding. I know that Oliver and I have some unfinished business to talk about, but Staci—*one of my best friends*—has never hidden anything from me.

That I know of.

"I'll call you later." She smiles sweetly at me.

I let her take a few steps before calling her back. "Freeze." My voice is stern and startles Oliver; a wicked grin paints his lips, but I don't have time for his cuteness right now. "Turn around and tell me what's going on." I wiggle my finger around in a circle until she turns to face me again. "We aren't having any more secrets between each other; do you guys understand that?"

Oliver pouts. "Hey, I'm just the fiancé here—don't drag *me* into this drama."

I shake my head. "What do you even mean by that?"

"He means that your brother and I are dating," Staci blurts. "Randy and I have been seeing each other for a few weeks. That's *my* big secret."

My gaze finds Oliver and he nearly spits out the water that's just passed his lips. "You knew about this and didn't say anything?"

He holds up his hands. "It wasn't my business to tell you. Randy wanted to tell you himself, but that was a week ago." He grins at Staci because he's amused. "But it looks like he didn't get around to it. Tell you what... why don't I go find him and give you two some privacy? I need some dry clothes anyway and something tells me he's not asleep yet."

Staci growls. "Don't act innocent—I'm surprised you didn't run to her and tell her the first chance you got. We all know you're not forthcoming with your *own* information."

Oliver's eyes grow dark and he locks them onto her like I'm not in the room. "You better fucking watch it."

"Would you two stop it?" I scream as loud as I can to shake them up. "I'm sick and tired of the fighting! Grow up! Why do you always have to stir things up?" My chest heaves up and down as I glare at Oliver.

He looks at me and his eyes fill with sadness. He puts the cap onto his water bottle and glides toward me, kisses me on the forehead, and leaves the pool house. The rain has stopped enough for him to get to the main house without drowning; I know I have to apologize, but that can wait until later.

My eyes find Staci's. "Spill."

She sighs and puts her bag back down on the sofa. "Okay, here it goes. Randy and I have been seeing each other for a few weeks. It's nothing serious." Her face darkens and her head full of newly ruby red curls bounces as she shakes it. "I mean, it's not serious *yet*. I really like him, Julie, and he likes me too. I've never met anyone like him. He's just so…gentle."

I pretend like I'm gagging. "Oh, okay. You can stop with the details. That's my brother, remember?"

She doesn't laugh with me; I'm sure she's still figuring out how upset I really am underneath my brush-off, but she's wrong. I'm happy that they each found someone they can feel something magical for; it's not every day that kind of thing comes along.

The smile that was meant for her turns into a smile for Oliver.

A man that drives me crazy a million ways to one.

"So, are you pissed?"

"Huh?" My throat is dry from taking in so much air to clear my thoughts from naked Oliver. "Oh, are you serious? Of course I'm not, I'm happy for you two. Let's just keep the PDA to a minimum when I'm around, okay? As much as I'm okay with this, it'll still be weird for a while to see my brother with someone—*anyone*, regardless of who it is—because it's been forever."

She sucks in air through her perfect white teeth. "Not *forever*…"

"Dude!" I groan. "That's really none of my business!"

Staci giggles and throws a sofa pillow at me. "Oh, come on! You know I'm not one for subtle things in life. I'm a firecracker and I always have been. It's nice to have someone calm to be around without the awkwardness of trying so hard, you know? I've been through some boyfriends, trust me—"

"Staci." I narrow my eyes. "I get your point. Let's just leave it at that, okay?"

"Okay." I can tell she has more to say and letting the air around us be so still and silent is a new thing for her. I'm sure Randy has his reasons, but they couldn't be more different. She's right, he's calm—for the most part —and doesn't like attention or loud places. The last time I checked, she basically lives at nightclubs and her laugh is so loud that it shakes the walls.

Opposites do attract sometimes.

I mean, Brandon and I were different too. I was a cheerleader running from her past, and he was a loner with publicly horrible parents who was trying to escape his miserable life. I guess that maybe in retrospect we weren't so different after all. When two people are scratching and clawing out of a dark hole of life and they find each other, it's natural to latch onto something they've been desperately seeking without even knowing.

"So, can we talk about it a little, though?" Her fingers pinch the air. "I need someone to talk to about this stuff. Nora has abandoned us for some new dick she just met, and I don't know where the hell Amber even moved to—she just up and left us. You're all I have left, Julie."

Guilt. Trip.

I sigh. "Okay, but spare me embarrassing details and don't use his name so I can pretend it's someone else. It's still new and weird for me."

She doesn't hesitate. "Okay, so he took me on our first date last week, right? Spared no expense and reserved like, the *best* table at Dilaggio's. He ordered expensive wine and he talked *to* me and not *at* me, which made everything ten times better. Even though we've kissed before—" Her lips turn into a grin when she notices the green look on my face. "—even after dinner, when he took me on the swan boats, he didn't try anything other than holding my hand. Then when he dropped me off, he walked me to the door and kissed my cheek before making sure I got in okay."

I have to admit, I'm impressed. I never imagined Randy dating because he never expressed an interest in it before, at least not to me. Then again, I haven't exactly been available much to him lately.

Or Clyde.

I wonder how he feels about this.

But, back to her problem. What *was* her problem?

"Sounds like a nice first date, what's the issue?"

She squeals and jumps up and down. "Nothing! That's the issue! There was absolutely nothing wrong with the entire night. Isn't that weird?"

I snort. "No, sounds like a dream come true."

Her eyes lower to the ground. "Oh, I forgot about what Brandon did to you."

I wave my hands in the air. "No, don't let that get

you down. Look, if you overthink this, you're going to do something to ruin it. Randy is like a bunny rabbit; he'll run away the first time he's startled. You'll have to be yourself for it to work...you don't want to become someone you're not just to keep him."

I feel sick.

I didn't change myself: Oliver changed my *outlook* on life.

That's different.

"I guess." She shrugs. "I just feel like this silly little kid next to him."

My laugh booms through the pool house. "That's the age difference, I guess. You'll have to get over that— that's something you can't change."

The questions brewing in her eyes are making me uncomfortable. "So...how is that, anyways?"

"How is *what*?"

She wiggles her manicured finger in between us. "You know, he's so much older than us. Were you a surprise?"

"No, Randy and I don't share a mother, but we share a father. Randy's mom, Aunt Helen—she's my mother's sister. My father cheated on Aunt Helen with my mother, and well...here I am."

I can tell she doesn't really want to know about those things right now. The sour look on her face makes it known that she's got bigger problems inside her head.

"I just don't want to get bored and screw everything up." Her fingers wiggle in between us. "What if Randy and I decide not to see each other and our friendship gets fucked up?"

"It won't." I smile to reassure her. "We'll keep it

separate. Trust me, if there's one thing I believe in…it's other people not getting into other's relationship business. I don't like it when people question what I have with Oliver, and I'm not about to do it to someone else."

I may be a liar, but I'm not a hypocrite.

My phone buzzes on the nightstand so I climb over the messed-up blankets to grab it. The reason the blankets are tussled up makes me smile until I see Brandon's name flash across the phone. My smile fades quickly.

"It's Brandon," I tell her. "I shouldn't answer it, right?"

"Maybe it's important." Her eyebrows rise. "I'll give you some privacy."

I want to scream for her to stay, but she's gone before I can open my mouth. The phone feels heavy in my hand; it's weighing me down into the darkness inside myself.

"Yes?" It's all I can manage to spit out.

His breath is heavy in the phone. "It's Brandon."

"I know."

"Okay. How are you?"

I look around nervously; I don't feel right about this, but I'm still the same person I've always been. As I sigh into the phone, I lock the pool house door so no one can interrupt. "I've been better, but I'm okay. Just a bruised eye and some scratches. How are you? You got most of the injuries."

He laughs and I've never realized how cold and short his laugh is compared to Oliver's warm, honey-down-the-throat laugh. "I'll be okay. Look, my boss found out about our marriage, or whatever you want to call it. He expedited the hearing. It's Monday at three."

"And I have to be there?"

"It's uncontested, so no…you don't have to be there. I thought you might want to be for peace of mind that it's finally over."

He's right. I didn't think about that. I still don't trust him, no matter how hard he and Heather tried to redeem themselves by attempting to rescue me. I hardly trust them any more than I did before, but he's still holding my secret close to his chest so I have to try.

"I'll be there. Meet me outside and we can go in together."

"Sounds good. See you then." He rushes and then hangs up. I'm thankful for the shortness of the call because when I open the door to the pool house, Oliver is walking back toward the now-open door. When he sees me, even though it's starting to get dark, a fire lights in his fierce, emerald green eyes.

A fire that burns for me.

The thief that stole his heart.

FOUR
BRANDON

I FUCKING HATE FRIDAYS.

I mean I really, *really* hate them.

Everything bad—since I can remember—has happened on a Friday.

My parents were arrested for drug trafficking on a Friday.

They were sentenced to fifteen years in state prison on a Friday.

I was taken into social services custody on a Friday.

I aged out of foster care and got put on the street on a Friday.

Julie and I broke up on a Friday.

I found out she was sleeping with Oliver on a Friday.

The list goes on and on.

Nothing could've made that phone call any more awkward. I hung up on her so fast, she might've even still been talking, I don't know. Things in my life haven't exactly been top-notch since we escaped Oliver's crazy mother and her equally as fucked-up boyfriend. I put Heather in danger just to redeem myself in the eyes of someone who loves her better than I ever could, and that doesn't sit well with me now that the dust is settled.

I love Heather.

I love everything about her.

I love that she's a fragile little bird who needs me to help her find her way. I love that she knows how to handle me at my worst and put shit back into perspective. I get so lost in my own head sometimes and dwell on my past mistakes that it's hard not to fall back into that hole again.

But she won't let me.

The phone rings almost immediately after I put it down on my desk. It startles me; I don't want to talk to Julie again—or Oliver if he's calling to scream at me. I can't even look at the phone as it rings over and over right beneath my eyesight. It's tempting, but I've had enough for one day.

I read the email on my computer one more time.

To: Brandon Whitehouse
From: Vernon Trumbull

Brandon,

I just caught wind that you have applied for a divorce. This concerns me because I was never notified of you getting married and you know how much I like to get to know my employees.

I'M A LITTLE BESIDE MYSELF WONDERING HOW YOU COULD TIE THE KNOT AND NOT SAY A SINGLE WORD TO ANYONE.

NOT TO MENTION THE RUMORS THAT WENT AROUND THE OFFICE ABOUT YOU AND ANOTHER WOMAN.

I'D LIKE TO MEET YOUR FUTURE EX-WIFE AND APOLO-GIZE FOR THE FACT THAT WE HAVEN'T MET SOONER. I'VE HAD YOUR HEARING EXPEDITED TO THIS MONDAY AT THREE P.M. AND I EXPECT BOTH OF YOU TO BE THERE. AFTER THE HEARING, I WILL BE TREATING YOU AND YOUR THEN EX-WIFE TO A LATE LUNCH AT NEWSON GALLERIA IF THAT WOULD BE ACCEPTABLE.

I WILL BE BRINGING A GUEST WITH ME AS WELL.

I LOOK FORWARD TO SEEING YOU AT THE HEARING.

BEST,
VERNON TRUMBULL, ESQ.

FUCK.

I'm *so* fucking screwed.

I should've taken more than three days off of work to heal myself; the bruises are fading and the deep gashes Mac gave me with his fist are closing up already, but I should've taken more time. I passed out from the searing pain in my head when his fist kept meeting my skull, but other than that...I'm lucky I got out of there alive.

At least I got Julie to believe that she needed to be there by playing the trust card. I know she doesn't trust me—and probably never even will—even after I helped rescue her from being kidnapped. In Julie's eyes, Oliver will always be her one and only hero. I know Heather wanted the chance to do the right thing, and we did. Still, it's annoying that no one notices the break-throughs we've had or the people we've become because Saint Oliver shines over the entire world.

I click my tongue against my teeth. I don't bother answering Vernon; he knows I'll show up because I'm loyal…and I don't want to lose my job. The hardest part of not knowing how this will end is wondering how Heather is going to react if I *do,* in fact, lose my job.

I won't be able to take care of her and she'll leave me.

My fists slam down on the table as the phone rings again. Heather's name flashes on the screen and it freaks me out now more than if it were Julie calling back. I have to answer her call, I know I do, but it's going to take me a few seconds to cool my shit.

I pick the phone up and stay silent.

"Brandon? Hey, are you busy?"

The air I'm holding in seeps from my lips slowly.

"I was thinking about making something special for dinner tonight. Something romantic so we can start a tradition to make Friday our date nights."

The air catches in my throat.

Friday date nights.

Friday.

I open my mouth to answer, but she gets there first. "What's your favorite thing to eat?"

Okay, I can save myself here.

I snicker into the phone and she gasps softly. "You know the answer to that one. You're my favorite thing to eat."

She snorts. "Gross...but kind of sexy. I mean *food*, dummy."

I lick my lips and think about burying my face between her legs, and she doesn't skip a single beat even from the returning silence.

"Okay, how about meatloaf and mashed potatoes? My grandmother taught me how to make this delicious recipe and I've never made it for anyone before. This'll be my first time."

All I hear is her last sentence and it sparks my insides.

"Whatever you want, baby."

Her giggle reaches for me through the phone. I want to spread her across my desk so fucking bad it's killing me not to tell her to just forget the fucking grocery store and come straight here. I'm already in hot water with Vern—I don't want to introduce him to my current girl-friend before he meets my future ex-wife.

I put my head in my hands. "A quiet night at home actually sounds really good right now."

"Should I pick up some wine? You sound like you're having a hard day."

A wicked smile creeps across my face. Something fresh about Heather punches me in the gut and releases the butterflies that zip around my stomach when she shows her sensitivity.

"Bourbon."

She smacks her lips together. "Oh, it's been a really,

really bad day then. No worries, I will take care of everything. I'm just getting out of class, so dinner should be ready by the time you get home."

"You don't have to do all of this." I check the clock on the wall for the time. "I'm not expecting you to make me dinner and have it ready by the time I get home, Heather."

"I know." I hear her car start. "And by the way, I'm still loving this car."

Last week—after we returned safely home—I was wracking my brain trying to figure out a way to make up for the danger I put her in. I thought of three pages full of ideas, but nothing was even close to what I owed her. She swore up and down that she didn't want anything until we passed a used car lot and I noticed her checking out a maroon-colored SUV. Three grand later and I felt like I'd redeemed myself for ever taking her out into the woods in the first place.

"I'm glad you like it, babe."

"I'm still going to find a way to pay you back." Her voice is quick. "I don't like that you have to pay for everything. I really should get a job."

"No." A twinge of annoyance packs itself in my voice. "I want you to finish school. That was the deal."

"I know, I know."

I roll my eyes at her silliness. She's exactly what I needed to spice up my life enough to pull me out of the dark Julie funk I'd been in. I'm so mentally exhausted that I can't stand it; the clock ticking loudly on the wall puts me in a deeper trance and I almost fall asleep sitting at the desk.

"Well, I guess I'll let you get back to work. I'm sure you're busy, right?"

I frown as I look at my desk full of files and paperwork. "You could say that."

"I'll see you later tonight." Her voice penetrates deep inside my mind. "I love you."

I let out a moan and quickly regret it. "I love you too."

It's like night and day, being with Heather after being with Julie. I never had to question anything with Julie—it was always automatic and I didn't have to try hard at all to keep her.

Well, until the very end.

Heather makes me wonder about *everything*. She's gorgeous—so is Julie in her own understated, vanilla way—and she knows that men know it. We can't go anywhere without some loser checking her out, and it freaks me the hell out. I'm trying so fucking hard to let it go and not worry about it since that was one of the reasons I lost Julie, but it's hard. It's hard to watch someone you love get excited about another man looking at her.

Dammit.

"See you later," I mumble, and she hangs up the phone. I throw the device back down on the desk and it makes a hard thump when it hits the surface. I'm not bothered by the fact that Heather wanted to hurry up and end our call; I'm bothered by the fact that she's not smothering me like she was a few weeks ago. Maybe I'm getting bored of her, I don't know.

…No, that's not it.

I groan out loud and stand up from my chair,

looking around the room. My office is smaller than Vern's, of course, and I don't have diplomas on my wall like he does. I have old mint-condition movie posters that Julie had framed for me when I first got promoted and earned this space.

That's it.

Julie is everywhere.

She's on my office walls; she's even in the fucking picture frame that sits on my desk, staring at me. What is wrong with me? Why haven't I cleansed myself of her by now?

You know why.

You're still in love with her.

You can love Heather and still love Julie.

I know I'm supposed to be making things work with Heather—and I want to—and I'm supposed to be moving way far along from Julie—again, I want to—but there's something wicked inside of me that won't let her go. It's different now; I don't feel like she belongs to me anymore, but I do feel like I'm responsible for her somehow. Maybe it's because of the way I treated her when we were together, maybe I feel guilty for making her feel so small that she's become a soft-spoken anti-socialite.

Maybe.

I bend over my computer and send a quick email to the secretarial pool, hoping that one of them will find a box and bring it to me like I've asked. I'm ready to purge myself of all that is Julie from this office, and even though my space will be bare…at least I'm making good strides toward trying to get over it.

A few minutes later, a small knock at my door rings

through the office and Carlie, a small-framed, red-haired young secretary pops her head through the door-frame and looks so nervous I think she's going to wet herself all over my floor.

"Mr. Whitehouse?" She clears her throat. "Here's the box you've asked for."

I swiftly take the box from her and frown. "Is this the biggest one you could find?"

She nods. "Yes, sir."

I wave her off. "Call me Brandon."

The flush on her cheeks makes me smile; it's nice knowing that I can still make a woman nervous. She touches her cheek and feels the heat, making them glow even more. "Is there anything else I can do for you, Brandon?"

I shake my head. "I'll let you know if I need something. Thanks, Carlie."

Shocked that I even care to know her name, Carlie leaves the office and shuts the door behind her. The box she found isn't big enough for the posters on the wall, but the picture and knickknacks around the office that remind me of Julie fit perfectly inside of it. I don't know what the hell I'm going to do with this shit, but it's better off out of here than constantly punching me in the face with reminders of what a fucked-up person I'd been.

I take the box into the elevator with me and nod toward Carlie as the doors close. She doesn't bother asking me questions or looking too long at me; she knows I'm a private person and if she wants to stay on my good side, she'll look the other way. Maybe that's how I got into this mess. If I had one person—besides my only friend left, Nate—telling me what an idiot I was being, maybe I'd still have Julie.

But now I have Heather.

And she's better for the person I am now.

Leaving work early usually isn't my forte, but if Vern finds out…I'm sure he'll understand why. I can't shake the feeling that he knows more than he's letting on, but there's nothing I can do about that now. All I can do is enjoy this weekend with Heather before getting divorced on Monday. The sick feeling grows in my stomach when I replay the night I dragged Julie into that twenty-four-hour chapel and kept her liquored up enough to say "I do." A pain stings in my chest when I pass the security guards downstairs and see Julie's face in my memory.

She's miserable.

I can't fucking dwell on this anymore.

The box sits in the passenger seat, staring at me like it knows all about me and my faults. It haunts me and taunts me into opening it and looking at its contents one more time before I throw it all away. I don't want Julie like I used to, but that doesn't mean I never loved her. She was my best friend for a long time and I drove her away…that stain on my heart will never fade.

I take out her picture and toss it to the side. After that, I look at each individual thing like it's the last time I'll ever see it.

It is *the last time you'll ever see it.*

None of this shit matters to me anymore. I don't feel anything when I sift through the pieces of my former life because that part of me is dead.

Dead and gone.

I turn the car on and hit the call button on the dashboard and tell the robotic woman who comes over the speakers to call Heather's phone. It rings a few times before she answers, out of breath and people talking in the background.

"Hey, sorry, I'm at the store—"

"I want to take you out to dinner tonight." I look at my dark gaze staring back at me in the rearview mirror. "Can you cook tomorrow night?"

She hesitates. "Sure, why the sudden change?"

"I want to take you out, does there have to be a reason?"

She swallows loudly into the phone. "I guess not."

"I love you." The words fly from my lips. "I love you and I want to show you that."

She says nothing.

I almost hang up the phone before I hear her softly breathing. "I love you, too. I'll pay for these things and head home to meet you."

Just like that.

Smooth and serene.

For now.

FIVE
CASEY

I WAS a damn fool to think Julie would ever choose me over Oliver.

I wouldn't even choose me over Oliver.

Still, I thought we had something, but that was apparently all inside my twisted mind. Man, these women and their mind games are really starting to piss me off. Nora won't answer my calls and I hear she has a new boyfriend. It's interesting how quickly she can move on from me, even though the things she said to me felt like forever. Lucy hates my fucking guts and I don't blame her. I ruined a perfectly good thing with her by being the biggest jerk on the planet...besides Oliver.

And Julie.

The unicorn.

She makes me feel alive and peaceful and like candy wrapped around a cloud.

I groan and click the TV in my apartment off. She's made it perfectly clear she's done with me and we can't even be friends. If I was really honest with myself, I would admit that I don't blame her. I hate that I know she's just protecting herself from the ones who are supposed to support her and I've screwed everything up.

Again.

The apartment is silent and dark; it's nearly nine but I don't bother turning on any lights. The darkness consumes me and I like the feeling of quiet and still air; it clears my head and helps me forget my inner monster for a little while. A series of electronic noises rings through the quiet space and my phone goes off in my pocket.

HARLEY

> Hey man, Victor and I are down at The Tavern. Haven't seen you in a long time. Catch up?

I sigh. I can use a drink to drown myself in.

> Be there in fifteen.

I'm not in any rush to meet up with Harley or his twin brother, Victor, but any company is good company right now. I only live a few minutes' walking distance from The Tavern, so I change my clothes and run a comb through my thick sandy blonde hair before squinting at my reflection in the mirror.

I don't recognize myself anymore.

Tomorrow is Halloween and the chill in the air nips your skin like needles; it takes a few minutes for me to find my leather jacket and I'm almost late getting to the bar. When Harley sees me, he gives me a quick and silent look to confirm that I won't spill my guts to Victor about Oliver taking Lucy home from here only weeks before.

I grit my teeth and nod.

Julie deserves to know.

Oliver doesn't deserve to win.

"Casey!" Victor's high-pitched voice finds me. "Man, I haven't seen you in months!"

I scoff as I sit down on a stool across from them and gesture for a waitress. "That's because you've been balls deep in some actress in the city. How is your little one-hit wonder?"

He laughs like I've just said the funniest thing in the world. "She's good! She's sleeping with her friend Anna, though, so that's a plus for me! Sometimes they let me watch—"

"Jesus…" Harley shakes his head and slaps his brother on the arm. "Have a little couth, will ya? Leave a little to the imagination? Women aren't only objects, douchebag."

"So, where's Oliver's stupid ass?" Victor smirks and winks at a woman passing us by.

I clear my throat. "He's laying low with Julie after everything that happened."

They look confused and I realize they have no idea what I'm talking about. I start telling them the story from beginning to end and by the time I'm finished, their jaws have scraped against the floor and we have a table full of empty beer bottles.

"What the hell? Why didn't anyone let us know?" Harley growls. "We're your friends, too, man."

"I *know* that," I snap. "I'm sorry we didn't think to call you up when we were trying to rescue Julie...or when I got my leg fucked up...or when Lucy left me..."

He holds up his hand in the air. "Okay, I see your point. Still, next time."

Victor's infectious laugh fills the air. "Let's fucking hope there's not a next time!"

We each hold up our remaining bottles and clink them together. "Let's toast." I wipe the wetness from my lips and my gaze trails around the room. "To fucked-up families, loves we've lost, and friends that have gone down the rabbit hole of marriage."

The sound of the bottles hitting each other makes me smile. "What happened with this Lucy girl?" Harley asks as Victor ignores us and starts chasing tail around the bar. He shakes his head at his brother before looking back at me. "He's going to stick his dick in the wrong place one of these days."

I nod. "At least he's getting some."

Harley smirks. "Ah, come on, man. You get plenty."

A tall, dark-headed woman with curves and a handful of tits slows down at our table and smiles at Harley. She wants to strike up a conversation with him but he's clearly not interested, so she frowns and leaves the table without even giving me a look. I shake my head and point to the now-empty space she was just in and frown.

"See that? She didn't even look at me."

He laughs. "I'm actually with someone right now. Plus, I'm pretty sure I've already fucked that one and I'm almost positive it was in the bathroom here."

"You remember all the names and faces of the women you sleep with?"

He swigs the last of his beer and snickers. "Uh, that would be a negative. I remember her ass and her legs, that's enough for me."

I think of Julie and my face flushes with heat. "What do you think about Julie?"

"I think she's Oliver's girlfriend and I think she's cool, why?"

I shrug. "Just wondering...don't read into it. The one that just left me, Lucy...she was a firecracker."

Changing the subject...good thinking, Casey.

"Don't look now, but there's trouble heading your way." He shakes his head and looks behind me. I feel a cold breeze hit the back of my neck before the person gets to our table. "I thought I told you the last time I was here to fuck off? I don't want anything to do with your kind of trouble, you hear me?"

"I'm not here for you, asshole," a familiar voice says. "I'm here for him."

She comes around into my view and I nearly choke on my own breath.

Lucy.

Harley growls. "He sure as hell doesn't want what you're selling."

She glares at him. "I'm not *selling* anything, and it's none of your business."

"Lucy, what are you doing here?" I look around to make sure Oliver and Julie aren't following her around. I know she's been taking classes with Julie and they've become friends. "It's actually great to see you, you've been avoiding me."

She opens her mouth to answer me, but Harley gets there first. "You know this chick?"

My gaze snaps toward him and warns him to watch his mouth. "This is the girl I was telling you about, the one who left me." I blush and look at her. "Where have you been?"

"Casey, we need to talk." Harley's voice is flat. "*Now*."

Harley is the last thing on my damn mind right now, but he's being so persistent, tugging my arm to get my attention. I break my gaze to snarl at him and Lucy sighs, sitting down on the stool where Victor left minutes ago. He nods to his right for me to get up so we can talk in private. I look at Lucy and point my index finger right at her face. "*You* don't go anywhere. I want to talk to you."

She salutes me and laughs. "Yes, sir."

Harley pulls me from my seat and pushes me through the crowd completely out of earshot from Lucy. His face is so red, it's a wonder how he's not exploding all over the place.

"That's the girl." He nods back toward Lucy.

I snort. "Yeah, I already told you that. Come on, stick with me here." I shake my head and start to walk back to the table, but his massive arm stops me.

"No, *that's* the girl Oliver went home with."

Something inside me clicks and a smile creeps over my lips. "I know that already."

His eyebrows rise. "You do? Why did you say it like that? What are you going to do?"

"Nothing." I shrug. "But, that's the girl I'm taking home with me tonight, so don't try and stop me."

He knows I'm a damn liar.

"Don't do this, man." He blows air from his lungs and it moves my hair. "Don't play Oliver against this, just let it go."

"I've known about this for a while now. I think it's about time pretty-boy Oliver Jackson gets a taste of his own asshole medicine, don't you?" I chuckle.

Lucy comes up behind us and I smell her sweet perfume before her heavily lined eyes meet mine. A crooked smile and a hand tug later, she's walking out the front door with me and I can feel Harley's disapproval the entire way back to my apartment.

She giggles when I smash my lips against hers as I open the apartment door. "Oh, are we having another slumber party?"

"We can do whatever you want to." A steady growl rumbles from my throat. "How about we talk about what your fucking problem is?"

She acts offended. "*My* problem? You mean, besides the fact that you're clearly in love with Julie and embarrassed me in front of her and Oliver? Or maybe the fact that you haven't called me since I walked away from you in the parking lot?"

"You haven't called me, either." I shut the door and take a few steps toward her trembling body. "Why should I try when I know it wasn't worth it?"

Her fingers touch my leather jacket and she slides it from my arms. It hits the floor behind me and her olive-green eyes light with fire. "It might've been worth it if you tried."

It weirds me out to even think about it, but I wonder what sex with Lucy would be like. It creeps me out even more to let my mind wander to Julie and how her curves meet her thighs like velvet and her pink pouty lips would look tucked around my—

"Whoa, there." Lucy giggles and points at my hips. "What's that all about?"

I look down and see what she's talking about, my jeans have a very noticeable bulge where my dick is trying to escape. I blush and clear my throat, looking around the room so I can figure out what I'm going to say to get out of this.

"Is that for me?" She looks excited.

I'm going to hell. I'm definitely going to fucking hell.

"It's for you." I smile. "I think we've done enough talking for tonight, don't you?"

Her body is wrapped around mine within seconds and I take her to the bedroom. Her thighs tighten around my waist when my lips touch her neck.

It's going to take everything I have not to think about Julie.

It doesn't stop me from getting what I need from Lucy.

And she lets me have what I want.

SIX
JULIE

"HAPPY HALLOWEEN, SUNSHINE." Oliver kisses my cheek as he puts several bags of candy on the counter. I let him talk me into coming to the new house for the trick-or-treaters because he knows that Halloween is my second favorite holiday—next to Christmas, of course. He brought me here because we wouldn't exactly get any trick-or-treaters in our apartment, and that's the part he's looking forward to the most.

Plus, I haven't had the nerve to move out of the apartment and into the house yet...Mostly because I'm scared that when we *do* make the move, every single thing will change again.

It's been hard to think about anything else besides meeting Brandon on Monday since he called me, but Oliver's sure trying hard to get my mind to stick onto him.

I examine the candy on the counter. "Candy bars,

chocolate, caramels. Where's the licorice and the hard candy?"

He frowns. "No, we're the cool house. We don't give out the grandma candy here."

"What's grandma candy?"

He opens one of the bags and pops a mini candy bar into his mouth. "You know, the candy you'd find at the bottom of a grandma's purse or in her candy jar. Hard candy, peppermints, gross bubblegum that won't chew right…that sort of stuff."

"Halloween is a big deal to you, huh?"

The thick index finger on his right hand twirls around the handle of one of the shopping bags. "You could say that, I guess. I never had a real trick-or-treat experience until I started living with Mrs. Atchley, and even then, we only went around her neighborhood. I always wanted to be the house the kids always talked about until the next Halloween." A broad smile pops up on his lips. "Don't act like you're not equally as excited."

I giggle as he playfully pokes my sides. "Okay, okay. I'm excited."

"You seem distracted. Are you okay?"

I nod. "I'm just nervous about finals on Monday."

I'm such a liar.

I'm nervous about seeing Brandon alone on Monday for our divorce. My stomach hurts when I think about it.

"Do you need help studying?" he asks and pops another candy bar into his mouth. "I have to stop eating these. I haven't worked out in a long time."

I scoff. "I'm pretty sure you'd be equally as sexy even if you never worked out again."

He blows a raspberry and picks me up, my legs dangling from his arms. "You're the sexy one around here, Miss Remington. That's why you're so desirable around these parts." He winks and twirls me around the kitchen. He's in such a good mood lately that I don't want to do anything to burst his happy bubble...especially tip him off about the dark cloud looming over me until Monday at three.

I can't even find the marriage license. It's not where I put it in my drawer, and it scares me half to death to think that Oliver found it and he's waiting for me to disclose my secret. It stresses me out too much to keep thinking about it, so I tell myself I put it somewhere and forgot about it to ease my mind. I assume that Oliver would have a hard time keeping something like that in, and he's not showing any signs of anger toward anyone other than Casey, so what else is there for me to do but just keep moving on?

"Hey, let's get ready for the kids." A twinkle in his eye shines as he kisses my lips. "I want to be ready. Next year, we can decorate the house all creepy and have a haunted house in the garage, don't you think?"

His boyish grin makes me laugh. "You are absolutely everything I love about life."

When his forehead meets mine, he sighs deeply. "Likewise, baby."

I have to tell him.

I really, really—

His lips find mine again and he slowly puts me back on my own two feet. "I have something to tell you." His voice is low and scary. "I've been keeping this a secret for a few weeks now, and I can't stand it anymore. I feel like it's time for you to know."

My stomach burns. "Know what?" The dryness of my throat catches my words and I have to push them out with force. "Is something wrong?"

A faint smile touches his lips. "I bought a commercial space for the bar."

"The bar you've always wanted to open?"

Our excitement twirls around each other and I jump into his arms. "I'm so happy for you! When can I see it? What's it going to be named? Where is it?"

He laughs and puts me on my feet again. "Whoa, slow down, slow down. One question at a time. Here…" He pulls a black binder from a drawer. "Read this."

I instantly open the binder and start frantically scanning through the contents. By the time I reach the end, I have so many feelings and emotions running through my veins it's hard to catch one and keep it.

His eyebrows rise. "Questions?"

"Why did you name this JJ's Tables and Taps?"

"Because you're my inspiration, sunshine. Of course it's named after you…well, what your name will be once we get married. Julie Jackson…sounds good, doesn't it?"

I am the biggest jerk of all time.

I have to act like nothing is wrong. "I like it, thank you."

He pulls the ends of my purple sweater toward him. "No, thank *you*. You've given me the fire under my ass to get this done. I've wanted this for a long time and now, thanks to you, I can have it."

"I didn't do anything."

"Oh, but you did. You've showed me that I'm not worthless, baby. That's everything."

My cheeks heat with embarrassment. "What does this page mean?" I point to a spot on the paper where a pink arrow Post-It is stuck that says, "Sign here."

"That means half of the bar is yours once you sign your name."

I shake my head. "No, this is your dream, you're not handing half of it over to me. Oliver, we aren't even married yet and what if something happens—"

He growls. "Nothing is going to happen. I'm not allowing anything to fuck this up."

"But you're not in control of *everything*, Oliver. I'm not saying I don't appreciate this, but this is yours, not mine."

"What's mine *is* yours, Julie."

I know he's not going to give this up.

"Can I think about it before I sign that?"

He nods. "I don't know what there's to think about, but you know I'm behind you one hundred percent. Anything you want or need, is yours." He's in tune with my emotions enough to know that I want to stew on this for a few days. So much is happening all at once; I don't know why we're in such a hurry to get everything done. I want to be engaged for a long time…I never got to enjoy my first engagement since it was apparently only a few hours old.

"You're overwhelmed." He nods and folds the binder back up. "We can talk about this later, it's not that important right now. For now…" The smile returns to his face and I know he's up to something else. "…we're going to talk about our plans."

"And that's not overwhelming?" I laugh as he pops a third candy bar into his mouth. "Can we just slow everything down? So much has happened these past few months…I just want to take a deep breath and actually enjoy some time with you."

Light shines in his eyes. "Oh, shit."

"What? Did I say something wrong?"

He violently shakes his head, takes the binder back out, and opens it. He sifts through some pages and taps his finger on the paper. "Boomerang."

"Boomerang?"

"There's another proposal in here for a restaurant in the space next to the bar. I was going to outsource it and team up with someone in the food industry but this is it —*this* is what I've been looking for. This is the missing piece to the ultimate dream."

"Oliver, you're not making any sense—"

He closes the book and looks directly into my soul. "I want you to create a restaurant and we're going to call it Boomerang."

And we're back to the overwhelming—and nail-biting—conversation. I actually like his idea since I've always wanted to take part in something like that but, again, this is too much too soon. The hope in his eyes and the quiver in his lips shoves me back down into an alternate reality where I feel safe and know that no matter what, Oliver will always come back to me.

Like a boomerang.

"That's it." He takes mental note of the questions

I'm answering inside my head. "We always keep coming back to each other. Hence…Boomerang."

"Get out of my head," I joke and he hands me the binder.

"Take a look at this when you have a chance and tell me what you think. I want you to make your own decision and take the path you want to take. Don't do this just because I want you to—do this because you want to do it with me."

He makes a compelling argument, I admit. There's not much Oliver can't say to make me swoon over him, even today, but there's a little voice in my head that keeps telling me not to do anything until we talk about the secret I'm keeping.

I don't know whether to tell him before or after the hearing.

"Hey, you okay?" His warm hand rubs down my arm. "Don't let this scare you. Take your time."

"I'm not scared," I blurt out. "I have to tell you something."

No, Julie. Don't ruin his Halloween, this means something to him.

"What's that?"

"I want to do this with you." That's all I can think about saying to save myself. "The bar, the restaurant, the marriage, and the new house. All of it."

He chuckles. "I kinda figured that already, baby."

The conversation halts for a quick few seconds and I know I have to stop talking or the truth is going to come out. I plan on telling Oliver about the marriage Brandon forced me into, but not until after it's over and he can't just show up to the hearing—which I know he will do. He can't help himself from hovering over me and trying to stick his hands into everything and I understand why. It's not that I can't take care of myself and it's not that he thinks he can do a better job at running my life than I can. Oliver is the way he is for one simple reason: He's scared to lose me. I'm not saying it's right and I'm not saying that it doesn't get mentally taxing at times; it's different than anything I've ever experienced. He doesn't want to cage me, he just wants to know I'll be by his side no matter what.

And I will.

The doorbell rings and a fire lights in his eyes. "Kids, already?" He squeaks and quickly dumps the bag of candy bars into a large orange bowl. "Let's do this." He flashes me a smile and takes my hand before pulling me out of the kitchen and into the foyer. It's dusk already and when he opens the door and sees three children dressed as superheroes, the fire in his heart only burns deeper.

Watching him interact with the countless children ringing the doorbell over the next three hours is amusing and heartwarming. He plays with them and talks to them like an adult should talk to a child, giving them way too much candy and telling them to make sure they come back next year for bigger candy bars and a haunted house in the garage. I warn him that inviting them into the garage is a little creepy, but he doesn't care. He's having the time of his life and he deserves to smile after everything we've been through together.

The doorbell rings for the last time at the end of the night and Oliver frowns at the empty candy bowl.

"Damn, I forgot to turn off the light. Do we have any candy left?"

I shake my head. "No, you've given it all out."

He opens the door anyway and I skirt off into the kitchen to make sure all of the bags are empty and we don't have any candy lying around that we missed. Once I step over the threshold into the other room, Oliver's voice gets dark and loud, pulling me back into the foyer.

"What the fuck are you doing here?" he snarls. "You're out of your damn mind if you think I'm letting you get near her."

When I enter the room again, Casey's frowning face comes into view. Oliver isn't letting him pass—and that's okay with me—and he puts his arm across Casey's chest to stop him from coming inside. Casey doesn't look surprised as he pleads with Oliver to just hear him out and calm down.

"Just listen to me, man," Casey says. "I have something I need to tell you."

"Nothing you have to say is anything we want to fucking hear," Oliver snarls, taking a step forward. "I guess I wasn't clear enough the last time. Get the hell out of here and don't come back. We don't want to see your face or listen to anything you have to say."

He starts to shut the door in Casey's face when Casey sticks his arm inside and winces at the pain it causes him when the door tries to close. Oliver growls and steps outside, making Casey take a few steps backward. His eyes find mine and I can tell he's lonely and scared; he just wants someone to talk to and maybe a little normalcy in his life. That's something we can all hope for.

"I know something he's not telling you," Casey says to me. "Julie, let me in."

A shiver runs down my spine. "No, Oliver's right. You should leave."

"You know nothing, now leave," Oliver snaps. "Get the fuck out of here."

Casey begs and pleads for Oliver to let him in, but Oliver isn't budging. I'm glad he's here because I'm a pushover for people and Casey fits into that category of people I want to save from themselves. There's nothing I can do for him now, though—he's made his bed and now he's the one who has to deal with it.

"I know about Lucy." Casey's voice turns dark. "I know *all* about Lucy."

Oliver scoffs. "I'm sure you do."

"No." He looks directly into Oliver's eyes. "I *know*."

The tone in Oliver's voice changes. "You want to talk? We can talk. Let's do it outside."

"I'd like to talk in there, please." Casey smiles because he knows he's won the battle. "Julie should hear this, too."

Oliver slams his hand on the doorframe and the steam from his hatred sizzles in the air. "You and I will go outside and talk and that's fucking final. You're not getting within ten feet of her, you understand me?"

Casey might have won the battle, but Oliver has won the war as he agrees to speak outside and away from me. I'm curious what Casey meant about Lucy, since he dated her for a little while, but I'm thankful Oliver pulled him outside and away from me. I thought

Casey was a good guy; he seemed genuine when he helped me through Oliver's accident.

Then, he turned.

He blames it on me—*apparently*, I'm this magical unicorn that makes everyone feel good—but I didn't do anything to lead him on and Oliver knows it. Somehow, it's okay for everyone to attach themselves to me and stake a claim like I don't even own my own soul.

I watch them bicker through the window and once Oliver pushes Casey to the ground and he runs off with his tail between his legs, I open the door and step outside. "What was that about?" I look down the road where Casey is burning the rubber off his tires as he drives off. "What did he want?"

Oliver shakes his head. "Nothing. He thinks he has something over me and he doesn't. Lucy broke up with him and she's not calling him back or something, I don't know." He brushes off my question and looks down into my eyes. "Don't worry yourself with Casey. He's not worth it."

"He acted like he had something to say that I should know."

He shakes his head and gently pushes me back inside, shutting the door. "He's grasping at straws. He thinks he has some information on me that will push you closer to him, but he's wrong. Nothing's coming in between us—I won't allow it."

"*What* information, Oliver?"

He picks up the empty candy bowl and frowns. "I said it's nothing. I handled it, isn't that enough?" The dark clouds that form in his eyes are enough for me to back down and let him have his space. He's obviously torn inside and he's hiding something; I can't say I blame him for not speaking up since I'm lying to him just the same.

I force a smile on my face. "Okay, you're right. You handled it."

"Thank you." He kisses the tip of my nose and takes the bowl back into the kitchen. I don't follow him right away because I need some clear air to think. I step back outside and turn off the light that illuminates the front of the house. The cold October air captures my body and makes me shiver.

A dog howls in the distance and it's not long before I hear something shuffling on the pavement of the road. I can't see through the darkness, but as the figure passes underneath the streetlamp a few houses down...I see her.

Veronica.

She's coming back for me.

SEVEN
JULIE

I'M FROZEN.

I don't know what to do. I can't get my legs to work so I can run back into the house. I can't speak or scream for Oliver to come and help me. All I can do is wait for her to turn into our driveway and notice me standing on the dark front porch. Her outline glows with the remainder of the streetlight and she stands in silence, waiting.

"Oliver." I finally force from my throat and manage to turn my neck to see that I closed the door behind me and he can't hear me. As she stands at the end of the driveway and stares at me, the air outside gets extra icy and blasts through every inch of my skin. I'm so creeped out that the wind rustling the leaves on the oak tree in the front yard makes my insides squirm.

Move, Julie.

You have to move!

Veronica takes a few steps toward me and stops again. She's baiting me to say something—to scream and cry for Oliver so they can hurt him too. I don't know how she got out of jail so soon, but something isn't right here.

Is her boyfriend with her?

I look around and don't see anyone else. He must be hiding somewhere, ready to pounce on Oliver when he comes to rescue me.

Not this time.

"What do you want?" I whisper into the breeze. "You should leave before I get Oliver."

I'm not sure if she hears me, but she takes a few more steps forward and stops again. "I'm not here to hurt you." Her voice is sad but ominous. "I'm just here to pick something up and I'll be on my way."

"You're not getting a fucking thing!" My voice grows louder. "He doesn't owe you anything!"

"I'm not surprised that you're angry, Julie."

"Don't use my name like you know me!" A warm liquid feeling washes through my body and my legs unlock themselves from the anger de-icing them from the ground. I feel brave enough to step toward her and as I step off of the front porch, the streetlight illuminates her in my view better.

She looks horrible.

"What happened to you?" I tilt my head so I can see her better. "Why do you have bruises and cuts all over your face? What happened to your hair? Why aren't you wearing a sling for your shoulder? You got shot, remember?"

She shrugs slowly. "I was in jail, kid. That's what happens. They ain't rushing to give us proper medical care exactly."

She's trying to make me feel sorry for her.
Don't fall for it, Julie!

"Well, you belonged in there so you won't get any pity from me." My lips curl into a frown. "How are you even out?"

"I got a deal for agreeing to testify against Mac."

Taking a deep breath, I try to calm down, but her presence isn't allowing that to happen. "I want you to go back the way you came and never come around here again. You don't deserve to even speak one word to Oliver."

"I know that."

"Then why are you here? He already brought you money and you got caught."

Her tongue peeks out from her mouth and it sounds like sandpaper when she tries to lick her lips. "I'm not here to cause trouble. Oliver told me when I got out to come to this address and he would give me some money to go away and never come back."

I scoff. "So, it's always about money with you two."

"You don't understand how deep greed runs in the Jackson family, kid." She snickers. "Those who crave it, they will always want a piece of it."

I shake my head. "That's disgusting. Oliver isn't like that."

"Maybe not anymore. You've changed him."

"Excuse me?"

One of the small bags she's carrying hits the ground and makes a hard thud. "You've changed him, girl. I've watched him over the years and Colin would tell me things when he paid me off, and he's not the same little boy I knew years ago. I guess that's my fault, but at least you helped him get to the man he wanted to be."

"I did nothing."

She snorts. "Keep telling yourself that. No matter how much you wanna deny it, you're just like me. Well, maybe the old me before I met Mac. I loved life and it was simple; I loved every minute of working at the Inn. Then, Colin Jackson swept me off my feet and showed me a world I never even dared to dream of. I didn't want that life but I wanted him. It's a horrible war between your head and your heart, dontcha think?"

The front porch light turns on and the door opens.

"Why are you telling me this?" I whisper so Oliver can't hear.

She smiles and it's actually filled with warmth and invites me into her dull eyes. "Don't make the same mistakes I made. You can be independent and strong with him by your side, you really can. Don't keep secrets, let him take you as you are. You won't regret it, I promise."

My eyes widen and she looks behind me. "Hello, Ollie Bear."

Oliver comes up behind me and slides his arm around my waist. "Veronica."

She winces a little and frowns. "I didn't mean to cause trouble, I just came here because you said to and I just got out—"

He hands her a large envelope and says nothing.

She puts it in the bag still hanging on her shoulder and looks hopefully at him for a moment, but he doesn't budge. His arm tenses around me and hurts a little, but I know he needs me right now. Veronica picks up the bag from the ground and tries to hand it to me, but Oliver intercepts.

"You're not to speak to her, and you're sure as hell not *giving* her anything."

She puts the bag on the ground in front of me. "These are Colin's journals from the cabin that went missing. I snuck in and took them because there's things in those books that I didn't want known. I trust you, Julie, so I'm giving them back to you. Take care of him." She nods toward Oliver and turns to walk back down the driveway. She winces in pain each time she takes a step and I feel the sorrow rising in my throat, ready to call after her.

Oliver pinches my side because he knows me too well. "She's fine, let her go."

"She can barely walk!" I hiss. "This is so fucked up."

He knows I'm right. "I don't know what to do here, okay? She's a terrible fucking person, how can I just jump and help her when she's done so fucking much to hurt me…and you? She just fucking kidnapped you, did you forget that?"

My stomach sours and I have to close my mouth so I can breathe through my nose and calm down. He doesn't deserve to be attacked by me and I know that; it's hard to find the fine line between helping someone and being your own person.

"I didn't forget." My gaze goes back to her as she makes her way down the street from the direction she came. She's dragging her left foot a little and that's the source of the scraping sound from before. "We can't just let her wander around Rockford, Oliver."

"Julie, she *kidnapped* you."

"I know that! I was there!" I snap. "You keep bringing that up and we're never going to be able to move past it. Don't you want to make sure she's okay? She's still your mother."

"No, she's not." The hollowness of his voice echoes around in my mind. "She was dead to me the moment she left me. You're *not* to follow her or help her, do you understand? I just handed her money to walk away and never come back, so don't go looking for her."

I open my mouth to counter his offer, but he shakes his head.

"Don't. Go. Looking. For. Her. Tell me you understand me. Never go looking for her. Promise me."

Figuring out which emotion and argument I want to go with is wearing me thin. I don't want to upset him but I can't let her walk the streets alone and hurt no matter what she's done to me. I like to find the good in people and there's more to Veronica than meets the eye.

And I want to know more about what she knows.

I have to respect him. I have to show him that I'm there for him.

"I can't let her be alone—she's *hurt*, Oliver," I plead with him. "Just let me get her into a hotel room for the night and a doctor can look at her tomorrow before she leaves town."

"No," he growls, gently grabbing my arm and pulling me back into the house. "You're not going."

Stop, Julie. Think about things before you say them.

My lungs expand with a deep breath. "Okay, I won't go after her. She's made it this far on her own…she can handle it, right?"

70

He doesn't smile. "Right. Thank you for making the right decision and not running after her."

Well, you sort-of made the decision for me, didn't you?

His eyebrows rise. I know he can read my mind sometimes and now…I'm in trouble. "I'm also thankful that you love me enough to respect my final decisions and do as I tell you when it really matters."

Oh, Oliver. I thought we were going to get out of this without your foot in your mouth.

"You don't own me." The surprise in my voice makes him let go of my arm and take a few steps backward. "You shouldn't order me around like I don't have a mind of my own."

"You're killing me." He exhales and rubs the bridge of his nose. "Baby, I love you, but you're acting like a child. I asked you not to go and yet you kept telling me you were going."

"No, you *told* me not to go." My eyes narrow up at him. "And I'm not a slave."

I want to stop this. I want to stop this now, but I don't know how to…

He holds up his hands and waves them around quickly. "Whoa, wait a minute here. No one said you were a slave and you have free will—don't play that game with me. You're doing this because you can't help yourself. You have to *fix* everyone. Guess what, Julie? That wretched, twisted excuse for a mother *cannot* be fixed."

Darkness has completely consumed the light in his emerald eyes; he can barely stand to look at me because the tears forming in the corners might fall. "Not to mention all the fucked-up shit she did to me when I

71

was a kid. She's not a good person and she can't be trusted. That should be enough for you, Julie. Me *asking* you to not do this to me should be enough for you."

Oh, no. He's right.

"Oliver, I—"

He kisses my forehead and turns to leave the room. He leaves his pain and hurt behind to suffocate me, reminding me of what a horrible wife I'm going to be. He's activated a headstrong quality in me and it's such a new feeling that I haven't mastered it yet.

I don't know how long I stand in the half-lit foyer in silence while I hear him shuffling around upstairs. My feet follow the outline of the carpet as I walk the stairs slowly, one at a time; the shower starts when I hit the top and a door slams, making me jump out of my skin.

He's never been this angry with me before.

The bedroom feels tense even though he's in the shower, but the anger he's left behind isn't pleasant to be alone with. I don't bother knocking on the bathroom door before walking in; the steam from the shower fills the space enough that he can't see me.

"I *feel* you." His voice is small. "I know you're in here, baby."

I hoist myself onto the sink and lower my head in shame. "I shouldn't have argued with you. You're right, she's not a good person. I don't know what I was thinking."

He sighs. "You're not flawed, baby, your heart's in the right place. I know the goodness inside of you wants to find the good in other people. You did that with me."

"Your mot—Veronica." I blush even though he can't

see me through the shower door. "She said that I changed you, that you aren't the little boy she knew."

Oliver scoffs and sticks his head out of the shower door. His chocolate brown hair is matted around his forehead and his bright green eyes shine like gemstones. "Of course I'm not, I haven't really seen her for twenty years. She's right about one thing: you *did* change me. It's a change I needed and I'm glad to have."

"How can I make it up to you?" I bite at my fingernails. "What can I do?"

An ornery grin lifts the corners of his mouth. "You can join me, for starters. The water is nice and warm, ready for you."

Oliver wants to put away the pain I caused him and focus on something else. Usually, and this time is no different, that something else is sex. Not that I blame him, since the sight of his naked god-like body melts whatever defense I have left against him.

"Are you sure that shower is big enough for both of us?" I joke.

He opens the door wider so I can step inside. "Get undressed. One of the main reasons I *bought* this house was the size of this shower. You know I like seeing you naked and wet, sunshine."

I chuckle as I undress and don't even think twice about standing in front of him naked. I got over that weeks ago, even though the feeling of his body pressing against mine makes me feel a hundred pounds heavier than I am.

His eyes never leave my body as I undress and saunter toward him; I slip past his body and make sure every part of me that can rub against him touches him in some way. He barely gets the door closed again before his hands are cupped around my neck gently, pushing me against the wall and devouring my lips with his.

"Oliver," my voice is scratchy from the steam, "is your knee strong enough? I noticed you were rubbing it earlier—"

His warm syrup laugh makes my body shiver. "Again, don't worry about me. I've been doing my own rehab work and that's why I'm stronger than I should be."

"But—"

"You frustrate me more than anyone I've ever known." He smiles into my skin when his lips reach my collarbone. "Sometimes it's hard to control my hunger for you."

I snicker. "You mean you've been holding back?"

The soft nips that his teeth make at my wet skin ignite the flame in my stomach. "Oh, there's plenty more than what we've been doing, don't you worry about that. There's things I want to do to you that would make you blush to hear me say out loud." I blush and he laughs. "See?"

Confidence, Julie. Find it and own it. You can do this. Be the woman you know you want to be.

"I already blush. Why don't you show me what you mean?"

Yes! There you go!

He growls and sucks on my shoulder; his tongue flicks across my skin in a circular motion. "Don't *tease* me; I have a rough side that you don't want to see."

My mouth finds his and I make a point to bite his thick bottom lip just enough to tantalize him. "Who's the one teasing now? *Show* me, Oliver."

The slow hiss that escapes his lips as he picks me up and wraps my legs around his waist echoes between the glass walls of the shower. He groans as his thick, hard flesh enters the space it owns inside of me, and he doesn't waste any time ripping through the barrier to get where he wants to be. His body pounds into me and I have to hook my nails into his back to keep from bouncing away. He snarls when my nails pierce his flesh and catches my lips with his and kisses me so hard that I lose all the breath I have left. The world goes fuzzy for a few seconds as he pulls out of me and slams back into my flesh so hard that I feel disconnected from my body.

It feels amazing.

Somehow, I manage to scream his name and he clutches onto me, pumping harder with each second that passes. He's holding me against the wall so he can do what he wants, and I'm so helpless to his touch that I don't even care.

"I told you…" He tries to catch his breath and runs his tongue along the outer rim of my breast. "…and this is just the beginning."

I lick my lips and the world is full of bright colors dancing around the walls of the shower. "More," I breathe, and his wicked laugh snakes into my ears. "I want everything."

He moans as he pushes back inside of me. "What's mine *is* yours, Mrs. Jackson."

I don't remember much after that as he takes my body to another plane, through space and time.

There we are.

Pushing aside our problems to get to what we truly want.

Oliver and Julie.

The Rulebreakers.

EIGHT
HEATHER

I MAKE it home before Brandon does and I know I don't have much time to spare to get ready for dinner. After I shove the last of the groceries in their places, I quickly wipe down the counters and tidy up around the house before changing out of my sweaty clothes. I don't have time for a full shower, so I freshen up in other ways and open the closet to try and find something to wear. Since Brandon and I are sleeping in the same room, we don't have much closet space for both of us to share. I took the closet in the purple room because of the full-length mirror behind the door for convenience.

The front door opens and adrenaline rushes through my veins. I manage to bend over and feel my legs for stubble before he leans in the doorframe with his tired eyes fixed on my half-naked body. "Is it okay if I change my mind again?" He yawns and I drink him in during his vulnerable state because I don't get to see this side of him too often.

I let out a sigh of relief. "Yes, that's totally okay."

He playfully smiles. "I don't know about you some-times, babe. I mean, I think about you all day long and I dream about you and you're doing…what? Planning meals and running errands? If I didn't know better, I'd say you were reaching some sort of normalcy."

I snort and my cheeks heat with embarrassment. "I haven't even thought about my quest for normalcy in weeks. I guess I'm just comfortable enough to forget about trying so hard and just let things be. I know Oliver and Julie aren't chomping at the bit to be our friends, and I'm okay with that. They don't hate us anymore, and that's a good start."

He swoops me into his long arms with grace. A few strands of his long, midnight black hair tickle my fore-head when he dips me low and slides his lips across mine. "I'm exactly where I want to be right now. My life is honestly so fucking perfect it's unreal. I thought I knew love before but this is…" He takes in a deep breath and smiles. "…so much more than that."

I feel his forehead. "What's gotten into you? What happened?"

He kisses me again and places me back on my feet. "Nothing happened…*yet*. Let's pretend I'm not offended for a minute that you questioned my inten-tions, but you'll need to know this. Trumbull knows about the divorce to Julie."

I blink a few times in confusion. "So?"

"So…" He steps backward and blows out a long tunnel of air from his lungs. "He expedited the hearing to Monday at three, and he expects Julie to show up so he can take us out to a late lunch."

"Why is he in your business like that?" I sit in the

chair at my desk and frown. "He shouldn't be able to just butt in like that."

Brandon laughs. "Vern Trumbull can do whatever the hell he wants. He's high and tight with a lot of New York's politicians and business leaders. He's pretty much untouchable."

"Well, he's a horrible boss for prying into your personal life."

He nods in agreement. "I think he's planning something, I just don't know what. I can't imagine he'd just want to meet Julie. He wants to get to the bottom of it."

I gasp. "Do you think he knows about you sleeping with his daughter?"

"I don't know, but that's what I'm afraid of." He notices the horror twisted on my face and frowns deeper. "I shouldn't be talking to you about this...it's not fair to you."

I stand up and cross my arms over my chest. "Hey, once you say those three little words, your problems become my problems."

"Is that so?" He pulls me back into his grasp. "I knew there was something I loved about you."

I groan. "Enough with the mushy stuff. We said I love you and now we can say it when it's appropriate, end of story."

He laughs. "When is it appropriate, exactly?"

"I'm not having this conversation." I shake my head. "You're fishing around to see how I'll react and I've already said the words to you. It's not like I can take them back now. Stop doubting yourself."

"Do you *want* to take them back?"

"No."

"Are you sure?"

I clap my hands in front of me. "Get over it and move on. I love you, Brandon Whitehouse, and you hold a special place inside of me. Let's not get too crazy too quick here."

"Okay, okay. I get your point. It's new and still in the baby stages. Which by the way, do you want any?"

I glare at him and try to play dumb. "Do I want any what?"

"Babies. Kids. Children."

I breathe in deep and let it slowly back out to calm my nerves. We just made the pact to wait a year to even talk about marriage and now he's asking about kids?

"What is all this about, really? You're testing me and asking me questions…are you really unsure that I'm being real when I say I love you?"

He shakes his head and looks down at me. "No, I'm not unsure. I'm just a little…unsure of what will happen on Monday if I lose my job."

I blow a raspberry and breeze past his body. "If you're asking if I'll leave you if you lose your job…then you don't know me well enough to say you love me." Before he can argue, I leave the room and lock myself in the bathroom with the sink faucet running. I look at myself in the mirror and frown.

I thought we were taking it slow.

Saying I love you is a huge step.

But I said it. I told him I love him.

And I do.

But I knew it would backfire on me and make things go in the wrong direction.

This is all too much, too soon.

I wanted to slow down; I wanted to feel it in my bones.

Brandon knocks on the door and calls for me. "Heather, come out here, please." His voice is steady and smooth. "I don't want to fight. I want to apologize."

The magic words make me unlock the door and his gray eyes instantly meet mine. "I'm sorry for making you upset; I don't like seeing you like that. I'm sorry if I offended you…I guess I'm just worried I can't take care of you if I lose my job."

"I don't *need* you to take care of me."

He lightly smiles and brushes hair from my cheek. "But I want to."

"We're in this together, you're not responsible for everything. I can get a job if you lose yours and it shouldn't be too hard for you to get another job."

He chuckles. "Vern will blacklist me. I'll never work for another lawyer again."

"Then you'll find something else to do. Brandon, I believe in you. You've become a person even better than what I'd imagined. Karma is going to take care of you on this one, you've done a lot of good these past few months and it's gotta count for something."

He snickers and pulls me from the bathroom. "You're starting to sound like Julie and trying to see the good in everyone. That's a good trait to have."

I blush and let him lead me into the kitchen. He points to the island counter where all the ingredients for the meatloaf are laid out and two aprons are hanging on the back of a chair. He slides one around me and ties it in the back, putting the second one around his tall body and brushing his hair back.

"So, let's make this meatloaf."

I giggle and open the package of raw hamburger meat. "You're helping?"

"Yeah, I can cook better than you, which isn't saying much. Between the two of us, we should be able to come out with something decent to eat." He laughs as I poke him in the arm. "Hey, I speak the truth and you know it, babe."

Babe.

I still cringe at that word.

I shake the negativity from my head. "Okay, here's the recipe." I point to a piece of white paper on the other side of the island counter. "It's my grandmother's, so it's pretty old. We may need to improvise."

He snorts. "I thought you went to the store for all this shit?"

"Well some things I couldn't find or didn't know what they were." I blush. "At least I'm trying something new!"

He rubs my back and my anxiety retreats back down in my stomach. "I get it, and I appreciate what you're doing. Let's try this out, okay?" He starts reading the recipe and together, we mash and stir and knead and roll the ingredients together to make something that sort of resembles a meatloaf in a small pan. He steps back to examine our work and smiles.

"I think we did okay."

I laugh hysterically. "Look at that thing! It's leaning over!"

He acts quickly and catches the meat stack from toppling completely over and we laugh so hard that it's hard to return it to its original state. He stands it back up the best he can and throws it into the oven. When he shuts the door, we both look at each other and frown.

"We didn't turn on the oven." He coughs from the laughter in his throat.

"Pizza?" I pick up my phone and quickly order a pizza online before catching his gaze again.

He still looks worried.

"Are you worried about the late lunch thing on Monday?" I ask. "Who cares what that old, fat geezer thinks? He wasn't in your shoes and he doesn't walk in your life."

He groans. "I screwed his daughter while I was married to Julie. He's going to kill me."

"Maybe he won't even know."

"He'll know."

I don't know how to get him out of this funk. Not even a proposition of sex can break this mentality. All I can do is stand next to him and cling to him and hold on. Eventually, his arms slide up my back and he squeezes me into him.

"I'm glad you're here," he whispers into my hair. "My fuck-ups keep coming back to haunt me in the worst ways and it's eating me alive."

I stroke the back of his head and he snuggles deeper into my hair. "You know what I thought about the other day? I wish that you and I could move far away from here and escape all the bad things we've done. It seems like everywhere I go, people only see me as Oliver Jackson's ex. I've been blacklisted from a lot of places around the city; it's exhausting."

"We may have to move if I get blacklisted from

another law firm." He groans. "I wish I would've never met Rachel or fucked her."

I snort. "You wish that now, but at the time you were sleeping with her it seemed like what you wanted to do."

"You're right." He laughs and kisses my head. "*I'm* to blame for my mistakes. Maybe one day we can move to another country and start over."

"Our problems aren't big enough to move entire countries." I shake my head. "Maybe California or Florida. That seems like it's far enough where people won't know who we are or what we've done."

"Hmm…" His arms let go of me and he rubs his chin in thought. "I've always wanted to move to Seattle. They have some pretty decent law firms there, and that should be far enough where Trumbull won't have anyone to sink his claws into."

I smile and kiss his cheek. "Everything is going to be fine, you'll see. There's nothing you can do about it right now, anyway."

"Besides freak out, you mean?"

"You just need to calm down and breathe. Nothing is as bad as it seems, you know? Whatever that asshole has to say to you, it's really none of his business. It's no one's business who you sleep with and you could sue him for getting personal information on you."

He laughs and pulls me into a bear hug again. "I love you, do you know that? Thanks for trying to make me feel better, I'll try not to ruin our weekend."

I let him hold me for as long as he needs because the truth is: I'm scared too. I'm worried that he'll lose his job and we'll be homeless again—that's something I'll never go back to. I make a mental note that I'll need to start looking for a job, and I may have to put school on the back burner again.

This time I'll make a smart choice and do what I have to do for my relationship to grow, not just agree with someone so I won't lose them. I smile at my newfound glory and when he parts his body from mine, I'm ready to tackle whatever sadness he tries to throw at me next.

The doorbell rings and saves the day as Brandon opens it and pays the driver, bringing the pizza back inside. He smells the air and moans a little too loudly for it not to be noticeable.

"Is something wrong?" I take the box from his hands and open it. The delicious scent of the ham and pineapple pizza fills the air. "Did you want something else?"

He shakes his head and steals a slice before we enter the kitchen. "No, I like this kind. I'm starting to like a lot of new things because of you. Julie was somewhat of a vegetarian, so I'd only get bacon and shit when she was feeling down." Sadness fills his eyes. "Actually, toward the end I had bacon almost every day."

"Well…" I shove another slice into his hand and push him down into a chair at the kitchen table. "You don't have to worry about that anymore. I'm not down, I'm not sad, and I like bacon. I also like pizza, so eat up." I take my own slice and nibble at it while he finishes his first. "And I like beer and vodka and probably a million other things Julie won't touch."

He snorts. "I can think of one thing in particular."

I try and be a smart ass and think of something that

will change his mood. I don't like when he goes from one emotion to the next as easily as changing socks. It's weird that there's no lag time for him to process anything; it's like he dwells for a reasonable amount of time and then locks it away deep down in his mind and forgets about it until someone or something raises it back up.

I like to talk things out.

I don't like to fight and argue.

I like to come to mutual conclusions.

I follow the rules.

…*Now.*

That's me now.

That's the Heather I've become.

It's only a matter of time to see if Brandon can keep up.

NINE
OLIVER

I CAN'T FUCKING BELIEVE this is my life.

I have the most intelligent, sexy, amazing woman lightly snoring next to me and the world just stands still; If I move a single muscle, she'll wake up and all the peace that fills my head will be gone. I know I can't keep her locked up and I don't want to.

But she's mine.

I belong to her, that's no secret.

Julie was about to tell me her secret earlier—I could feel it. She knows it's wrong to keep something like this from me, but there's nothing I can do but wait for Brandon to hold up his end of the deal and take care of it. Preferably without making or causing a huge scene in the process.

I don't want to lose Julie to anything...or anybody.

She snuggles deeper into my chest and all I want to do in life is hold her.

I want to make her feel safe again.

My mind wanders to the first time I saw her,

huddled in the backseat of Randy's squad car. If I knew then what I know now, I'd never let him drive off with her. Her fierce, glowing blue eyes haunted me for so many years that I did whatever I could to forget about her.

And now I know.

All I need is her.

My mind wanders to Mrs. Atchley and I feel guilty because I haven't spoken to her much lately. I know she understands what Julie means to me, and I made a mental note to ask her the next time I see her if she recognized Julie from years ago too. I'm not sure she even knew Julie was hiding in the backseat...but I did.

I could feel her.

I can *always* feel her.

She's the best part of me.

Julie's naked body stirs next to me; the sunlight hits her face just perfectly and she smiles in her sleep. Regardless of our little argument, it's been the best Halloween ever. The picture perfect, white picket fence life is all I've ever wanted. I know it's crazy, but it's the small things that make life amazing: all of the small things combined into a huge, gaping hole of love and happiness.

My hand slides down her side and rests on her curvy hip. I have to fight the urge to slap her ass; it's so close to my fingers...just one good smack ought to hold me for a while. I grin and move my hand closer to the roundness of her backside when she turns onto her back and denies me access to what I want. Touching her isn't enough anymore—I have to really *feel* her.

"Denied." Her sleepy giggle reaches my ears. "I know *all* about you, Mr. Jackson."

"Good morning to you, too." I look down at her naked body and drink her in. "Aren't you just a little ball of sunshine this morning?"

She moans and stretches; her curvy hips flatten and my lips start to inch toward them. "After what we did last night, I could use a few more hours of sleep."

"It's Saturday; you can sleep in."

She groans and turns her body to face me again, snuggling in my chest. Her breath moves my chest hair and tickles my skin, but I hold her there and keep her near me. "I can't sleep in. I promised Staci I would meet her downtown...she needs a new dress or something. Plus, Lucy and I are getting together later to study. Is it okay if she comes to the apartment instead of here? We'll be more comfortable there, I think."

It takes everything I have to swallow the lump in my throat. "Of course, baby. What's mine—"

She snuggles deeper and her lips find my shoulder blade. "—What's yours is mine, I know. You've only said it a million times."

"Then when are you going to listen?" I scoff and tip her chin upward. My lips glide across hers and she gently sucks them in; I can feel her exhaustion through her kiss. "If you want someone to come over, you don't have to ask. I want you to feel comfortable treating our home like you belong there, because you do. You belong wherever I am, whatever house we are in and whatever city we live in."

She giggles. "Are we planning on moving?"

I kiss her forehead and stretch my legs. "No, we just

bought this house. Don't you want to give it a test run first before we decide we don't like it?"

"I love this house." She blushes and sits up, her sunshine-colored hair falling around her body in a thick, tangled mess from my fingers getting twisted in it the night before. "I love everything about this house. You found a good one, Oliver."

I stand up and her eyes widen as she realizes I'm still naked too. "Everything about this house made me think of you. The library, the kitchen, the master bathroom." I chuckle and look away; I know I'm blushing as I think about the amazing sex we've had and where I want to take her next. "Even the backyard and the gazebo."

Her eyes widen. "There's a gazebo?"

"Have you not seen the entire property? I thought when you and Casey were here looking around—before Veronica and Mac showed up—you took a good look at everything?"

Her voice lowers and she looks down into her lap. "I only got as far as the walk-in closet when—"

I pick her up and place her on the floor next to me, our warm skin touching and igniting invisible sparks as she pushes her hair behind her ears. "Say no more. Do you want to look around today? I have to meet some lawyers at the commercial space so we can go over some paperwork at ten, but after that I'm free."

She shakes her head. "Can we spend the day apart?"

My stomach drops into my toes. "Okay," I slowly say and try not to act worried. "Is there something you're not telling me?"

"No, no." She waves me off. "I just think we need

some time apart sometimes, you know? Absence makes the heart grow fonder?"

I narrow my eyes, because I don't believe her. "I already know you're going out with Staci today, but is there something else I should know? Anything about Lucy?"

Okay, man. You're digging and she's going to see right through you.

Julie looks angry. "Nothing is wrong. I just want to spend a day where I don't have to answer to you or think about what you'll say or do."

Ouch.

"What's *that* supposed to mean?" I growl. "You act as if you don't have freedom."

She quickly realizes what she's said wrong. "I didn't mean it like that. I love my life with you, don't get me wrong. I just think that some time apart will be good sometimes. I didn't get that with Brandon and I felt suffocated."

"Say no more, I understand." My lips purse together and they start to hurt from the pressure I'm putting on them to keep them closed. I don't want to say anything to fuck myself over with her again like I did when she told me she was late a few months ago. The thought of having a family—*a real family*—with Julie excites me. I've never been the kind of person who plans for the future and gets excited about what's to come, but with Julie…everything is flipped.

I can't imagine life without her.

"Oliver?" Her voice is faint and she's worried. "Is everything okay between us?"

I scoff. "Of course it is, baby. It just takes me longer

sometimes to realize the point you're trying to make. Your beautiful face distracts me." I smile and wrap my arms around her. Before, she would swat me away and blush when she'd remember she was naked, but not anymore. Now she welcomes my touch and aches for more.

I want to give her more.

I want to do more to her, with her, and for her.

"Do you think we can go on a date tomorrow night? Just you and me, maybe Dilaggio's?" She licks her lips before I can devour them. I know we have to start our day and standing here, in our bedroom, naked and will-ing...that's never going to happen.

I nod. "I'll take you wherever you want to go. We should spend a weekend in New York City sometime soon, too, before we start the bar. That will take up a lot of our time once it gets going."

She squeals. "I'm excited about that. I love that you wanted to name it after me, but Boomerang...that fits it perfectly. Do you have anyone else helping you?"

I let her go so she can pull on some clothes before examining herself in the mirror. I watch her smile and gawk at her teeth and lips, no doubt picking herself apart in her mind. I come up behind her and wrap my arms around her waist and smile into her hair. "Harley and Victor are going to help me do some construction work on the place so I don't have to have a contractor for very long. I thought you could come up with a menu for the restaurant, maybe some of the things you've made for me since we've been together? And some of your favorite dishes, too—nothing as fancy as Dilaggio's, but somewhere around that. You and Staci can decorate both spaces if you want, the bar and the restaurant."

She laughs. "I'm sure she will love that. That's more her forte than mine, though, but I'll be glad to help wherever you need me."

Oh, I need you to help me with this raging hard-on poking into your back, sunshine.

I clear my throat. "I know I can count on you, baby."

She smiles at me in the mirror and waves me off. "Okay, now get dressed and get your day started. You don't have much time before you have to meet your lawyers." Her grin is wicked as she sees my pout and growing rebuttal. "And if you don't get dressed, I'm going to get undressed again and then *both* of our days will be wasted."

"Oh…" I spin her around and pick her up, placing her on the dresser next to us. "*Trust* me. The day won't be wasted."

She giggles and pushes me aside, jumps down, and races to the bathroom. Before I can get to her, she's locked the door and laughs on the other side, mentioning something about blue balls and the water in the sink starts to run. I look down at my hard dick and frown. I wonder if I could get away with just taking care of it myself without her finding out. Not that she would be disgusted, but I don't want her thinking that she doesn't turn me on.

Because she surely fucking does.

"That's fine," I say loudly to the closed door, "but you're gonna get it later."

She shuffles around in the bathroom and laughs loudly so I can hear her. "Promises, promises."

Okay, you win. You're cute as hell and you've won me over.

After I find some basketball shorts hidden away in my suitcase, I pull them on and rush through various sets of push-ups, crunches, and planks until I can't take it anymore and collapse onto the floor in a sweaty mess. I packed some of our things to bring over to the new house, but there isn't much here and I didn't bring a suit, so I opt for a pair of jeans and a black sweater. I know I need to shower, though, and she's still locked away inside the bathroom.

I knock on the door. "I need to shower, Julie."

She waits a few seconds before answering. "You just woke up, you haven't done anything to even sweat. Why do you need to shower? You shower more than three people do."

I snort. "I just worked out, I'm sweaty."

She groans and opens the shower door and her small feet pad toward the door. When she opens it, her smile widens as they fix on my flushed cheeks.

She's wet.

…and naked

She's wet and naked.

I almost reach out to grab her but restrain myself at the last minute. "Can I shower with you?"

She shakes her head. "I'm already done and I have to meet Staci. I'm sure you can manage to shower by yourself. You need to take care of that, after all." Her small fingers point down to my dick and she has a hard time wiping the smirk off her face. "I'm sure you don't want to walk into a business meeting with an erection."

I growl. "That's what you do to me, Julie."

She shrugs. "I was in the shower, how did I do that?"

"I was thinking about you."

She makes a small noise and steps out of the now-open bathroom door. As she saunters toward the bed, I notice that the towel she grabbed is only covering her front and her bare, wet ass is staring me straight in the face. Her sexy eyes glance back at me to make sure I'm watching, and she smiles when it's clear that my gaze is fixed on her ass.

Oh, I'm fucking watching, all right.

"Like what you see?" She laughs. "I could show you more and it could be our little secret."

The air I'm holding in my lungs starts to hurt my insides, so I quickly blow it out and take a step backward into the open bathroom doorway. I know that if I don't keep myself from wrapping her legs around me, I'll never make it to that meeting.

I fake a chuckle. "I get it. That's what I said to you our first night at the cabin when we met."

She giggles and wraps the towel fully around her so I'll retreat into the bathroom and leave her alone. I'm not sure how, but I manage to close the door and step into the shower to wait for the water to get warm enough to relieve myself in.

I think about her round, thick curves and how they meet her ass with perfection.

I think about the way her lips suction with mine and it sends shocks down my spine.

I think about her long, sunshine-colored hair and her strawberry shampoo.

She's taking over every single thought I have and

it's like I can't focus on anything else. She doesn't have to be naked for me to want her; I'll always want her no matter what she looks like.

She was made for me.

My mind races back to her again like it's never felt more at home.

Her finger skims the rim of a silver mixing bowl and she licks batter from her finger.

She looks up at me with wide, bright blue eyes after she's been reading for a long time.

Her innocence is in everything I see, everything I touch.

Lucy.

Fuck.

Then there's Lucy.

I have to play by the rules on this one.

I have to remember that Lucy isn't out to get me and she doesn't want Julie to know.

But Casey does.

I'll kill him if he tells her.

TEN
CASEY

I EXHALE everything I'm saving in my lungs. I want to have fresh air flowing through me when I bring Oliver's world to a screeching halt. Lucy told me everything and I have so much leverage over him now, his life is going to become mine without anyone even knowing.

Their voices waft through the closed door and flashes of what happened last time I was at this house buzz through my skull. I let her down here; I couldn't save her no matter how hard I tried. I punished myself for days after that, wishing that I did more or trying to think of what I could've done better so they wouldn't have taken her.

Oliver would've saved her.

My eyes narrow at the light pouring from the top of the door. Julie is in there and he's touching her; the anger rises in my throat as I ring the doorbell before I can stop myself. I know I'm stupid for even thinking I have some sort of claim over her, but she never gave me a chance to show her the man I can be. Well, the good parts of me, that is.

"What the fuck are you doing here?" he snarls. "You're out of your damn mind if you think I'm letting you get near her."

I frown. Oliver has no intentions of letting me pass and he puts his arms across my chest to stop me from just coming inside on my own accord. Julie comes into the room and her fear scratches my flesh so much that it burns.

"Just listen to me, man," I say. "I have something I need to tell you."

"Nothing you have to say is anything we want to fucking hear." Oliver snarls and takes a step forward. "I guess I wasn't clear enough the last time. Get the hell out of here and don't come back. We don't want to see your face or listen to anything you have to say."

He starts to shut the door in my face, but my arm jolts out from the side of my body and obstructs him from being able to shut me out. He swings the door open and steps outside, making me take a few steps backward. My eyes find Julie's—who hasn't said anything since Oliver answered the door—and she waits a few long seconds before averting her gaze to Oliver.

"I know something he's not telling you," I say to her. "Julie, let me in."

Her body shivers. "No, Oliver's right. You should leave."

"You know nothing, now leave," Oliver snaps. "Get the fuck out of here."

I don't know what else to say for him to let me inside.

"I know about Lucy." My voice turns dark. "I know *all* about Lucy."

He scoffs. "I'm sure you do."

"No." I look directly into his eyes. "I *know*."

The tone in Oliver's voice changes. "You want to talk? We can talk. Let's do it outside."

"I'd like to talk in there, please." I smile and I know I've won the battle. "Julie should hear this, too."

Oliver slams his hand on the doorframe and the steam from his hatred sizzles in the air. "You and I will go outside and talk and that's fucking final. You're not getting within ten feet of her, you understand me?"

I decide not to press my luck and I let him shut me out from Julie once again. His body revs like an engine that's ready to roar. "What the hell do you think you know about me?" He crosses his arms over his chest— no doubt so he won't haul off and punch me in the face. "I'm curious to see what you think you know."

I try to swallow the lump in my throat. "You're not winning this one, asshole. Lucy told me all about you taking her home from The Tavern and what you two did."

"I don't know what she told you, but she's a fucking liar. I didn't take her home with me and I didn't even know her before you introduced us."

The tone of his voice even makes me believe him for a second. I know him better than this, though. I know how hard he worked to be someone else at the drop of a hat and now he's perfected living a lie of a life. He painted himself a good person from the very moment he could.

"What exactly do you think I'm lying about now?" he snarls. It's like he read my mind and he's trying to snake his way out of this one like I'm going crazy.

"You took her home and slept with her. You cheated on Julie when she was worried about being pregnant or not. Once she finds out, she'll hate you and be rid of you for good."

He throws his hands into the air. "Are you forgetting that we're together *because* of you? You and Nora, to be exact? I'm sorry things didn't work out for you but Casey, you *have* to leave this delusion alone. It's eating you alive."

"I'll get her alone and I'll tell her. I don't know when, but I will," I call after him as he walks back into the house and turns the light off on me. I stick around for a few silent minutes and try to hear their conversation inside, but I give up after I realize I didn't win after all.

I lost again.

I scream into the air and rush back to my car. The cold air whips through the inside of the car as I speed away and roll the windows down. I need the whip of the icy wind to bring me back to life. Every time I try and go up against Oliver, I lose. He hardly even tries—that's what pisses me off so badly.

I want what he has.

I want it all.

At the end of the road, I slam on my brakes after nearly hitting someone crossing the street. Their tattered clothes and pale, cold skin reminds me of someone who I'd rather forget. Her electric green eyes stare at me through her limp hair, and even on the dimly lit street, her wretched snarl makes me uneasy in my own skin.

Veronica.

I roll down my window and hiss, "What are you doing out? Don't make me call Oliver and warn him, or better yet...the police."

She shrugs her bony shoulders. "He knows I'm coming. He invited me."

A sour burning in my stomach bubbles and makes me nauseous. "Oh, he did...did he? And the fact that you just fucking kidnapped the love of his life escaped his decision-making? What a fucking idiot! He has no regard for her safety and puts her in danger every chance he gets! I'm tired of him making stupid plays with her life!"

I can feel her disappointment from a distance. "You'll never compare to your brother. Oliver may hate me just as much as you do, but there's something off about you, kid. You're turning out just like me, no matter how much you don't want to admit it."

I scoff. "I'm not a drug-fueled pathetic waste of life."

She shrugs and adjusts the small bags over her shoulder. "There are many ways you can take after me besides that. You think you're owed something when you're not. Or maybe the fact that you let jealousy over-power you and take your freedom?"

I growl and hit the gas pedal, peeling the tires out in the street and leaving her behind. She's wrong; I'm nothing like her. A quick drive around Rockford and it hits me that I don't really even know her to believe that isn't true. I know I want answers from her and I've probably lost my only chance to know anything about her…or who my father truly is.

I need to distract myself.

"Hey, you." Lucy picks up the phone and coos. "If I didn't know better, I'd say you were addicted to my wicked ways now."

"Don't flatter yourself." I snicker and pull into my apartment complex parking lot. "I'm just looking for some fun."

"I told you when we first met that I'm not a whore."

I snort. "Since when does casual sex make you a whore?"

She thinks for a few moments in silence. I hardly care if I offend her—since I don't even *think* about her when we're together, anyway—but she's my ticket to easy sex without any strings attached. Lucy knows she wants to come over; she's just scared of what people will think if they find out.

"If people ask, you can say we're dating," I assure her. "I know you care about what people think for some fucking reason."

She scoffs. "Uh, I care if people see me as loose, thanks."

"It's literally 2018, Lucy. It's not like casual sex was born yesterday—it's more common in our youth than it was twenty years ago. Not to mention you shouldn't fucking care what other people think."

"Like you don't care what *Julie* thinks?"
Shit.

My throat tightens.

"I know you're in love with her."

All the air in my lungs evaporates and I'm left gasping for air. "I'm not in love—"

"You are."

"You don't know what you're fucking talking about."

"I don't?"

I shake my head and open the car door, taking in as much fresh air as I can handle. "I don't know what to tell you. I'm *not* in love with Julie."

"So, you'd be okay with never seeing her again?"

My fist slams against the dashboard in the car. "What is this? Have you already talked to Oliver?"

"No, why? Should I?"

I want to hang up on her, but I still want to unwrap her body in my bed. "Just...come over. I'll give you what you want if you give me what I want."

She makes an agreeing noise. "Oh, answers for sex, huh?"

I chuckle. "It's a fair offer."

Lucy isn't one to shy away from a challenge, and she's not going to run away from an opportunity that we both clearly know that she wants. After agreeing to meeting me in an hour, I'm in no rush to get upstairs to my apartment. I don't give a shit if I smell good or if my hair is clean; I'm going to fuck her, let her ask a few questions, and then make her leave.

Mac, on the other hand, has another plan for me.

My phone buzzes in my pocket and I don't recognize the number. I answer it because it could be Julie...I want it to be her so damn bad. "Hey, you little jerk," Mac snarls as I get the key into the apartment door. "I think it's about time we talk, don't you?"

I laugh into the phone. "You used your one phone call on *me*? How did you even get my number? Haven't you done enough damage to me already?"

He laughs. "I'm not callin' to fight. I'm callin' to talk about your good-for-nothing mother."

"What about her? Shouldn't you two just steer clear of each other until all of your legal bullshit dies down? You just fucking *kidnapped* someone."

He coughs and it sounds like a hollow drum in his lungs. "Your piss-ant brother made some kind of deal and got that bitch out for narcing on me for other shit."

"Sounds like a bad fucking deal," I snarl, starting to take the phone from my ear.

"I think it's time you learn the truth about your whore of a mother." He lowers his voice. "Got the time?"

"I have company coming." I suck air in through my teeth at the information I shouldn't have given him. "Maybe another time."

"Fine," he growls. "But you're gonna wanna know sooner or later. You're entitled to more than you realize."

ELEVEN
VERONICA

THE NIGHT SKY TAUNTS ME.

It hates me too, and I guess I don't blame it. Every-thing around me has fallen to pieces and I have no one to blame but myself. I can't even blame Mac because all he did was pretend to love me when I thought no one else really did. Colin always loved me; from the moment he looked at me, I knew my entire life was going to change. I didn't care about the same things anymore, I didn't enjoy life like I thought I would.

Oliver and Julie are talking about me as I walk away from them; Julie wants to find it in her heart to help me but honestly, I can't be helped. I've tried to help myself —Colin tried to save me and even Colin's father, Vic, wanted to keep me around. They hiss at each other and once I hit the dark pavement of the main road, my left foot is barely usable from being caught in the crossfire of a prison fight. It drags behind me a little, creating a scraping sound on the pavement.

I keep thinking Julie is going to call for me and the

sun will come out, shining down on the three of us and angels would sing.

Hallelujah!

But they don't.

None of that happens.

Oliver rushes her inside and I know I have to hold up my end of the bargain. I told Oliver I would be leaving town and I intend to do right by him at least once in my life. Once I'm far enough away from their eyesight and I find a bright streetlamp, I take the thick envelope from my bag and start to count the money inside.

Twenty thousand dollars.

That's exactly what he offered me.

He must really want me gone.

My heart burns and I shove the money back into the white envelope. I want to be the kind of person to march right back up there and stick it in his mailbox, but that's not even close to who I am. I want this money and I still feel like I deserve it. Colin promised to take care of me for life and that means something to me even after his death.

I see Colin Jackson everywhere I go.

For the first few years after he died, people on the street looked like him. I couldn't walk in the French Quarter without him haunting me. He followed me everywhere I went: every city we moved to and every town we passed through. He would wave at me from the side of the road, pass me in the grocery store, and find me in my dreams to tell me how ashamed he was to even know me.

I'll never forget the last thing he said to me before he died. A week before his accident, we met at that ritzy place, Dilaggio's, for our annual payment dinner. I agreed to have a nice dinner with him in exchange for that year's payoff money. The last dinner we had, he announced that since Oliver was old enough to make his own decisions about me, he wouldn't be providing any more money.

———

"YOU'RE FUCKING KIDDING ME," *I growl at him. "You've been paying me to stay away for ten years."*

Colin shrugs and picks up his wine glass. "Oliver is old enough to make up his own mind now. I haven't spoken badly of you and neither has Mrs. Atchley."

"What about your father?"

"I'm not sure I can say the same about him." He sucks in air through his teeth. "I hate to be so cold about this, but I can't keep giving you money. My father has frozen everything we both own and I'm left with my savings, which can't cover a yearly agreement anymore if I want to send Oliver to college."

I smack my hands on the table. "You can't do this to me! Mac will be pissed if I come back empty-handed, don't you care about me? I thought you loved me?"

"I did love you."

My heart burns in my chest. I fucking hate this sometimes but, in the end, I get what I want.

Always.

"Don't you care about Oliver?" He coughs and drinks from his wine glass again. "If you insist on taking this

money, his life will change and he won't be able to attend college."

"Your father will give in by then."

Colin shakes his head. "No, he won't. He's made it perfectly clear that unless I stop giving you money, Oliver and I will be cut off. I can't do that to my son."

I take a drink of water to chill my insides. "Our son."

"You can't claim him if you wouldn't be able to recognize him in a room full of people."

"Why are you doing this, really?"

He taps his fingers on the table. "I met someone."

A fire burns inside of me and I feel guilty for being jealous. I don't have a claim on him anymore, and the ten years I've spent apart from him haven't exactly been kind to me. Three hospital trips, six arrests, and a handful of dark secrets I'll take to my grave can make a person look mangled and torn.

That's me.

Veronica Anastacia Bennett.

"She hasn't met Oliver yet, but we're headed that way. I met her in Florida on business and we've been dating for almost a year. Not that I have anything to explain to you, but I wanted you to know."

I take another drink of water. "You mean, you wanted to rub it in my face."

"You left me. Let's not get it twisted around here."

His voice is so calm and unnerving that it pisses me off. "I bet she's the typical Colin Jackson type."

"And what does that mean?"

I take in a deep breath, ready to throw daggered words at him. "You know, blonde and willing with fake boobs and a red-lipstick smile."

"Like you, you mean?"

I lick the water from my dry lips. "Maybe in my younger days. I don't have fake boobs, though."

"I know that." He smiles and looks down at his empty plate. "But your smile was captivating."

The hardness of his voice shakes me to my core. "There must be something about me that you still love, Colin."

He shakes his head. "You're a stranger to me now. I'm still in love with the old you and I always will be. You pulled me from a life of greed and privilege and showed me the real side of things. You showed me true love, no matter for how long, and there was a time when I really felt like you weren't like everyone else. You showed me different. You wanted what I could buy you, not what was inside my heart and soul. Our life would have been perfect if you hadn't done what you've done."

"So it's all my fault? I'm to blame for everything?"

He stands up and hands a few bills to the waiter to pay for dinner. He knows better than to leave it on the table because I'll snatch it before I run. When his dark brown eyes look down at me, for the first time since we've met, he looks ashamed of me.

"Yes." His hands shove into his pockets. "You've created this mess, now you deal with it."

———

To be fair, Colin wasn't always this cold toward me. He was right—I created the mess and instead of dealing with it, I went to his father to get what I wanted. I had to do some pretty unimaginable things to and with Vic before he gave me triple the amount I usually got from

Colin to leave until he died. His clear instructions were that he would leave me more in his will so I could leave and never come back. I was never to speak of what we did to anyone—or the fact that we did it more times after that—and there's no way in hell I would want to. Vic died taking our secret to the grave...*all* of our secrets.

I'm too chicken to end my misery.

But I don't want to be this complete disaster anymore.

I'm done with excuses and I'm done with pity. No one owes me anything and the sooner I start to realize that, the better. I have to stand on my own two feet and stop blaming Colin for dragging me into this mess when I know damn good and well Mac and I were snorting shit before Oliver even came about.

Kissing him for the first time was magical.

Sex with Colin Jackson was...*cosmic*.

He always wanted more and the hungry look in his chocolate eyes melted me every single damn time. I know what it's like to not be able to resist a Jackson man; Julie has her work cut out for her in the future when Oliver starts working around beautiful women and jealousy roars its ugly head.

Maybe she won't. Maybe Julie isn't like me at all.

I see myself in her innocence and it's heart breaking.

Not realizing how far I've hobbled, the lights of a strip of businesses still open burns my eyes. A salon with multiple women underneath hair dryers is the first building I pass. I decide not to go in because I'm almost positive I look homeless or like I just got out of prison.

I *did* just get out of prison, thanks to Oliver.

He got me a deal to narc on Mac so I'd go free with a lesser charge and fines, then gave me money to run away.

That's what I'm the best at.

The next space is a karate school and my heart starts to burn again. I lean against the cold wall and watch my faint breath in the icy air, remembering the time Mac and I sat outside Casey's karate class and the first time he made me feel actually less than human.

———

"THAT'S THE KID?" Mac points across the parking lot from the dojo several ten-year-olds are piling out of. Their parents are smiling and having wonderful, comedic conversations about their children and trying to one-up the other people's kids. "He's fucking short."

I scoff and light a cigarette. The smoke fills my lungs and stings, burns then goes ice cold. "Who cares how tall he is? You're short and he's just like you."

"He ain't mine."

I throw the lighter at him. "He's yours, asshole."

"I know you were fuckin' Colin Jackson, I know that little jerk-off ain't mine. He's either his or—" Mac snorts and unzips his pants, letting his pudgy limpness fall out of his tattered jeans. "—why don't you show me how you fucked Grandpa Jackson?"

My entire body shivers. "What the hell are you talking about?"

"I seen you and I know it wasn't just once."

The shame that consumes me nearly bursts from my skin.

"You're disgusting, put that small dick away and leave me be. I didn't do anything like that, you sick fuck."

Mac snorts and pulls me toward him, his rough hands gripping the back of my hair and tugging backward. "I know you fucked him for more money, don't fucking lie to me anymore. If you wanted to be a whore, why didn't you say so? I would've put you to work a long time ago."

My fist meets his mouth and I grab as much cash from the glove box as I can before I run.

I don't realize what I've done until I'm halfway through the parking lot and I'm running toward the group of parents, screaming and flailing my arms. A sandy-haired man stops me and notices Mac running up behind me with anger bursting from every surface of his face.

"Give her back to me," he growls. "Don't be messing in other people's business."

The man pushes my broken body behind his. "Look, man, I don't know what's going on here, but she looks scared and you look pissed. Why don't you just walk away and give her some space?"

Mac steps forward and his fists clench into tight balls.

He's going to swing on him. This is all my fault. He's never spoken like that to me before; he's been rough and annoying at times, but he's never treated me like a piece of trash on someone's freshly cut and manicured lawn before.

"Mind your fucking business, jackass," Mac snarls. "Don't make me fuck you up in front of all these kids and make you look like a loser."

The man scoffs. "Walk away, man."

Another man steps up and crosses his arms over his chest. "Do what he says, prick."

Three more men puff out their chests toward Mac and

finally he backs down. The look of death he gives me makes me shake to my very core. I know this isn't the last I've seen of him, but the man who's guarding me makes me feel safe after what I've done.

"You okay?" He turns and looks down at me. "What happened?"

My body doesn't feel good. Once I hit more adrenaline, I'm able to force a smile and shake myself from the man's grasp. "Just a little spat, that's all. No need to worry. Thanks for the help." I start to walk off but he holds out his hands to stop me.

"That looked like more than just a spat."

I frown. "I'd rather just forget it ever happened and run off, if you don't mind."

He looks at me like he knows me. "Can I take you somewhere? I can give you a ride if you need to get to a safe place." A dirty blonde wraps her arms around his, but he doesn't miss a beat. "I don't think you should be walking around Rockford with that crazy jerk on the loose."

"We can give you a ride." The woman nods and smiles. "I'm Elena and this is my husband, Rodney. Oh, and this is our son, Casey." She broadens her smile and the same ten-year-old I was watching earlier wraps himself around her lower torso in shyness. "Casey, can you say hi?"

"Hi," he mutters. "Can we go home now? Oliver said I can come over and play."

My body ignites with curiosity. I know I shouldn't, but I get into the front seat next to Rodney, and Casey and Elena get into the backseat. They giggle and play games as we pull from the parking lot, and I notice that Mac is still seething in our van, creeping out of the parking lot after us.

I'm in for it now.

I can't let these innocent people pay the price for my mistakes.

"I really don't need to go that far," I say and look into the side mirror. Mac is directly behind us and I swear I can see his evil smirk from this far. "You can drop me off there." I point to a gas station across the road and Rodney pulls into the lot. Before he comes to a complete stop, I hop out and try to save them from Mac. "Thanks for the ride." I stick my head into the open window once he stops the car. "I appreciate the help."

Before any of them can reply, I scurry off into the gas station and wait for them to pull away. Poor little Casey in the backseat is so confused, and he should be.

His real mother was just two feet from him without him knowing it.

Without any *of them knowing it.*

Mac pulls into the parking lot and I step back outside. I wonder if I should've brought him something from inside to ease his mood, but he doesn't look all that pissed.

"No more spying on your demon spawns," he grunts when I hop back into the van with him. I wait for his hand to crash down on me. "Nothing good is coming out of spying on those little jerks. Look what happened just now."

I nod. "Okay."

"Good. It's just easier if you do what I say."

"Okay, Mac."

"That's more like it. The sooner you learn that I'm in charge here, the better."

He's in charge.

He's taken what's left of my freedom.

I'm finally a slave to more things than just cocaine and cigarettes.

I'm a slave to the one person in this world I shouldn't be around.

———

I PUSH myself off the dojo's outer wall and keep slowly walking down the street. I pass a laundromat, an insurance place, and the final building I come to is a place called The Tavern. It's a large bar with people standing outside smoking and laughing. The burn of alcohol has been absent in my throat for a few days, and I could use something to take the edge off right now.

Pushing the door open, the place is only half-full inside and I'm able to reach the bar with ease. The cocky, tattooed, and pierced lady bartender eyeballs me but never asks for my order. She keeps passing me by and ignoring me on purpose.

I snort. "I guess I look worse than I thought."

An old, scratchy woman's voice cuts through my ears. "You do look like you just hopped off the train transporting mental patients. Hello, Veronica."

When I look over at her, I can't believe my eyes.

Mrs. Atchley.

"Oh, it's you." I cough and tap the bar top with my fingertip. "Don't worry, I'm leaving town. I just need to wait until the morning when all the buses are back in business."

"I know. Oliver called me and asked that I look after you."

I blush. "He did? How did he know where I'd be?"

The older woman downs her double shot of whiskey and glares at me. "He's a smart kid. I always knew I raised him right. A water for this one." She looks at the bartender and nods her head toward me.

"You don't have to rub it in." I grind what's left of my teeth. "I'm trying to be different."

Mrs. Atchley laughs loudly. "Same story you've had for over twenty years…why is it any different now?"

"I don't know, it just is."

She looks into my eyes and frowns. "Dammit, I believe you."

"You do?"

She gulps down another double shot and sighs. "For some reason, I do. The look in your eyes isn't a look I've seen on you before when you'd try and come crawling back. I see truth in your eyes."

"That's because for once I'm being truthful."

The old woman stares at me with knowing eyes. She knows all the horrible things I did to Colin and Oliver; she knows my most shameful moments of my entire life. She's been there for them when I should've been, and I'm actually thankful that Oliver had her in his life when he couldn't have a real mother to love and nurture him.

That's all my fault.

She groans and stands up to stretch out her legs. "All right, come on. You're coming with me."

"I told Oliver I would leave town."

Her frail fingers wag at me, back and forth. "Not like that, you're not. I don't blame him for letting you walk away looking like that." Her cold eyes look my body up and down. "But I can't let you walk out of here without a clear conscience."

I sip the water the bartender puts in front of me.

"You've already done more than enough for me over the past twenty years. I hardly think you owe me anything else."

"*You* owe *me*, that's why I'm helping you. You owe me more than just humoring an old woman, let's not forget that." Her eyes narrow at me. "First, we need to get you into a hotel for the night and get you cleaned up. Then we can make a plan and I can let you go without feeling horrible about myself."

I frown at the water glass. "I don't want Oliver to hate you too."

The old woman scoffs and picks up a bright pink walking cane. "Grab my purse and let me tell you a little something about the son you left behind. He's loyal and I treated him well—he'll never forget that. What you couldn't give him, I tried my best to do. There isn't much I can do to make him hate me."

A smile finds my lips and I don't hide it. Mrs. Atchley is actually a remarkable woman, but I never gave her the chance to hear that from me. All I felt for her was betrayal because I thought she'd brainwashed Oliver against me and ripped his soul from mine. As time wore on and wore me down, though, I realized... she was the mother I couldn't be.

I owe her everything.

"If he finds out I didn't leave town—"

"I'm not scared of him." She gestures for me to follow her. "There's a middle-class, three-star hotel just around the corner. Where's your stuff?" She looks around and frowns at the lack of luggage trailing behind me. "It doesn't matter, we'll get you fixed up. We'll make a few stops along the way to pick up some clothes and shampoo…" She sniffs the air around me and shakes her head. "…and soap that doesn't contain someone else's DNA."

I blow out air from my lungs, making her short, gray, and curly hair blow in the light breeze. "Are you sure you want to do this? Why are you trusting me? Most people don't even want to be alone with me."

She hobbles out of the building and into the quiet, dark night. Once she hails a cab on the side of the road, she turns to me and wipes a tear from the corner of her eye.

"You missed out on raising a hell of a kid. I feel sorry for you that you didn't get to see it. Oliver is one of the best people I know, and it's just a tragedy that you had no part in that."

"This isn't comforting."

"It's not meant to be. I'm giving you a chance: a chance to make things right."

I snicker and she flips her coat over her small, fragile body. I shiver in the icy October air and hand her the purse she ordered me to grab. "He doesn't want to see me. He won't even speak to me like a human being, let alone forgive me and live happily ever after."

"Some things are never as they seem. He may surprise you…you have to try."

I think of Mac and what he would always say to me when I was feeling down.

Get over your bullshit and stand up for yourself. No one else is going to take better care of you than you. You know what you need and you know what you want.

Now go and get it.

TWELVE
BRANDON

I BARELY GOT any sleep the entire weekend; I was too busy worrying about the hearing and watching the minutes tick by on the clock as they counted down to the time I had to leave for work today.

Monday.

I hate Mondays now too.

Jesus, my palms are sweating and I'm so nervous that the next eight hours are going to be fucking torture. Heather tries her best to make me more comfortable, and I fucking thank her for that, but damn it if I'm not freaking the hell out.

I'm nothing more than what I am now.

"Hey, it's going to be okay." Her smile reaches me before she does. I let her wrap her arms around my neck and kiss my lips before faking a quick smile. "No matter what happens, I'll be here waiting for you. I got Rita—the owner of the dress shop—to give me an interview for some part-time work, so don't worry about things, okay?"

I growl. "I don't want you to get a job."

She scoffs because she doesn't care what I think about that. "Well, get over it. I want to have some money of my own and I want to help out around here. You don't get to just decide that you're the sole bread-winner of the house, do you? What am I even going to school for if I'll never work?"

She's right, but I don't fucking like it.

"Fine." I give up and put my hands into my pockets. "But only part-time. I don't want anything getting in the way of your bigger dreams, okay? You're going to school to get a better job than working part time in a dress shop, that's why you're going."

Her grunt makes me think she's accepted that this conversation is over.

As she leaves the room and doesn't bother looking back at me, I know she knows it's over.

When I shove my feet into the nicest, slickest black dress shoes I own and the smoothest gray suit that I've hardly ever worn, Heather's eyes light up when I enter the kitchen behind her. She shakes her head at my tie and runs back upstairs to fetch a darker version of the one I just had on.

"Thanks, babe." I smile and peck her lips. "What would I do without you?"

She snorts. "Crash and burn. Listen—" She snuggles into my chest and I like the way her body fits against the silky fabric of the suit. "—I meant what I said. No matter what happens today, I love you and nothing is going to change that. I don't care if we have to move to California or Florida or wherever we want...I'll always want to go with you."

I kiss the tip of her nose. "I love you too. I have to get going."

She narrows her eyes at me. "I mean it, Brandon. Walk tall and proud."

A chuckle escapes my mouth as I quickly kiss her cheek and grab my car keys. The drive into the office was normal but I sure as hell don't feel normal. It's like I'm hovering over my body in someone else's body and I'm screaming to get the hell out.

This is going to be a damn disaster.

I sit in the car for what seems like forever; my co-workers pass me and give me slight waves and nods as if they know the feeling of needing a fucking second before going into this place. No matter how I look at it, I agree with everyone. Heather is right, I don't need to work for a man who thinks it's his business to be up in my business like Vern is.

Speaking of…

A loud knock on my window startles me. Vern's round body leans down as I roll the window down and put the fakest smile on my face I have, but he isn't as fake about it as I am. His frown reaches eye level with me, but I keep my smile painted on my lips as much as I can.

"Something wrong?" His eyebrow rises.

I shake my head. "No, sir. Just soaking in the quiet before heading inside."

He grunts and pats the top of the car. "Are you sure that's it? You sure you're not nervous about your hearing?"

I scoff. "Why would I be? Julie and I want to be divorced, it's amicable. She'll be here and we aren't fighting, so really there's nothing to be nervous about."

"I guess we will find out." His expression is cold and he walks off without saying another word. The tension doesn't automatically leave with him and it holds onto me as long as it can before blowing away. He knows more than he's willing to tell me, and that scares me to my core. I want to be the man who doesn't care if he loses his job…a man who's confident enough to say that he'll be able to work it out and find a new job quickly, but that's not going to be the case.

I'm not a lawyer; I just pretend to be one.

Blowing out the air from my lungs, I watch Vern greet some of my co-workers and then enter the building. I give him another five minutes to get to his office before I slide from the car and slowly make my way inside. My office is on the third floor so it doesn't take long to get to and honestly, I thought something would jump out at me once I opened the door.

I half-expected to see the rest of my shit packed in boxes, waiting for me to arrive. Instead, the office is quiet and people will hardly look me in the eye. Even Carlie, my favorite secretary, can't stand to be near me for more than thirty seconds.

"Hey, what's going on around here?" I pull her aside after my second cup of coffee. "People are acting really fucking weird."

She blushes. "I'm not sure I know what you mean."

"Carlie." I jab her name at her. "Just tell me."

The small-framed woman pushes me inside of my office and closes the door behind her. She's nervous; the words that want to escape her mouth know better because the look on my face isn't the friendliest I'm sure. She pushes her black-rimmed glasses up her nose and finds the courage to look at me, her eyes are wide and unsure.

"There's a rumor around the office that you're getting a divorce." She bites her bottom lip and searches my eyes for answers. "Everyone is talking about it."

"Fucking office gossip," I groan and find my desk chair to fall into. "I can't believe this shit. What exactly are they saying?"

She shrugs. "Just that. Oh, and that you've cheated on your wife with someone in the office."

Shit.

"Who? Who are they talking about?" I demand.

Carlie is uneasy and quaintly sits in the chair across from me. "They aren't naming names, I don't think anyone knows for sure. Is it true?"

I run my fingers through my hair and lean my head back on the chair. "Just the part about my divorce. I didn't know it was public knowledge and I definitely didn't fucking know it was an obligation to tell the entire world about it."

She blushes. "I think people should mind their own business."

I smile at her because I'm thankful for her words, regardless if they're true or not. "Thanks, Carlie. I appreciate that. Is there a rumor that I'm getting fired by chance?"

She shakes her head. "I haven't heard that one."

"Good."

Her smile is small and dorky but it comforts me just the same. I feel bad that I haven't taken the time to get to know her better—not that I was doing much of getting to know anyone except Rachel around here—and I find a smile to suit hers.

"You're a good person," I say. "Most people around here would join in the gossip and twist and turn it into something ridiculous."

She giggles. "It already is something ridiculous. I just know how the rumor mill around here works and it hurts people. I nearly quit last year when that rumor went around about me and Kate down in the mailroom, I couldn't take the stares and the talking behind my back."

I scratch my chin and kick my feet on the desk. "What rumors about you and Kate?"

She laughs. "Seriously? Well, I can't blame you for not knowing...you had your own drama going on it seems. Before it was public knowledge that I'm gay—" I don't mean to, but I gasp and my eyebrows rise. "—Kate and I were seeing each other. No one knew about either one of us and it was still pretty new to the both of us too. It got so bad that Kate left and works for the post office now."

I snort. "At least she found a job."

Carlie shakes her head. "Yeah, but at the expense of what? Other people's entertainment?"

"Jesus, I didn't think of it like that. I didn't even know you're gay...where was I when this happened?"

She laughs again and smooths out her pink dress. "Wrapped up in your own rumors, I guess. It doesn't matter, I just know how these things can hurt someone.

I didn't feel like I had a place for an entire year and then something else happened and Kate and I weren't a hot commodity anymore." The smile brightens on her face as she thinks about her girlfriend. "I'm not sorry it happened, though."

"You're not?"

She smirks. "No, I'm not. It brought Kate and I closer together and now we're talking about moving in together. It's funny how these things can make or break a relationship."

"You can say that again. My current girlfriend is being way too cool about this, it's freaking me out."

Carlie's head vibrates from the new information. "Current girlfriend? So, you're with the person you cheated with?"

"Hell no," I blurt out, "that one is long gone from my mind. I messed up my marriage with her and sent her on her way. I'm a different person now and I'm still paying for who I was back then. Julie and I—Julie is my wife…soon to be ex-wife—we're in a good place and she gets along with Heather, my current girlfriend, just fine."

Carlie blows out air from her lungs. "That's quite a lot to process."

The moment our eyes meet, our laughter fills the room. "It's all fucked up." I hold my stomach and she continues to laugh with me. "It's crazy how much one bad decision fucks up our entire life."

"That's life, though." She stifles her laughter. "You can only be as good as you are today."

She's right.

She's absolutely fucking right.

You can only be as good as you are today.

And today I'm a fucking warrior.

"You can get through this," Carlie's voice breaks through my thoughts. "Mr. Trumbull is a scary guy, but he can't take your love from you."

I narrow my eyes at her. "Did he try and take yours from you?"

She smiles and stands up, smoothing out her dress again. "He gave us an ultimatum. Kate had to find another job or else he would fire us both."

"How can he just do something like that?"

She walks to the door and turns to smile at me before leaving the office. "It's his building, it's his company. He's a powerful guy, Brandon, you know that. Kate didn't want to work for him if he was going to be that way anyway."

"I'm sorry that happened to you guys, Carlie. You're a good person." I smile. "Thanks for taking the time to talk to me about your situation."

"Anytime." She winks and shuts the door behind her. I don't know if it's because I know she isn't into men or what, but her wink means nothing to me. If anything, it makes me feel better about upcoming events rather than turning me on. I want Heather to be here and make everything okay so badly that I think about calling her and asking her to tag along to the hearing, but I decide that would make things a lot more complicated to have her hanging around while Vern is grilling me about Julie.

It's going to be awkward enough having *Julie* there.

The clock fucking hates me too. It's ticking away so damn slowly that it's killing me. I can't nap on my sofa because there's no way I can sleep; I don't want to work because I'm not giving Vern any of my time until I know I have a job to come back to; I search the internet on my computer for various things to try and keep my mind off of the hearing.

I check my social media accounts and text a few people, but no one responds. My groan echoes in the room and comes back to haunt me...I'm literally alone right now.

Lost in my thoughts, two o'clock finally rolls around and I told Julie I'd meet her in fifteen minutes in front of the courthouse. Vern's building is only three blocks from there and I hardly want to see his fucking face before the hearing, so I sneak out of my office and give an assuring nod toward Carlie before stepping on the elevator to head down.

"Brandon." Vern's rough voice finds me in the elevator. "Funny meeting you here."

Oh, fuck you, Vern.

I fake a chuckle. "Yes, sir. Are you headed to the courthouse too?"

"I am, indeed. Care to join me?" The elevator doors open and he steps out first, gesturing toward the employee parking lot where his Mercedes is parked.

I look around to see who is watching us. "No, thanks. I was planning on walking over to clear my head and all that."

"It's November, kid...it's freezing out there."

I smile. "I know, I have an overcoat in my car. I'll grab it and meet you there, okay?" He accepts my bullshit and waddles to his overpriced car. Once he's sped off, I reach my car and open the trunk to take out the dry-cleaning bag with my overcoat inside. It's black and long and suits me well—at least for my current mood. I'm hovering over my body as I throw it on and lock the car back up...the time isn't creeping anymore and in just under an hour my life will come to a screeching halt.

The walk to the courthouse isn't peaceful. It's filled with questions zooming around inside my head that I know I'll have the answers to shortly, but damn if it doesn't fuck me up in the meantime. My phone buzzes inside my pocket and I quickly check it just in case it's Vern—by some grace of a fucking miracle—canceling the lunch and wishing me good luck.

Heather's name pops up and it excites me that she's worried just like I am.

HEATHER

Good luck today. I love you.

I smash my fingers on the phone as quickly as I can.

I love you too. I'll call you after.

She doesn't answer back and I'm okay with that. The less distraction for me right now, the better. As I walk up to the steps of the building, I see Julie walking up in the opposite direction looking just as nervous as I am. When she sees me, I force a small wave and wait for her to join me. I know she's pissed that she even has to do something like this and no amount of apology is going to suffice for this shit now. I've exhausted every angle of getting her to forgive me that I know...now it's just going to take time.

Fuck time.

Time hates me.

Time is what got me into this mess.

Well, that…and breaking the rules of protecting the one you love.

I didn't protect Julie.

I preyed on her.

"Are you ready?" Her voice catches me.

I clear my throat. "Not really."

Her giggle makes me feel a little better, but the image of Vern smashing my head in with his fists kills the mood. Julie notices my hesitation and surprisingly takes my hand into hers, tugging me up the stairs behind her.

"We can do this." She smiles and looks around the lobby of the courthouse once we're inside. "Why isn't Heather here?"

"I told her not to come," I say. "She doesn't need to be here for this. I'm closing a chapter in my life I'd rather not have follow me into this life, ya know?"

She sighs. "As much as I don't want to admit it, and not that I'm thrilled that this happened…" She puts her things into the small gray bin to be scanned by security. "…think about what our lives would be like if this *didn't* happen. Think about what it would be like if I never left, if I never met Oliver or you never met Heather…in some sort of messed-up way…this is where we're supposed to be."

"You don't have to try and make me feel better, Julie: I know I did a fucked-up thing."

She shakes her head. "I'm *not* trying to make you feel better. I'm trying to be a good friend."

A good friend.

That's all I ever wanted her to be.

Now here we are.

Standing in front of our past and struggling to keep our future in our hands.

THIRTEEN
JULIE

THE COURTROOM IS stuffy and full of people—people who look like they're tired of fighting and can't stand the person next to them—and Brandon and I still hold hands as we sit down and he nods toward an older, bald man like he knows him. The man looks at me and smiles, but I act like I don't notice him and he goes back to his business at the front of the room. Brandon squeezes my hand to let me know everything will be okay, but this is awkward and embarrassing.

"All of these people are getting divorces?" I whisper toward him.

He nods. "Yes, they are. Today this particular judge only sees divorce cases."

I gulp. "What if he denies our divorce request?"

Brandon snickers and shakes his head. "He won't, it's just a formality. He's just the mediator to make sure both sides are fair and amicable. It's harder when there's children involved, but thank God we don't have that issue."

I glare at him. "That would've been a hard trick to come back from."

"Jesus, Julie." He lets go of my hand and scowls. "I was a dick back then but I wouldn't have tricked you into getting pregnant. I just wanted to marry you, not be your baby daddy."

Before I can argue with him, the bailiff enters and everyone stands while the judge gets situated. He starts calling names from the top of his docket list and two by two, people skulk toward the lecterns and their entire lives are laid out for everyone to see and hear. I wish Oliver were here with me, but Brandon is doing a pretty good job of calming me down, even though he's the reason I'm here in the first place.

"Brandon Whitehouse v. Julie Whitehouse." The judge calls out our names.

Brandon curses underneath his breath and stands up, smoothing out his nice suit. He looks down at me and frowns because he knows I can't move my feet. After tugging me upward, he holds my hand down the aisle and places me at a lectern opposite of him.

"Brandon Whitehouse?" The judge looks at Brandon and he nods.

When the judge looks at me, there's pity in his eyes. "Julie Whitehouse?"

I cringe and nod. I don't know about what else was said after that because I zoned out on a crooked painting on the left side of the room. I hear Brandon conversing with the judge and then the old, bald man that he nodded at before steps up beside me and smiles.

"Mr. Trumbull, nice to see you again." The judge smirks. "Are you the counsel for Mrs. Whitehouse?"

The old man nods and straightens his jacket. "That I am, Your Honor. We're asking for spousal maintenance and for property as well, sir."

Brandon gasps and his knuckles are white from hanging onto the lectern too hard. "What are you talking about? We never discussed this." He looks at the judge and frowns. "This is uncontested, and Julie isn't asking for anything—right, Jules?"

I nod and say nothing.

"Well, then, if that's the case then we can proceed," the judge says, and my mind goes blurry again. I think about Oliver and imagine him sitting in the chairs behind me, waiting for me to come back to him. This is crazy, I shouldn't have come. I should've let Brandon take care of this like he said he would. I don't belong here.

"If I may—" Mr. Trumbull starts to say, but something inside of me clicks.

"I don't want you to speak for me." I look at him and frown. "I don't even know who you are."

The judge's eyebrows rise. "Is that true, Trumbull?"

"I'm a last minute change of counsel, sir. Mrs. Whitehouse has never met me."

"I don't have a counsel," I tell the judge. "What is going on here?" I look to Brandon for help, but he shrugs his shoulders and hangs his head. "Can you please sit down? I don't want you up here with me," I say to Mr. Trumbull, and he does what I ask without question. I look back at the judge and get nervous again.

What would Oliver want me to do?
Fight for yourself!

I clear my throat. "May I speak to you?" I ask the judge. He nods and waves his hand for me to proceed. "This is a big mess...I just don't want to be married to Brandon anymore. Nothing bad has happened, I don't want anything of his...I just want to be free."

Brandon smiles at me and the judge starts listing off legal jargon that makes my head fuzzy. Before I know it, he's taking me by the arm and leading me out of the courtroom and back into the main lobby.

"What's going on? Is that it?" I look back at the closed door behind us. "What happened?"

He laughs. "We're divorced, that's what happened."

"Just like that?"

"Just like that. Well, once the judge signs the paper-work and I do a few more legal paperwork things then yeah, just like that."

"Is it weird that I feel a little sad about it?" I chuckle. "I mean, it's an odd feeling but I feel like a part of me is missing now."

"We were best friends before all of this, Jules, it's only natural to be sad." He looks at the door opening and Mr. Trumbull emerges from the courtroom and smiles at the two of us like nothing happened.

"Well..." Trumbull claps his hands together. "A little unorthodox, but you got what you wanted, right? You two are single again. How does it feel?"

Brandon scowls at him. "What the fuck was that in there?"

Trumbull doesn't bat an eyelash. "I figured the least I could do for this poor girl was help her out, but if she doesn't want anything, she doesn't want anything."

"I really don't." I narrow my eyes and cross my

arms over my chest. "I think you owe Brandon an apology."

Trumbull laughs loudly and several people stop to stare. "Let's just get to lunch, shall we? My guest should be meeting us soon and I'm famished."

To my surprise, I shake my head and refuse. "I'm sorry, but no thanks. I have somewhere to be."

"Jules..." Brandon smiles at Trumbull and takes me aside. "You gotta come to lunch. Trumbull will fire me if he doesn't get what he wants. He's my boss."

"It sounds like he's going to fire you no matter what," I hiss. "This is too jacked up. At least let me call Oliver—"

Trumbull clears his throat behind us. "Ready, kids?"

Brandon nods and tugs me beside him, tucking my arm around his and holding me so I can't run. I didn't tell Oliver where I was going and a late lunch with my now ex-husband and his boss isn't exactly going to make him feel very good. I know Oliver has a secret understanding with Brandon about something to do with me, but they are getting along so I know not to push it.

He tucks me into the backseat of Trumbull's black Mercedes and slides in next to me. We don't drive very far, and he pulls the car into the parking lot of Dilaggio's and parks in a spot near the front doors. Trumbull turns to us and grins. "The original place I wanted to take you kids has a private party booked, so this will have to do. Do you like the chocolate cake here?"

He's looking at me so I sweetly smile and nod. He grunts and turns the car off and Brandon unbuckles my seat belt, nearly pushing me out of the door. I feel like

I'm walking on air as we follow Trumbull inside and get seated at a table near the windows. Trumbull orders a bourbon but Brandon tells the waiter that he and I will have water, nothing more.

"So, how does it feel to be divorced?" Trumbull laughs. "I'm sorry we never got the chance to meet, honey. I'm Vernon Trumbull."

I nod. "I know who you are. Thank you for lunch."

He purses his lips. "Oh, she's a little firecracker, Brandon. How did you lose this one?"

Brandon coughs into his hands. "I cheated on her with someone who doesn't matter to me and pushed her away. I lost a good thing." He smiles over at me. "But we're still friends and that's all right by me."

Trumbull grunts. "I see. I don't take kindly to cheating, Brandon."

Before I know it, I shake my head and scoff at the man who is berating my friend. "Excuse me, not to be rude but—" Brandon squeezes my leg underneath the table to get me to shut up. "—how is this any of your business?"

Vern's eyes darken as the waiter brings his drink and he gulps it down, gesturing for another. "Oh, Miss Priss, it's my business. Don't you worry your naïve little head, I know what he's done to you and I intend to make him answer for his bullshit."

Brandon gulps loudly next to me. "What do you mean? What do you think you know?"

Trumbull looks past us and I smell a suffocating amount of designer perfume. Heels click against the floor like a clock ticking: methodical and with purpose.

"Daddy?" a woman greets Trumbull and he stands up to hug her. "What's this about?"

Trumbull clears his throat and pulls out a chair for her. I look over at Brandon and his face is so pale I think he's going to pass out. My eyes follow where his gaze ends and I instantly share his fear.

Rachel.

As she nervously chuckles, my eyes fall to her bulging midsection.

Rachel is *pregnant.*

"What the fuck?" Brandon hisses next to me, but only I hear him. I grab his hand underneath the table and he squeezes the life out of it. I want Oliver so badly right now; he's always good in situations of this…*caliber.* Even *Heather* would be a better choice than me. I just want to cry and scream and pull Brandon away to save him from this.

He looks over at me and tears form in his eyes.

"So, let's have it." Vern downs another bourbon and Rachel can't look at me or Brandon. "Help me understand how this happened."

Brandon growls. "How *what* fucking happened?"

"I know your entire story, Brandon. I know what you've done and I know what resulted from it." Vern looks over at his daughter's growing stomach. "And now I want to know what you intend to do about it."

I can't listen to this.

My legs won't work to stand up and run away so I'm trapped next to Brandon—who is losing every inch of his freedom and life as the seconds tick by—and there's nothing I can do for him. Rachel looks nervous as Vern leans into the table to spew his hate toward Brandon more.

"Let me tell you how this is going to go," he scolds. "You're going to marry my daughter and do right by her, like you should've done to your *actual* wife, or I'll make your life a living fucking hell."

Brandon scoffs. "I fucking quit, then, before you go any further and threaten to fire me. Who the fuck do you think you are coming here like this and accusing me of...*that*?" Brandon's voice rises and people start to look around to see us.

Vern looks directly at me. "Tell me the truth. You have no loss in this since I know you've moved on and got rid of this pathetic waste of space."

"And just how do you fucking know that?" Brandon's ears are steaming and he lets go of my hand because he knows his grip is cutting off my circulation.

"Oliver Jackson is a client of mine—he's put her name on everything he owns." Vern laughs and sizes Brandon up with one look. "She lucked out, too, because I would've advised him against it until he told me her story and how much he loves her. I put two and two together, mentioned your name, and he spilled his guts about everything." Brandon growls and looks down at me like it's my fault. Vern laughs harder and Rachel shakes her head. "Looks like Miss Priss traded up...way, *way* up."

Brandon stands up, ready to pounce. "You son of a bitch."

"Brandon," I calmly say his name and pull him back down next to me. "Don't cause a scene." The hate and anger that seeps from his skin is burning me, but I grab his hand again anyway and squeeze it as hard as I can to let him know he's not alone. I turn to Vern and shake my head. "After I tell Oliver about this, I'm sure you'll be losing him as a client."

"Not if I tell him your little secret." Vern's lips curl into a snide smile. "He doesn't know that you two were married, does he? I mentioned your hearing and he didn't know what I was talking about."

Panicked, I squeak and start to reach for my phone to call Oliver. "Don't worry, Miss Priss, I didn't spill your secret. I have leverage against you now—that's how the real world works."

I narrow my eyes. "Are you *threatening* me?"

Vern smiles. "I'm just stating a fact, little girl." His dark eyes go back to Brandon. "As for you…You're fired. So fucking fired. You seduced my daughter and ruined her life. You're never going to work for another firm again as long as I live, and trust me, you'll be paying for this fucking kid."

Rachel whines. "Daddy, let's just go."

Now it's *my* turn to stand up. I don't care who's looking at us or who can hear us. I don't even care if Oliver is standing behind me, because he's going to be proud of what I'm about to say.

"Don't *ever* call me little girl again. Don't call me Miss Priss or any other vulgar, bullshit, and chauvinistic name. You don't know me and you sure as hell don't know your own daughter. Yes, Brandon cheated on me with Rachel. Yes, it was more than once. It destroyed me and it took a long, long time to rebuild myself. But if you think your slutty ass daughter wasn't part of that, you're a fucking waste of space yourself."

Brandon stands up and throws his arm over my shoulder. "Listen to the woman, she knows what she's talking about. Your daughter fucked half of the office— maybe you should spend more time on who she's opening her legs for instead of accusing only *me*. If that kid is mine…" Brandon points to Rachel's stomach. "I'll step up and do what's right. Either way, I fucking quit like I said before."

"I already fired your sorry ass," Vern growls. "You'll be hearing from me for a DNA test, boy."

Brandon scoffs. "I'll be by to clean out my office in the morning." He takes my hand and starts to tug me away from the table, but I have a chance to glare at Rachel as we pass. She still looks nervous and I know it's because she doesn't know who the father of her baby is herself.

I don't have any more room inside of me to worry about any other lost cause.

Halfway down the sidewalk, Brandon stops and tips his head to the sky and screams loudly into the open air. People walking the other way stop and stare at us but I don't care; I join him for a few seconds until our eyes meet and we start laughing.

"What are you going to do?" I say through my laughter. "You're so screwed."

"That kid isn't mine, Jules." He holds his stomach. "Well, I'd be surprised if it is. Anyway, I'll honor what I said if it's mine, don't worry about that."

"I'm not worried." I smile at him. "I know you're different now."

He nods and wraps his arm over my shoulders again, leading me back toward the courthouse. "When we get back, I'll give you a ride home. I have to get home to Heather and tell her what's happened."

"Is she going to be upset?"

I feel the love he has for her burst into the air, replacing his angst in front of us. "Nah, we've already talked about this. The baby thing will be new for her, but…" He stops and stands in front of me, looking down into my eyes. "She loves me enough to stand by my side. We don't have secrets; that's what I love most about her."

My heart sinks.

I have to tell Oliver where I've been.

I have to tell him *everything*.

FOURTEEN
HEATHER

THERE'S nothing I can do but sit in the house and quietly wait for Brandon to come home. I try not to bite my fingernails in suspense and I really, *really* try not to blow up his phone looking for answers. It's been hours since the hearing and he hasn't sent me a single word of how thing are going. I think about texting Julie and asking her but refrain from damaging that relationship too. Dozens of fireflies are buzzing around inside my head right now, and though they're harmless...I can't save myself from *myself*.

Finally, three hours after the hearing was scheduled for, Brandon calls me and I can't answer the phone quickly enough.

"Hey," he greets me, "what are you doing?"

"I'm waiting for you," I say quickly and jump up to look outside. "Where *are* you?"

He groans and I hear Julie talking in the background. "Well, shit sort of hit the fan. Can you meet Julie and me at Berk's Café? We didn't exactly get to eat lunch and we're starving...Julie asked if you wanted to join us so I can tell you everything, because we know you're dying to know."

I blush and I'm a little jealous. "I guess...are you there now?"

"Yeah, we're here. You want something to drink? I suggest something with alcohol in it."

The air I'm holding in my lungs is spent, so it leaks into the space in front of me. "Oh, it's going to be *that* kind of news. I'm not sure we both should be drinking, so you go ahead and I'll come down as soon as I get ready."

He scoffs. "Babe, come as you are. You know I love you no matter what."

I blush because Julie heard him say that to me. I expect his tone of voice to change and get all squirrely like he's embarrassed, but he coos on. "I want you here, Heather. I missed you like fucking crazy today. I almost called you like seventeen times."

"Me too!" I smile and start undressing while cradling the phone. When I reach the purple room, I drop the clothes into the wicker laundry basket and sift through my drawers for skinny jeans and my favorite blue blouse. The silk against my skin will make me colder since the weather's fallen to subzero temperatures, but that's what they make cute black pea coats for.

"Hi, Heather!" Julie squeals in the background. "Come join us!"

I laugh instead of scowl, which is still a new feeling for me. "I'm getting ready—I'll see you in ten minutes. Don't do anything fun without me," I warn him. I hang up before I say "I love you" and I know I'm going to regret that later. I find a pair of brown leather knee-high boots and smash them on before grabbing my handbag and car keys.

My phone rings as I get into my car and buckle my seat belt. It's a number I don't recognize, but I get a stinging feeling in my stomach that I really shouldn't ignore it.

"Hello?" I turn the car on and place my bag in the seat next to me.

"Heather Michaels?" a woman on the other end says. "This is Rita Pardue, the owner of Rita's Boutique downtown. Is this a good time?"

Not really!

I swallow hard. "Yes! How are you, Rita?"

Her laugh is big and boastful. "Oh, honey, it's been a day. I hear you're looking for some part-time work? I'd like to talk to you about that if you have the time tomorrow."

"Yes, I absolutely have the time. When do you want to meet?"

She shuffles papers around for a few seconds and hums to herself. I like that she's loose and free when talking to a complete stranger. "I can see you around three if that works for you."

"I don't have classes tomorrow, so that works. Thank you so much, Rita!" My smile is big and almost embarrassing if anyone were around.

"Well, thank you, darlin'." It sounds like someone walks into the shop when a bell dings. "I'll be right with you!" She comes back to me and sighs. "I really need the help, as you can tell. I'll see you tomorrow!"

"Yes, ma'am." I hang up before I can embarrass myself any further. I turn the radio up as loud as I can and sing loudly the entire way to Berk's Café to meet Brandon and Julie. I hate being so upbeat when he might not be, but I can't help it…things are finally starting to come up Heather for once.

Julie waves me over to their table when she spots me nearly fifteen minutes later. Brandon stands up and wraps his arms around me, holding me so tightly it hurts to take a deep breath. He doesn't want to let go of me and that's a little concerning; it's like he's holding onto a butterfly so it can't fly away.

"I missed you," he whispers in my ear. "I love you."

I clear my throat and sweetly smile as he pulls away. I'm still a little awkward about returning those words to him and it's not like I don't feel it the same way he does…it's just different when his perfect ex-girlfriend— no, *ex-wife*—is sitting at the table cooing at the two of us.

"It's so great to see you!" Julie giggles and stands up to greet me. Her small body clutches onto mine for a weird, quick hug. "Here, sit down."

I sit down next to Brandon and he calls the waitress to our table. "What do you want to drink?" His eyes burn into mine. He's trying to get me drunk and I want to know why.

"Just water." I nod at the girl who steps to us and then steps away just as fast.

Julie takes a swig of a brown beer bottle and her smile shines at me. "Did you have any finals today?"

I shake my head. "No, I stayed home all day."

Brandon's face falls. "Oh, hey, I'm sorry for leaving

you alone all day. I just thought it would be weird if you tagged along to that divorce hearing—"

My lips smack together in annoyance at how much the two of them are dancing around the information that I want to know. "And how did that go?"

Julie and Brandon look at each other but neither one of them answers me.

"Brandon?" I glare into his gray eyes. "How did it go? What happened?"

He takes a drink of his dark liquor and frowns. "Well, we're divorced now." He nods at Julie and she raises her beer bottle toward him. "So that's over. Trumbull took us to that late lunch bullshit and we got into an argument. I quit my job."

I know he's waiting for me to throw a tantrum.

I have a better idea.

My hand finds his arm and squeezes. "Are you okay?"

He looks a little surprised and glances over at Julie, who excuses herself to the bathroom to give us some much-needed privacy. "You're not pissed?"

I shake my head. "I just care if you're okay. What did you argue about?"

He downs the rest of his drink and motions for another one. "Rachel is pregnant."

What. The. Hell.

"Rachel...the girl you cheated on Julie with? How far along is she? Is it yours? Is that why your boss fired you? Why didn't you tell me this before?"

He holds up his hands in defeat. "Whoa, slow down. I don't know how far along she is, but she was definitely showing. I don't know if it's mine and Trumbull threatened me with a paternity test, but I don't fucking care. Oh, and I quit, I didn't get fired."

I lick my lips and try to understand. "What are you going to do?"

He sighs and rubs the bridge of his nose. "I'm going to do the right thing and take that paternity test, and if the baby is mine, I'm going to help take care of it."

"And if it's not?"

His lips turn into a wicked grin. "How do you feel about California?"

"Like, moving there?" I start to panic because I haven't told him my good news about Rita's yet, and I don't want to ruin whatever mood he's currently in. He's not going to like it if I get a job when he's just lost his, especially if he didn't really want me working in the first place. I pocket my good news for later so I can see what's going to happen before I throw a dagger and burst his happiness bubble.

"Yeah, like moving there. I can poke around for an entry-level job at a firm out there and we can just pick up and leave. I'm on a month-to-month lease at the townhouse, we both have cars so we can drive across county, and I have enough money in savings that we could find a place and live for a few months if I can't find a job before we go."

His fingers intertwine with mine and there's so much hope in his eyes it's hard to say no. "You've thought a lot about this...you've got an entire plan worked out."

He shrugs. "It's not a perfect plan, but it's a plan."

I know he wants me to say I'll go with him, no questions asked.

I know what he wants from me.

Say it, Heather. Say it!

"I'll go wherever you are." I smile and let him wrap his arms around me, squeezing me into a bear hug. I can't let him down, not when he's done nothing but be good and kind to me. What kind of horrible person would I be if I took this away from him? I told myself that I would treat him differently than I treated Oliver and I meant it. "But, what about school?"

"You can transfer."

"What about all of our stuff?"

"We can hire a moving company to bring it out."

"What about Julie and Oliver? Harley? Your friend Nate?"

He grunts and leans back in his chair. "Oliver will understand. Julie said she'd talk to him about getting my job back for me, but I don't want him to."

"How can he get your job back for you?"

Julie comes back to the table and eyeballs us to make sure it's safe to return. "Oliver does business with his boss, I guess," she says. "At least, that's what that jerk said."

I laugh and welcome her back with a smile. "Brandon wants to move to California if Rachel's baby isn't his," I tell her, and she doesn't look surprised that he told me all about Rachel and her surprise bundle of joy growing inside of her.

"That sounds fun." She giggles and checks her phone. "Oh, Oliver is wondering where I am. I better get going soon." She turns to Brandon and nods. "Thanks for taking care of everything today. I know it was your fault to begin with but still, you stepped up and I'm thankful for that change in you. I could count on you today and that means something to me. Take care of him, okay?" Her gaze is on me now, and Brandon and I both sit with open mouths looking at her. "What?"

Brandon laughs. "You're fucking crazy, you know that? She told off my boss, first of all, and stuck up for me, which is something the old Julie never would've done. Old Julie didn't like confrontation."

Julie stands and puts her bag over her shoulder. "I guess none of us are the same people we were six months ago, are we?" She winks at him and pats me on the shoulder as she passes to leave. We watch her go like a sunny day has just turned into a thunderstorm.

He claps his hands together. "Hey, wanna go home? I want to veg out and watch stupid movies with you on that big ass TV I just bought."

I groan. "Sounds like a perfect night."

"Hey, I'm sorry you don't get to go to that fancy Children's Gala thing for my work. I know you were looking forward to bumping elbows with some of the rich and semi-famous of New York." His laugh is genuine as he throws cash on the table and leads me out of the café. The waitress waves at us and Brandon returns it as he guides me outside. I didn't get a chance to even take off my pea coat so I'm instantly warm, and as his overcoat swirls around him, I can't help myself but blurt out my good news.

"I have an interview at Rita's Boutique tomorrow at three."

He fixes his collar and smiles. "That's great! Is it part time?"

I nod. "Yes, it will work around my classes."

He kisses the tip of my nose and leads me to the parking lot where my car is parked next to his. When he opens my door for me, I expect an attitude of some sort, but he never lets it free. "I'm happy for you—things are looking up for you, babe. I guess we might have to stay in Rockford after all."

"What about you? I thought you said Trumbull would blacklist you?"

His eyes darken and it sends weird vibes down my spine.

"I'll talk to Jackson; maybe he has some ideas."

I let him place me in the car and shut the door behind me. I roll down the window and he kisses my lips before grazing my cheek with his fingers.

"You said you would go wherever I am, right?"

I nod.

His sexy grin quickens my heart.

"My home is wherever you are. If Rachel's baby isn't mine and you choose to stay here and work and go to school, I'll stay here with you. Don't worry about me. I love you and there's nothing that's going to take that away. I'll meet you at home, okay?"

He shuts the door and gets into his car, waving at me as he starts his car and drives off.

Love is making life complicated.

And I wouldn't have it any other way.

FIFTEEN
OLIVER

FINALLY.

Julie's name pops up on my phone and I waste no fucking time answering it.

"Where are you?" My voice is strained. "Why haven't you been answering my calls?"

"I'm almost home, I'm sorry. I wasn't paying attention."

Not paying attention?

Pushing my anger back down inside of me, I try to understand enough where I'm not snapping at her and causing a fight for no reason.

A door shuts and she's walking quickly, with purpose. "I just want you to be safe," I say and listen to her soft breathing in my ear. "Veronica's still out there, you know."

"She's not going to do anything to me," Julie says, and a faint ding enters the phone call. "I may have been wrong before, but I'm not wrong now. She's broken, Oliver—she's done being the villain."

"Baby, I know you want to believe that..." Someone's outside the apartment door shuffling around, so I get off the sofa to investigate. When I open the door, Julie is standing in front of me with the phone still to her ear.

She blushes. "I was going to surprise you."

I hang up the phone and shove it into my jeans pocket. "You're always a surprise to me." She beams as I tug her inside and wrap my arms around her. "How was your day?"

She pulls away from me and shuts the front door. "We need to talk about something."

Shit. I hate that fucking sentence.

"Okay." My lips flatten. "Do I need to sit down?"

She nods and leads me back to the sofa where she places her body dangerously close to mine and her strawberry shampoo is making me dizzy. I have to remind myself that she wants to talk about something and it doesn't sound good...but her electric blue eyes are calling to me.

Oliver.

Oliver.

"Oliver?" Julie giggles. "Are you with me?"

Oh, I'm with you, baby.

I clear my throat. "I'm here. What do you want to talk about?"

The air around us grows tense as she thinks about which part of her story she wants to tell me first. Carefully, her mouth opens and closes and a chill runs down my spine.

I know what she's about to tell me.

Except that she fucking *doesn't*.

"What are our plans for tonight?" Her milky skin flushes. "I want to spend the night with you doing something cheesy."

How about spending the night telling me all about your marriage?

I lick my lips and focus on her crystal blue eyes. "Don't you have more finals tomorrow?"

She shakes her head. "No, I made a special arrangement with my professors. I took all of my finals early this morning. I'm free until my next set of classes starts after Christmas."

Not really trying to hide it, the smile on my lips broadens until it hurts from how far I'm trying to stretch them. I have her all to my fucking self for at least two months.

Two glorious months.

"I was thinking maybe we could move into the new house before Christmas—you know it's my favorite holiday and I wanted to get a ridiculously large Christmas tree and decorate it…" She realizes that my eyes are following her every small move and the flush on her cheeks brightens. "I mean, we can move whenever it's good for us, I just thought—"

Screw her secret. I don't care about that shit right now. All I care about is wrapping her soft, small body around mine and breathing in her strawberry deliciousness. School plans, opening two businesses at once, secret marriages, and my secret with Lucy can all kick fucking rocks.

I've never wanted her more than I want her right now.

"I'll move in that house tomorrow if you ask me to."

My head dips down to catch her falling eyes. "Haven't you learned by now that I'm with you? If you ask me to move to France tonight, I would. Julie…" My too-long brown hair falls into my eye. "You are everything to me. Every. Thing. You want to move into the house before Christmas? Tell me the date and I'll make it happen. You want a huge ass fucking Christmas tree? I'll buy you two. I'm yours."

The way she bites her bottom lip is dangerous for me. "I know, you've told me." She blushes harder and looks down at her lap in embarrassment. "Maybe we can stay in and shop online for stuff for the house?" She yawns and finally relaxes into the sofa. "I'm mentally exhausted from today; it's been a long and interesting twelve hours."

I put her head into my lap and stroke her head gently. Her body vibrates and she sighs with satisfaction into the air. "Tell me about your day." My voice cuts through the air like a chainsaw. "What happened that was exhausting?"

Okay, Oliver, you dick. Do a little fishing for information.

She purrs beneath me and it takes every ounce of self-control I have to keep my dick from trying to escape my pants. "Well, I took three finals in five hours for starters." She yawns again and snuggles deeper into my lap, massaging places that I'm trying to not focus on right now.

"That would be frustrating." I lean my head back and focus on the softness of her honey blonde hair twisting through my thick fingers. "I don't think I had it that bad in college."

She snickers. "I'm sure you didn't, you probably breezed right through."

"What's that supposed to mean?"

Her head lifts beneath my touch and when I look down, her eyes are staring into mine. We lock together and her pouty lips turn into the sexiest grin this woman's ever shown me. "It means that you're smart and resourceful; you probably had no problems getting good grades. What did you think I meant?" The sexy grin widens and her eyes cloud over.

It's hard to fucking swallow. I want every inch of her body touching me and it's getting harder to resist the urge to take her on this sofa. I don't know how, but I'm keeping my dick under wraps for now even if she's playing me like a damn fiddle.

"Oliver?" Her silky voice tickles my ears. "You know that about yourself, right?"

Oh, fuck. She's going to say something to give my ego a super orgasm and I'm gonna lose control. I can't take her right now, not when I'm obsessed with what she's keeping from me. She's good, though; Julie's learned—and mastered—the art of seducing Oliver Jackson to the point of paralysis.

"Oliver, are you okay?" Her small hand touches my forehead.

It's just a small touch. Breathe, Oliver. No matter how good her skin feels on yours.

"I'm fine. Do I know what about myself?" I lean into her touch.

She knows what I'm doing but doesn't stop stroking my forehead. I can't fucking help it; when she touches me I just know that I'm...*home*. "That you're smart and resourceful. Plus, you're strong-willed and direct, which are two traits I've learned to love about you. It's sexy and exciting the way you take charge of things sometimes." She doesn't blush or put her head back down. "You're a good person, Oliver Frankford Jackson."

Her wink nearly sends me over the edge.

"Julie..." I grunt and move my leg so she'll sit up on her own, and I won't have to touch her and risk losing the millimeter of control I have left. "You're the only person in my life who sees me that way. I think you're looking at me with rose-colored glasses. I'm a fucking mess—"

Her lips press against mine and everything in my mind dies.

"I believe in you enough for the both of us," she whispers, sliding her body into my lap, facing me. "You're going to do big things, you'll see."

I snort. "Isn't that from a movie?"

She shrugs and giggles. "Who knows, maybe. I watched a lot of late night TV at Randy's when I was staying there." She licks her lips and I reach up to graze my thumb over them. A fire blazes in my stomach when she whimpers at my touch; she wants me to take her as much as I want to have her.

"I love you, sunshine." My mouth moves and words fall out. "You're the best part of me."

"I can't take credit for something that was already there." Her lips find mine again and they tuck them-selves into a soft kiss. I let her body and soul melt into mine; it's something I find myself craving hardcore each and every minute of each and every damn day. My hands slide up her back and my fingers find her jaw, gently holding her in place so I can devour her lips completely.

Her hands find my thighs and she rests them behind her to steady her body, making her mouthwatering C-cups graze against my chest.

I have to stop this. Now.

"Julie." My lips move against hers. "Hey, let's slow down."

She frowns and frantically jumps off of me, pulling up my shirt to look at the scar where my car accident stitches were. When she doesn't see blood, her eyebrows furrow and she glances down at my wounded knee.

"I'm fine." I laugh and wave her off. "You weren't hurting me. I just think we should slow down for tonight. You had a long day and if we start this, it's going to be a long *night* and we won't get to do anything for the new house."

She isn't buying it.

Fuck, she sees right through me.

No, wait.

She tugs her clothes around her and hides her eyes.

Shit. She thinks I don't want her.

"Oh, Julie." I brush her hair back from her eyes and tip her head up. "Trust me, it's not because I don't want you. It's because I want you too much, baby. Come here." I pull her back onto my chest and her arms snake around my body. "It's hard for me to resist you most of the time, sunshine, it really is. I just think we have some things to talk about before we keep pretending that nothing is wrong."

Her body tenses and she pulls away from me. "What do you mean?"

Hoping she can see the look in my eye and automatically know what I'm thinking about doesn't work out for me. It makes her withdrawn and angry that I'm stalling so she can fess up about her marriage to Brandon before I say something.

And it's on the tip of my fucking tongue.

"I mean, I think you're hiding something from me and I want you to come clean," I blurt out and I'm surprised that I don't regret it. "I just want you to be honest with me."

She groans and crosses her arms over her chest. "Oh, okay. So...what? Brandon's boss already called you, then? I'm sure he had a lot to say. Did you know that he also threatened me and tried to blackmail me?"

What the fuck? There's obviously more that's happened since I found out about this, so I make the wrong decision to play along instead of coming clean myself. "Why did he threaten you? What did he say?" I make this my main focus because *no one* fucking threatens her.

"He said he would tell you about the divorce if I said anything to you about what happened today and had you cut ties with him."

I nod like I know what she's talking about. "And did you ask me?"

"No."

"Why didn't you ask me, Julie?"

She throws her arms into the air. "Why would I? It's not like you would do that just for Brandon. Oliver, you weren't there. You don't know what happened, but I know you wouldn't help him because of why we were there."

"And why were you there? And where is *there*?"

She scoffs. "At the courthouse or the restaurant?" Two seconds after she finishes her sentence, she realizes that I have no idea what she's talking about. She knows she's said too much to stop now and I have a million questions, so she places her anger on me instead of the situation and it doesn't fucking feel good at all.

"You know." Her eyes narrow at me. "You know everything."

I can't pretend anymore no matter what happens next.

"Before you storm out and leave me, hear me out." I take her hand and hold it in mine. "Please just try and understand why I didn't say anything."

"You let me go through this alone!" She wipes away a few tears streaming down her face. "You let me worry about you finding out and what you'd do to Brandon when you knew all along? What's *wrong* with you?" Her breath is raspy and she's trying hard to calm it down. "I can't believe you would do this, Oliver. Not after all the fuck-ups you've already had—"

"Whoa, what the fuck? How did this become *my* fault?"

She lets go of my hand and stands up. "It's not. This is my fault for not telling you. I'm just sorry that you felt you had to keep it from me like you don't trust that

I could take care of something like this and had to wait in the background to clean up my mess again."

"Julie…" I stand up and catch her arm before she storms off. "It wasn't like that."

"Then what was it like?" she screeches and turns to face me. I'm waiting for her to clock me in the jaw but it never happens. "Poor little Julie, can't make decisions for herself; she can't live life properly, so let's walk two steps behind her and shield her from the world?"

"You're being irrational, just calm down."

The glare she gives me breaks my damn heart.

"Fine, you want to know where I was today?" Her voice calms down so much it's eerie. "I was with Brandon getting a divorce. He got me drunk a few years ago and took me to a twenty-four-hour chapel, I signed the paperwork, and we got married. I never remembered and I never knew, so imagine my surprise when I found out and didn't think you'd want me when I wasn't available."

As the last piece of my heart breaks, hers does too.

"There isn't going to be a time where I don't want you," I say flatly. "*Ever.*"

"I was embarrassed to tell you." Her voice shakes. "I didn't want you to think less of me because of how it happened, and I didn't mean to keep it from you for so long."

She lets me walk to her without running away. "Oh, baby." I tuck her body into mine and she starts sobbing into my chest. "It hurts me to know that you think you can't come to me with anything." I rub her back and let her continue to cry. "I'm here for you… with anything. You're my best friend, Julie—there's nothing you can say to me to make me turn my back on you."

"I'm sorry." She sniffles and wipes her eyes. "I should've said something."

I smile and wipe the remaining wetness from the corner of her eye. "I'm not happy that you didn't, but I *understand* why you didn't. That's why I didn't tell you that I knew. I trust you to make your own decisions, sunshine, no matter what you think. You're not hopeless or stupid; you're actually the best person I've ever met."

"Don't say things like that."

I pick her up and hold her in my arms, her small feet dangling in the air. "Oh, but it's true." She lets me kiss her before putting her back down. "We all have our secrets. I've been keeping one too."

I have to try and make this up to her. She can't be the only one getting caught in lies around here.

"Before we met Lucy, she came home with me."

The air is cold when Julie processes that information. "What do you mean?"

I take a deep breath and act like it's not a big deal. "I mean, when we fought about you being late a few months ago and you left me—or at least I thought you left me—I met Harley down at The Tavern. I met Lucy and I was already drunk and I brought her home with me."

She removes herself from my grasp. "You did *what*?"

"We didn't do anything; I was drunk and I kept talking about you the entire time. She slept in the bed and I slept on the couch because Veronica and Mac showed up and she was too scared to leave."

Her eyes get so wide I think they're going to pop out of her skull.

She turns and leaves the apartment without grabbing her bag, her keys, or saying a single word.

When I come to my senses, I follow her but she's already gone.

She's gone.

SIXTEEN
JULIE

I DON'T KNOW where I'm going but I know that Oliver isn't following me. Why would he? Of course he hid the fact that he brought another girl home when he knows I'm holding a secret myself. What is *wrong* with us? I don't have my phone or my bag with the car keys, so I'm left walking alongside the road toward Rita's Boutique just in case Lucy is working tonight.

I want to hear it from her.

How can she be friendly with me and keep this to herself?

After a few long blocks of cooling off, I realize I left the apartment without a coat and it's about thirty degrees outside. I can't shake the feeling of someone watching me, but that's normal for who I am and what's happened to me lately. It saddens me that Oliver didn't follow me and beg me to come back inside, but no matter how much I wanted him to...I *didn't* want him to even more.

"Julie?" a familiar voice wafts into my mind. "Hey...*Julie!*"

A rough hand grabs me and the last three months flash inside my mind like a flipbook of memories; before I know it, I'm swinging my body around and my fist meets someone's face.

He groans and whimpers away. "Fuck, Julie, what'd you do that for?"

Casey.

I blow out the remainder of air in my lungs and fall to my knees. He forgets about his jaw that I just sucker punched and catches me before I can completely hit the ground. I know he's talking to me but I'm shivering so badly that all I can do is let him pick me up and take me to his car.

The warmth of the running heater slowly brings me back to life as we sit in a dark parking lot and he frets over me. His sandy blond hair glistens from the faraway streetlight, but I can see the worry in his eyes better than anything.

I clear my throat and make eye contact with him. "I'm sorry I punched you."

He laughs and turns on the overhead light so he can see better. "Well, you owed me one."

Casey wants me to laugh, but I need to focus on Oliver and getting back home. "Can you take me back to Oliver's apartment?" I buckle my seat belt and look forward. "I left without my phone; he's probably worried."

Without hesitation, he puts the car in reverse and pulls back onto the main road. We aren't far from Oliver's apartment, but it seems like forever until we pull into the parking garage.

"Thanks," I mumble and put my hand on the doorknob.

"Hey, hold it." He locks the doors and a bolt of panic swells in my stomach. "What were you doing walking out there in the cold? Did you guys have a fight?"

I scoff, playing it off. "I went for a walk and he wasn't even home." I'm a horrible liar, but Casey, thankfully, doesn't know this yet. "I locked myself out and didn't have my phone so I went for another walk."

Crap.

His eyebrows rise. "In the cold?"

I nod.

"Without a coat, your keys, or your phone?"

"Yeah. All of that." I smile sweetly. "Well, thanks for the ride. I'm sure Oliver's back now—"

Casey takes out his phone and dials a number. "Let's just make sure before I let you go off alone without a way to get inside, yeah? I'm sure he'd be pretty pissed if I let you do that."

He's already going to be pissed knowing I'm in the car with you.

"Hey, are you home?" Casey says into the phone. "Well, Julie is with me and she says she can't get into the apartment. I didn't want to leave her alone without knowing she's safe. Did you guys have a fight?...Oh, I see. Okay, I'll tell her."

He hangs up the phone and my stomach does flip-flops.

"Oliver says he doesn't want to see you."

The tone of his voice scares me so badly that I instantly reach for the door handle, but he's locked me inside. He doesn't reach for me as I struggle to open the door, but when our eyes meet...he looks emotionless and dead inside.

"I guess you'll just have to go home with me," he says and puts the car in reverse.

"Casey, don't do this," I plead with him. "Let me out."

He doesn't unlock the doors, but he hits the brake and brings the car to a stop again. "Oliver said he didn't want you and I want you—what's the problem?"

I know I should be scared; I'm more pissed than anything that this is happening a second time. A growl escapes my throat and he flinches, prepared for a fight. "What is it about me that makes people think they can just kidnap me? Let me out of here this instant!" I scream and kick the dashboard. "Casey Anderson, you let me out of here right now!"

"I can't do that!" he screams back at me, and it echoes so loud in the car I have to cover my ears. "You won't see me otherwise! I tried, Julie...I tried really fucking hard to make you see what a bad fucking guy Oliver is, but you just won't listen. So, I have to *make* you listen." His voice goes low and it's barely above a whisper. "I can't let him keep putting you in danger."

"What do you mean? He isn't putting me in danger!"

"Yes, he is," he says calmly. "Letting you walk the streets at night without a phone or a way to defend yourself is putting you in danger."

"And you'd lock me inside an apartment, never letting me out?"

The look in his eyes sends a shiver down my spine.

"Casey, let me out. *Please*, let me out. That's not the life I want…doesn't that matter to you?"

"Of course it does." He turns to fully face me. "We can move away where you can be free again."

"Move away?"

This time, he doesn't say anything and he starts to put the car back into drive. The panic that's set into my bones has numbed and I'm ready to figure this out. I have to get the hell out of this car before he gets out of the parking garage or I may never have a chance.

"Can I at least go and get some of my things?" I ask, quickly, before he hits the gas.

"What kind of things?"

Think, Julie! Think!

"Some of my childhood things; they're sentimental and I don't want to lose them."

He thinks for a few seconds and pulls the car back into the parking spot. First, I think he's actually going to let me go upstairs alone, but he gets out of the car and pulls me out with such force I know there'll be a bruise where his fingers are gripping my flesh.

"I can go alone, you know." He pushes me into the elevator and there isn't a guard at the desk right now. Casey takes a mental note of this and pushes the floor of Oliver's apartment, letting the doors shut in front of us.

"I'm not stupid—I'm not letting you go up here alone. You're coming with me, Julie, don't forget that. You have five minutes to grab what you can and come with me."

"Is there an 'or else'?"

He nods and the elevator dings. I can see Oliver's

apartment door from here. I think about screaming out for him, but the grip that Casey has on me warns me not to. During the short walk to the door, I hope that he's left the apartment to look for me.

"Wait, we can't get in...I forgot I don't have my keys." I turn to leave the hallway, but he shakes a silver key in front of my face.

"I have one."

He starts to unlock the door when we hear laughing coming from Mrs. Atchley's apartment and it breaks his concentration on me. I'm able to wriggle free of his grasp and make a break for it, but he catches me against the wall near her apartment, accidentally slamming my head against the wall too hard. Things start to get fuzzy. I can't fight him now; my limbs are like putty in his hands.

"What are you doin' out here with her, boy?" Mrs. Atchley's scratchy voice booms when the door opens. "I suggest you put here down right this minute."

"Go back inside, old woman," Casey snarls, "this isn't your fucking business."

She takes a step forward and looks at me with sad eyes. He pulls me backward into him and I'm able to focus a little better. I think my eyes are playing tricks on me when Veronica steps out of the open apartment door and snarls at Casey when she sees what he's doing.

"What the fuck is this?" Veronica scolds him. "Boy, you better let her go. This isn't the way."

"It's *my* way!" he yells, pulling me backward toward Oliver's door. "Don't follow us or I *promise* you that you'll never see either of us again."

The two women gasp once we pass Oliver's door

and I think it's because he's opened it and he's waiting to save me, but once the cold metal of the gun presses against my bare neck, the panic returns to my body and I start to vibrate with nerves.

"Casey, please just let me go," I beg him. "I won't press charges, I'll let you run. Just leave me here."

"Listen to her, kid," Mrs. Atchley chimes in. "Put that damn gun down."

Veronica steps forward. "You don't want to hurt her, Casey. I *know* you don't."

He shakes his head and screams. "Everyone, just stop! We shouldn't have come up here and now we're leaving. She can get new things to replace what she's lost."

"Oliver!" I scream as loud as I can. "Help! Oliver!"

Casey backs us up before his body goes solid like a rock. "Tell me who my real father is."

The women stop and look at each other; Veronica takes a deep breath. "If I answer your questions, will you let her go?"

"No."

She takes a few seconds to think about what she's going to do. "Take me with you. I can answer your questions and know that she's safe."

"No, just answer the fucking question."

"Casey—"

"Answer the question!" he screams, and Oliver's door finally pops open. Instead of Oliver's tall body coming through the door, Lucy steps out and gasps loudly. Casey starts to laugh uncontrollably and tightens his grip on me. "Well, would you look at that."

His body heaves behind me. "It looks like Oliver misses you terribly, Julie."

Lucy's eyes widen when they meet mine. "I came over to talk to you, Julie, I swear. Oliver called me when you left so I could set the record straight and when I got here, you hadn't come back yet. I *swear* nothing happened, Julie—he was drunk and all he could talk about was you. I tried to kiss him, he didn't kiss me back, and all of this happened before I even knew you."

"Yeah, but Oliver knew he had a girlfriend," Casey answers for me. "He knew what he was risking."

"I'm gonna fucking kill you." Oliver's rough voice swoops around Lucy. He comes into view and so much anger has built up in his eyes that they turn black. "Don't you *dare* fucking touch her for another second— let her go. Julie, come here."

I start to go to him, but Casey pulls me back. "She's coming with me. You've put her through enough damage, don't you think, brother?"

Oliver's eyes fill with fear when he notices the gun pressed against my neck. "Casey, look, I know we have our problems, but I know you love her, okay? Put that damn gun down."

Veronica steps forward, thinking Casey isn't watching her anymore. "If anyone takes another step, I'm going to shoot them."

"Oliver, don't move!" I squeal and try to stand as still as I can. "Veronica, wait!"

Veronica stops dead in her tracks. The gun makes a clicking noise and the group gets more nervous, begging with Casey to let me go. All I can think about is what my life is going to be like once he puts me back into the car; I'm not letting him shoot anyone over me.

"Everyone, just calm down," I manage to say with a loud enough voice to shut them up. "Just let us go. I don't want anyone getting hurt."

Oliver wants to move so badly it's killing him. "I'm not letting him take you. That's not even a fucking question, are you serious?"

Oliver takes a step forward and Veronica follows next to him. Lucy cowers back inside Oliver's apartment, and I pray that she's calling for help. Mrs. Atchley scowls behind everyone; she knows she wouldn't be much help in this fight.

"I told you to stay put," Casey growls. "Now, instead of shooting you, I'm going to shoot Julie if you take another step forward."

"No, no, no! Please, Casey, *don't*!" Oliver's eyes meet mine and for a split second, I get a strange feeling that he's going to do something stupid. "Shoot me! Don't shoot Julie, shoot *me*!"

Tick, tick, tick.

Three small seconds.

That's all it takes to make everything come crumbling down.

One.

Casey thinks about what Oliver is offering him: a chance to get him out of the way so he can truly have me.

Two.

Casey makes his decision and loosens his grip on me to focus on what he's going to do next.

Three.

He shrugs his shoulders. "Okay." The sound his voice makes my body cold as a loud bang fills the hallway and people start to scream. There's so much commotion that all I can see is Oliver lying on the ground and Mrs. Atchley screaming for help. Everything rings inside my head and someone grabs my arm and pulls me away from Oliver as I'm screaming his name.

"Is he shot?" I shake Lucy as she shuts the door to the apartment behind us. "Where did Casey go?"

"*I don't know*! I called the cops before he shot the gun —who did he shoot?"

"We left them out there, Lucy!" I dash for the door and start to unlock it, but she wrestles me to the side. "No way! I dodged bullets just to pull you inside. We're waiting for the cops!"

I growl and push her aside, unlocking the door and peeking my head into the hallway.

He shot Oliver. He really shot him.

I feel weird and lightheaded and there's a pain in my chest that's so hard to ignore that it's blinding me. There's blood everywhere on the floor and Veronica lies next to Oliver, both of them with their eyes closed. It's hard to tell where the blood is coming from. Most of it is pooled around Oliver, and as I kneel down, I'm pushed aside by paramedics who arrive and start working on them. Someone shines a light into my eyes and it's like I'm in a tunnel.

"Hey, I've got a gunshot wound over here—they're about to pass out!" I hear someone say.

I close my eyes and drift away.

SEVENTEEN
BRANDON

HEATHER FLUTTERS AROUND THE HOUSE, picking up and putting away laundry while she hums. I like the sounds she makes, in and out of the bedroom—they comfort me in some small way. For two days she's reassured me that no matter what the paternity test says—the one I took two nights ago before we headed home—she won't leave my side. I don't expect her to help me raise a baby I have with someone else, but it's looking like she doesn't really care what I expect anyways.

Vern used some of his pull around town to get the lab results back sooner, and they promised him they would have them back to us by this afternoon. It's nearly noon and I keep checking the emails on my phone like it's life or death.

"Hey, do something to take your mind off of it." Heather hums around me and dusts the coffee table. "It's not going to do you any good sitting here worrying about it. You've made peace with what your decision will be if it goes either way…what else is there?"

"I wouldn't mind having a baby." I blush and she smiles at me. "I just don't want one with Rachel. She's immature, and it's going to be a fucking horrible eighteen years."

Heather laughs. "You made this bed, you gotta lie in it."

"I'm glad you're here with me, babe." I wink at her and playfully slap her ass as she passes me. "I better start looking for another job...something in another field."

"You can try for jobs at local firms—maybe Vern hasn't blacklisted you just yet." She tries to comfort me by looking at the bright side. "Maybe he's been too busy trying to figure out who the father of his slutty daughter's baby is to say anything."

I shrug. "I can try. I have some contacts I can reach out to." She kisses my forehead and I click a few buttons on my phone, looking up numbers of other law assistants I've networked with over the years. Of course, I don't have a good rapport with a lot of them, but Nate, my former best friend, would be glad to hear that I'm changing and becoming a better person...I hope. Maybe he can appreciate that enough to help me weasel into his level at Brown and Dickenson, the second-largest firm in the state of New York.

> Hey, can we talk?

I wait a few minutes and don't bother waiting for a response any longer.

> I wanted to catch up. Can you get together?

He replies almost instantly.

NATE

> What do you want? Chasing Julie again?

> No, Julie and I are friends. I'm with a girl named Heather now.

A few minutes pass before he replies, and I think that's fixed whatever problem he has with me.

> Good for you.

> I'm looking to change firms. Think you can put in a good word?

There. Straight to the point.

> No.

Well, he's straight to the point too.

I push the call button and let it ring a few times before calling right back. I know if I blow up his phone that eventually he'll have to answer and hear what I have to say.

"What, Brandon?" he booms when he finally answers. "What do you want?"

"Hey, ease up, man. I just want to talk to you." I look around to make sure Heather isn't listening; I don't want her to hear me beg for a job. "Look, I know I haven't been a very good friend lately—"

He snorts. "*Lately*? Try never."

I grit my teeth and do my best to stay calm and not tell him off. I need something from him, and the old me would've just berated him until I got what I wanted, but now, I want to do this the right way.

"Okay, that's fair. Things have changed, Nate. A lot has happened, and I'm not the same person I was when we last saw each other."

"I heard about what happened at Trumbull's place," Nate tells me. "*No one* is going to touch you after what you've done."

"What did he tell people?"

Nate hesitates, but some sort of loyalty apparently kicks in. "How much money did you steal?"

The burning in my stomach intensifies, and the anger bubbles harder. "I didn't fucking *steal* any money. Trumbull found out that Julie and I were getting a divorce and injected himself into my personal business. Oh, and Rachel is pregnant, so there's that."

Nate gasps. "She's *pregnant*? Dude, I told you not to go down that road with her. She's empty and cold-hearted; she's going to take you for everything you've got."

For a minute, it actually sounds like Nate feels sorry for me enough to help me out. I plan out the conversation as he's talking badly about Rachel—I should probably be upset that he's talking shit about the possible mother of my child, but I'm not because everything he's saying is true.

"I took a paternity test; I find out today if it's mine," I tell him. "That's not what I'm worried about."

"It's not? It fucking should be!" he hisses. "You don't want to be tied to her forever."

I rub my jaw and make sure Heather hasn't come in the room. "Yeah, I know. I'm more worried about work. I quit Trumbull's office and cleaned out my desk. Heather wants to say in Rockford because she just started school and she got a new job, and I want to stay with her."

Nate notes the change in attitude. "I don't know, man, you're going to be a hard sell. You're going to have to go far and wide to find a firm that Trumbull hasn't talked to."

"Can you try? Come on, Nate, we're still friends."

He takes a few seconds to think about it, and I can almost hear the discussion inside of his head. "I'll see what I can do, but don't hold your breath. Trumbull already has half the city against you, man…he's pretty pissed if he's making up stories about you stealing money."

I thank him and hang up the phone, never expecting to hear from him again. I hear someone outside and I hurry to look out the window. A courier is walking up the steps with a large envelope in his hands. I chose not to trust the lab that Trumbull was using, so I paid an extra five hundred bucks to use a private lab and get my own expedited service as well.

The courier doesn't have time to knock on the door before I open it and take the envelope from him. He looks shocked as he hands the clipboard out for me to sign and I put my name to it, closing the door on him before he can even speak. Not having any time to worry about formalities, I rip open the envelope and take out a thin folder of documents.

Scanning them takes a few minutes, but then I have my answer.

"Heather!" I call out for her. She answers from upstairs and I take the steps two at time, frantically searching for her until I see her black hair disappear into the master bathroom. I make a beeline for her and startle her enough for her to drop her toothbrush in the sink.

"Hey, slow down!" She laughs and picks the toothbrush back up, rinsing it off. "What's wrong with you? Is there a fire?"

I shake my head and thrust the papers toward her. "A courier came. I have the results."

She opens the papers and reads through them a few times before looking back at me. I'm not quite sure what I was expecting her to say, but her expression isn't giving away anything.

"What do you think?" I cock my head and stare at her. "Are you okay with this?"

She nods and smiles. "Of course I'm okay with this…is this from the lab you used?"

"Yes." I take the papers from her and stuff them back into the envelope. "Looks like Rachel is going to have to figure out who her baby daddy is, because it's *not* me."

Heather jumps into my arms and I admit…I want to fucking cry right now. It's not that I don't want to have children—I just don't want children with someone I only wanted sex from. I never intended on dating or marrying Rachel, and I sure as hell didn't plan on it when I found out her baby could be mine.

"So, she was screwing other guys when she was screwing you." Heather shakes her head. "Have you been tested for diseases?"

I feel disgusting almost instantly. "No, I never thought about it. Maybe I should get checked before we have sex again to make sure."

She blows a raspberry and starts to wash her face in the sink. "I'll make an appointment to get checked out too, just in case." I silently watch her rub her hands together to make the face wash soapy. She applies it to every inch of her gorgeous face and gently washes it back off. It's like a song, the way she does things some-times. She knows I'm watching her but she doesn't care; I think she likes having an audience fixed solely on her.

"I'm sorry you aren't able to go to the Children's Gala." I clear my throat and hide my hard dick inside of my pants by shoving the papers over it. "I know I already said that, but—"

She waves me off and dries her face. "I don't care about stuff like that anymore. There's more to life than money and fancy galas. It's just taken me a bit to realize what life is *really* about."

I let a low growl escape my throat. She's taken off her crimson tank top and leggings and stands in front of me in nothing but a matching pair of red lace panties and bra. "Like what, exactly?" I lick my lips and lean on the doorframe. "What's life about, Heather?"

"Life is about being with the person you can totally be yourself around...the person who accepts you fully for who you are and whatever bullshit that comes with you. That's why I'm not taking that job at Rita's and I'm moving with you to California."

I nearly choke. "I wasn't aware we were moving."

"I overheard your phone conversation with your friend. I don't know what your old boss said to make you untouchable, but it sounds like it worked. How bad is it?"

I lower my eyes to the floor. "Pretty bad. He told the community that I stole money from him."

She isn't surprised. "Well, I know that you didn't, and I'm on your side. If we have to move so you can continue working in the field you love...then that's what we're going to do."

"You'd do that for me? What about your job and school?"

"Of course I would. I'll go anywhere with you, Brandon. I love you. I can get another job wherever we go, and I'm sure my credits will transfer too."

I don't have to think about my answer.

"No, we're staying here. I'm not taking you away to a place where we don't know anyone just so I can run away from my problems. I slept with Rachel and fucked Julie over—now I'm paying the price for it. I can always try something new, right? I may even go to school too."

Heather giggles and pulls on a pair of jeans, making me frown. I try and hide my scowl as she finds more clothing and pulls a sky blue blouse over her head, laughing at my turmoil. "We're stuck in a bad movie or something, doesn't it seem like? Let's just get over ourselves and figure this out right here, right now. I don't want to regret our decision later, so let's talk about it."

"Like adults?" I snicker. "When did we become mature adults?"

She shrugs. "Let's just try it. Look, I don't want to move anywhere, but I will if you want me to without any resentment or regret. I really want something of my own, and my interview with Rita went so well she offered me the job on the spot. I guess Lucy stopped coming to work or something, I don't know, but the point is…I've never had something like this, just for me."

I hold up my hands to stop her. "You don't have to explain, babe. Decision is made: We're staying here. End of discussion as far as I'm concerned."

"Are you sure you won't regret that? What if, let's say ten years down the road, you're stuck at some crappy job you hate and resent me for making you stay?"

I glide over to her and scoop her into my arms. "Trust me, I won't regret it. You're my soulmate, Heather. I never want to be without you, therefore… we're staying in Rockford. A job is a job, but you are you."

She snorts. "Whatever that means. As long as you're sure…"

"I'm sure." I pin her arms to her side and kiss her lips. "I have enough money saved up for the mortgage for six months, and by then I should be able to figure out my life."

"Shouldn't be too hard." She rests her head on my shoulder. "Rockford's a big city, but it's *not* a big city at the same time."

I playfully groan. "Ah, I'll figure it out. Maybe I'll

talk to Jackson and see if he wants to team up on something. He's not exactly employed, either."

"Oh, something in common for the two of you." She laughs and pokes my side. "By the way, he hasn't made good on his promise to try and be friends with us. As far as I can tell, he doesn't really plan to."

"You let me worry about Oliver Jackson. You worry about what you're going to wear on your first day of work and the good grades you got on your finals." I wink and let her go. "I'll talk to Oliver and everything will be okay…okay?"

"Okay."

I blow her a kiss and leave her standing puzzled in the middle of the room.

Jesus, can I *be* any more pathetic?

I'm at the mercy of Oliver Jackson.

And I don't fucking like it.

EIGHTEEN
OLIVER

DARKNESS.

No! Not this again!

This feels like it did when I got in that accident.

A big vat of nothingness.

Wake up, Oliver!

Replaying the last few minutes like a flash of photos in my mind, I recall what happened very slowly.

Casey took Julie.

He *took* her.

———

"HEY, MAN, WAKE UP!" Casey shakes me from my deep slumber. "It's a brand-new day, Oliver. It's been a week since you kicked Heather's sorry ass out of here, man."

I groan and swat my arms around without opening my eyes. I remember going to bed with someone and I know it wasn't Casey, who's hovering over me like a motherfucking hen.

"Go the fuck away," I mumble into the pillow as I bury my face. *"I don't fucking want you here."*

"I don't care if you want me here." He scoffs and starts smashing pillows over the rest of my head. *"You don't even want to be here, so that's not a surprise. Now get the hell up and let's go do something fun. You need some fun."*

It's unsettling how much Casey acts like a fucking woman sometimes.

"Talk about your feelings."

"Be a different man."

"Get over the woman who shattered your fucking soul."

"Be happy, Oliver, just be happy."

"I know you loved her," he says and pops the top of a silver can of beer, handing it to me as I sit up to look at him. *"She knows you loved her. She just didn't love you the same. You gotta let that go, man, it's eating you alive."*

"Oh, like you're such a relationship expert, are you?" I snort and open the beer, chugging it. *"Have you even asked that girl from the library out yet? Forget that you even went to a library, but finding a hot girl there is pretty rare."*

Casey rolls his eyes. "Your outlook on women is jaded right now. This isn't you. But, for your information, yes...I asked her out. And she has a name."

"What is it, then? Do you even remember anything past her thick ass and tan skin?"

Casey shakes his head, but I don't give a shit what he thinks about me. Honestly, I don't give a rat's ass about what anyone thinks of me at this moment. What Casey doesn't know is that no matter how many nights I've brought a different girl home and tried to numb my pain...it never works.

I'm not pining over Heather, though.

The girl with the electric blue eyes…she keeps coming to me in my dreams. I thought I was over these dreams since they faded when I started high school, but they're coming back with a vengeance. I can't sleep anymore because it makes me jealous when I have to wake up and be without her.

Heather was just keeping the spot in my heart warm until I found her again.

I haven't told anyone about the girl with the blue eyes because she's all mine. I don't want to share her with anyone —no matter how small the memory might seem—and the need to find her and hold her close to me grows with each night I spend awake thinking about her.

"Hey, Earth to Oliver." Casey snaps his fingers at me. "What the hell is wrong with you?"

I clear my throat. "Sorry, what did you say?"

"Nora." He sighs and claps his hands together to keep me focused. "Her name is Nora?"

"Nora? Oh, the girl you're chasing, right." I leap off of the bed to get dressed. He turns his head because he hates knowing that I look like I do when he looks like he does.

I can't help how other people see me.

"Yeah, we're dating now…she laughs at my jokes, which is weird."

"Especially since you're not funny."

"Well she thinks I am, and I'm okay with that. Her laugh is cute—"

I look toward the bedroom door, because I really don't give a shit. "I'm going to take a shower—do you want to head out for breakfast after?"

He notes my annoyance and shrugs. "Sure, I'll wait for you in the living room."

I have to get him out of here so I can be alone with my thoughts. When he leaves, I shut the bathroom door behind me and turn the shower on in hopes that the steam will help clear my head.

Endless ocean blue eyes.

"Dammit!" I hiss, opening the shower door. I try so hard to forget her, but it's not working. No matter how hard I scrub shampoo into my shaggy hair or how rough I wash my body…she's not going away.

Would I know her if I met her?

What if I've already met her again and didn't know?

Should I research Officer Randy and call him up?

Do I really care about some little girl that I got a four-second glimpse of over a decade ago?

Yes.

She stole your soul and you're not complete without it.

———

ONE THING IS for fucking sure.

I'm going to kill Casey so fucking dead when I wake up.

Everything makes sense now that I've met Julie. My memories and dreams make more sense since I've been dreaming about her for several years.

I don't hear anyone around me, so I have no clue what's happening.

Am I dead this time?

———

I LOOK in the bathroom mirror and try to calm down.

Julie has no idea what she's asking of me. She wants me to put twenty years of tension with my mother—who just kidnapped the person I can't live without—behind me and help her?

She doesn't know what she's asking of me.

I want to make her happy, though. I want her to see a side of me that no one else gets to see. She didn't run after Veronica, but I know she desperately wanted to. That's just the kind of person Julie is; she's kind and full of so much infectious, upstanding goodness that it makes my jaw hurt.

I fucking found *her.*

I did it. I don't know how I did it, but I did it.

When Julie stepped out of Randy's house the first time I met her, I didn't know she was the one I've been looking for. It took a few weeks to realize she's the girl from the backseat of Randy's cop car. Her eyes have dulled since I first saw her years ago, and that's because Brandon has been sucking the life out of her slowly. I've tried my fucking hardest to put her life back together and mesh it with mine, and so far...it hasn't been a fairy tale, but it's been a ride that I never want to get off of.

I can't shake the feeling from my head.

I have to help Veronica. It's what Julie would want from me.

Walking back into the bedroom, I quickly find my phone and try to figure out what I'm going to do.

Should I call Randy and have him pick her up and take her out of town?

Should I call Casey and have him deal with it?

Mrs. Atchley.

That's who I'm calling.

"Hey, boy." Her scratchy voice reaches me on the second ring. "Long time no speak, kid."

I strip naked as I cradle the phone between my shoulder and ear. "I'm sorry, we'll be staying at the new house for a few days...can I bribe you into seeing it?"

"You know I'm not fond of fancy things."

I laugh. "I know. I actually wanted to talk to you about something else, but I wasn't sure how." I proceed to tell her the entire story as quickly as I can so Julie doesn't walk in and find out what I'm doing. I don't want her feeling guilty and thinking that she forced me into doing this.

I'm doing this because she's full of goodness and I love her with every ounce of love I have to give.

"So..." I take a deep breath once I'm done explaining. "Can you help me?"

"I'm proud of you, Oliver," Mrs. Atchley's motherly voice shines. "This woman hasn't been good to you a day in your life and you're still willing to help her."

I shrug, knowing that she can't see me. Reaching in to start the shower, I dodge the falling water and shut the shower door. "I just want to be the man Julie sees in me, that's it."

She makes an agreeing noise and thinks for a few seconds. "Where is she? Veronica?"

"I don't know, she took off walking toward the outskirts of downtown."

Mrs. Atchley snorts. "Leave it to me. I'm at The Tavern and she'll make her way here, I'm sure."

"She's a drug addict, not a drunk."

"Trust me, kid. She'll be here."

I WONDER if Mrs. Atchley found Veronica.

Oh, that's right. They were in the hallway with me when Casey shot the gun off.

Casey.

That fucking shithead.

Veronica never did tell him who his real father was, and it better not be *my* father.

Colin Jackson is my father, not his.

Mine.

————

THE PIANIST STARTS to play a soft, angelic melody, and everyone's eyes turn toward the white double doors that slowly start to open. They can't take their eyes off of her and this time, it doesn't piss me off that people are checking her out.

She's an angel.

Julie emerges from the double doors, white roses in her hands, and her eyes gravitate toward mine instantly. Just a few feet and she'll be here, next to me, becoming my wife.

My knees start to buckle and Harley pats my back from behind me to let me know he's there in case I give into my weakness and drop to the floor. It's a damn shame that Casey couldn't be my best man; he turned out to be the worst person in my entire life. Harley has always been there for me, no matter what bullshit I had to offer, and that speaks volumes larger than trying to fucking kidnap my fiancée and force her to be with him.

"Oliver?" Harley whispers behind me. "You good, man?"

I nod and say nothing. I'm intoxicated by Julie, and it's like her strawberry scent drifts all the way up the aisle and wraps around me, comforting my nerves and stopping my body from uncontrollably shaking.

I want her more than anything I've ever wanted before.

And she's about to fully be mine.

The white silk gown tucks around her curvy hips like butter, and she's showing so much skin that it's hard to concentrate on why we're really here.

She's going to be my wife.

I know she thinks she's too young, but I don't care.

She's. Going. To. Be. My. Wife.

The pianist plays a little louder, and everyone stands as Randy joins Julie and she snakes her arm through his. He beams down at her—I know he's proud of the strong person she's become just like I am, even though it's taken him a while to warm up to me. I know he's proud of the man I've become too. I haven't had a chance to talk to him about the night we met in the dark parking lot years ago, but honestly, I think letting it go would be just as fulfilling.

It's not going to change anything—it's already changed everything.

Randy walks her down the aisle toward me slowly; it takes forever for them to stop and become within arm's reach of me. He kisses her cheek and whispers something in her ear that makes her smile before the pastor asks who is giving her away.

"I am, sir. I'm her brother." Randy nods at me and places her hand in mine. She's warm and just as excited as I am about where we are right now.

I gently tug her small hand toward me and place her in front of me. Her smile lights up the entire fucking church and it takes everything I have not to devour her lips before he announces us as man and wife. The reception afterward is going to torture me; she's already jolting my insides by the way her big eyes are looking up at mine and she's biting her bottom lip.

I hear a snap, like a twig when someone's stepped on it, and I look over to investigate but when my focus returns to Julie, she's gone.

They're all gone.

No more bride, no more pastor, and no more friends and family.

I'm all alone.

NINETEEN
JULIE

I'M SCREAMING as loud as I can and it just keeps bouncing back to me against the darkness. This is such a weird feeling...it's like I'm here but I'm not here at the same time. I hear distant whispers—I think that's what they are—but I can't make out what they're saying.

Or if they're saying anything at all.

I focus the best that I can on Oliver. It's stupid to entertain the idea that he can somehow telepathically speak to me, but it's worth a try.

Oliver.

Can you hear me?

Waiting for him to answer makes me sad.

Like really, really sad.

Can you hear me?

Can anyone hear me?

It's no use trying to scream to myself inside my own head, so I try and calm down. I wonder if Oliver is sitting at my bedside, watching the orange line go up and down like I did when he nearly died.

The darkness gets cold and it hits me.

The orange line bounced when he heard my voice.

I don't hear him.

Panic flashes through the darkness and the last turn of events is behind a foggy glass that I can't make out clearly.

Casey.

He had his fingers around my neck.

He wanted to take me.

Anger fills the darkness and I hear a gunshot.

He shot off that damn gun.

Who did he shoot?

Oliver said to shoot him and Casey said, "Okay." Then, the gun blasted my eardrums and all I can remember is someone pulled me into Oliver's apartment, out of harm's way.

Lucy.

She pulled me out.

I ran back to save Oliver and he was lying on the ground, covered in blood.

But so was Veronica.

Then I blacked out.

Was it me?

Did he shoot *me*?

———

THE WICKED GRIN on Marianna's face sends shivers down my whole body. I know that she hates me; she's hated me since even before Randy married her.

She reminds me of the evil stepmother in the Cinderella story from that big, brown book Randy likes to read to me from. I used to laugh at her pointed nose and small, beady eyes until she told me she'd never wanted me to come here in the first place.

Now I just see her as a person.

A ghost of a person, really.

Maybe I wanted her to be someone else, I don't know. The people Randy is shipping me back to, they are the real monsters of my story anyway. I don't have room for any more monsters in my life.

Randy frowns as I step onto the Greyhound bus and turn back to say goodbye. A tear forms in the corner of his eye, but he doesn't let me see it fall.

"Hey, kid, you know I'd let you live here with me, but Marianna gave me an ultimatum—"

I shrug. "It's okay."

He shakes his head and sniffles. "No, it's not. I know how they are; I know what they want you for, and I'm just shipping you back to be lost up in all of that."

"They just want the money from the state to help take care of me, no big deal."

He chuckles and puts his hands on my shoulders. "You're way too young to be dealing with these adult problems. Let me talk to Marianna again. I'll make her see why you staying here is the best choice."

"Randy, it's okay, just let me go," I say. "I want to go."

He raises his eyebrows in suspicion and looks back at his wife, who can't even care enough to pretend to be sad that I'm leaving. "You don't mean that." He lowers his voice. "Just let me figure it out, okay? I promise you that I won't leave you there for long."

"Don't make promises you can't keep. They aren't going

to let me leave again. I'm sure they've run out of whatever money I left them."

"Jules, you shouldn't have to leave them money. You're not the adult."

The bus driver honks for us to hurry up, and I don't make eye contact with Randy as I hug him and put his arms back to his sides.

"I have to go." I turn to leave, but he pulls me back and hugs me harder.

"I'm coming back for you, Julie. I promise."

———

EVEN THOUGH THINGS didn't work out for Randy and his wicked wife, they still produced Clyde from the love they had for each other and I wouldn't change that for the world.

Oh, Clyde.

He'll be going on his first date soon. I know he likes the new girl that just moved in across the street from Randy's house. Even though Marianna left when Clyde was just a few years old, he still reminds me of her in every way except her attitude.

I wonder if Randy knows that I can't wake up.

As much as I don't like to admit it now, he's really the person who saved my life. Yes, he sent me back to my parents—two people that should never be allowed to be in the public—but he also kept his promise and came back for me.

———

There it is.

The old, rickety house I left behind.

I never dreamed I would have to come back here, but here I am.

Randy is right; I'm too young to be dealing with the things my parents make me deal with. They don't abuse me, but they aren't exactly fans of me either.

The entire bus ride home—the hours seemed like days—I drifted off and dreamt about that boy I met in the rain. What was his name? I can never remember that part when I dream of him. His green eyes were glowing in the night, and that's all I can ever seem to fully remember about him.

It's like he knew me.

The door of my parents' house is unlocked so I step inside, trying to be as quiet as I can so they don't notice that I'm back. Once they see me, their games will start again and my little mental vacation will be over.

Too late.

"What you doin' back here already?" Bob asks me. I call them Bob and Dianne instead of Dad and Mom because you're supposed to call strangers by their first names. "I thought that boy was keeping you longer?"

I shrug. "Marianna didn't want me there."

Bob snorts. "Well, since you're back, you can clean up the dog's mess in the backyard, yeah?" He cracks open a brown beer can and chugs the liquid inside. After burping, he scratches his stomach and disappears back into the living room where the television is blaring an action movie loudly.

Dianne emerges from the kitchen and frowns at me. "After you're done with the dogs, you can clean up that disgusting kitchen. There's weeks' worth of dishes in that sink because you haven't been here to do them. Did you have a nice vacation?" Her voice is too sweet and makes me anxious. "Did your brother treat you right?"

Does she want me to get excited and sit down to tell her all about my trip?

Her smile fades quicker than it started. "Well, we have work to do around here to get the rent paid. Miss Carter's house down the street needs cleaned and she offered you fifty bucks to do it. Get down there after you do the dishes and don't come back without a full fifty, okay?"

Her cigarette smoke fills my nose and makes it itchy.

I'm still only a child.

"Okay..." I look toward the staircase and back at her. "Can I put my things away before I start?"

Dianne pats me on the shoulder and squeezes my skin a little too hard. "Don't waste too much time. I want that money by the end of the night, and you've got other obligations tomorrow so you'll need a good night's rest."

I nod and run up the staircase, noticing that the door to my bedroom is cracked open. I push it open and scan the room for all of the contents that belong there.

My bed is missing.

My desk is missing.

A thin air mattress sits in the middle of the floor next to a now-empty bookshelf.

They even sold my schoolbooks.

Randy isn't going to come through on his promise, I know he won't.

I'm stuck in this cage forever.

———

It's like I'm sleeping and these old movies keep playing in my mind. I'm not scared or afraid; I'm more intrigued, like I don't know what's going to happen next and it's my own life. For the first time in a very long time, I'm at such peace that it's hard to believe it won't end.

Coming in and out of the movies inside my head is like gently popping a bubble and floating around in the dark night sky for who knows how long. It could be weeks, months…*years* before I open my eyes and wake up from these dreams.

It could be never.

———

"What the hell is this about?" Bob's voice booms downstairs. "You can't fucking do this!"

"Get off of him!" Dianne screams. "Julie! Run!"

I don't run.

I know what's happening.

They're getting what they deserve.

I found the credit applications with all of the fake names and stolen identities on them weeks ago. At the time, I wasn't sure what to do about it since I knew this would land them in prison, but where would it land me? I don't want to go to a foster home…or worse.

The screaming continues for a few minutes until my bedroom door opens and three pairs of sad eyes fall on me. Three young male paramedics gently make their way toward me, but I'm not going to run or scream. I'm not going to fight them and I'm not going to make this worse.

I haven't seen the sunlight in over a week.

"Hey, you," one of the men coos at me, "are you okay? My name is Chase, and these are my friends, Mike and Raoul." My eyes dart to the other two men; Mike is blonde and goofy and Raoul is dark-skinned and wide-lipped. He smiles at me and it makes me feel warm inside.

"Is it just you up here?" Mike looks around to make sure we're all alone.

I nod. "It's just me."

Chase brushes his wildfire red hair back toward his neck. "Hey, don't worry. We're going to check you out and then get you somewhere safe, okay?"

"Okay."

I'm used to people taking what they want from me.

This is no different.

"We aren't going to hurt you. What's your name?" Raoul asks, gently tugging my arm and unfolding it from my side. He examines my skin and turns my arm over to look at something else.

"Julie." I lick my dry lips. "Julie Remington."

Raoul smiles. "Nice to meet you, Julie. When is the last time you've eaten?"

I shrug my shoulders.

"Bathed?"

I shrug again.

"Been outside?"

I know the answer to that one. "Last Thursday."

Raoul's eyes widen. "How old are you?"

"Thirteen and three days."

Chase snorts. "That's precise. Do you have any other family nearby?"

I shake my head. "My brother lives in New York. He's a police officer."

"Is his name Randy?"

The ice around my heart starts to melt.

"You know him?"

Chase smiles. "He sent us for you. After he found out about the scam your parents were running, he contacted the authorities and they caught them. If it wasn't for your letter, no one would've known."

Mike pats my leg. "You're a hero to a lot of innocent people, Julie."

Hero.

Not me—I'm not a hero.

"I just want to see Randy." I shake Mike's hand from my ankle. "Is he here?"

"No, you need to get checked out at the hospital and released into social services." I start to protest, but Mike holds my ankle again to keep me from jumping up. "You're not staying there. Someone from social services will escort you to New York."

"You can't tell her all of this," Chase hisses. "Randy wanted us to be the ones to talk to you. His wife didn't agree to keeping you with them, so Randy's mother will be fostering you."

I've never met Randy's mother before.

"I don't know her." I bite the inside of my cheek. "Is she nice?"

Chase feels bad for my sadness. "Honey, anything is better than here, isn't it?"

He's right.

Anywhere but here.

TWENTY

VERONICA

SO, this is what dying is like.

I've been close to it before, but never somethin' like this.

This is…*empty.*

———

I HEAR someone in the distance, but it's too damn dark to see anything. I don't feel like myself; I feel healthy and vibrant.

My legs come into view and the room I'm standing in fades into view around me.

"Veronica?" Someone calls for me. "Hey, it's okay." His warm hand grips the back of my arm and squeezes gently. It's like it's really happening; I feel his touch like he's really there.

Colin Jackson.

"Are you nervous?" His voice whispers in my ear as he pulls me close. "There's nothing to be nervous about…my father can be a big teddy bear sometimes."

Vic Jackson.

This is the first time I met him.

"You look gorgeous." His lips brush my ear. "And you smell amazing."

A giggle flows from my mouth. I'm watching this from inside my body, but there's nothing I can do to change the outcome. All I can do is sit back and watch the trauma that unfolds with each ticking second.

"I love you, V," he whispers again. "Ah, here he comes."

Before I can say it back to him, Colin's pulled himself next to me and wrapped his long arm around my waist. I chose the fanciest pale pink skirt I own, and even though it's a little too short for my comfort, it's all I had to impress him.

"You look fantastic, baby, don't fret." Colin chuckles and swats my hands from tugging at the white blouse my friend Poppy lent to me. "Dad." He greets his father when Vic arrives and it takes a few seconds for me to get enough courage to look him in the eye.

His dark eyes are preying on me. "Who is this?" he demands of his son. "Colin, I don't have time for another one of your puppy love—"

Colin clears his throat. "This is Veronica, Dad. I love her."

Vic snorts and doesn't bother giving me any attention. "I'm sure you do. Just like the last one and the one before that."

This isn't going well. I'm getting angry at Colin each time they banter back and forth. I didn't want to believe that he was the womanizer everyone said he was. I thought he was different and didn't want to collect me into his scrapbook of women.

"I think I'm going to head home," I say and try to shake

Colin's grip from me. He made me think I was special, and I should've known better than to believe anything he said.

"No, V. Stay, okay? Dad, I love her and it's real this time."

Vic waves him off. "Whatever, I need a drink." He walks away from us and pours brown liquid from a crystal decanter into a scotch glass. "Where did you get this one? At least she's got a nice rack on her—the other ones you bring home look like cardboard cutouts."

Colin scoffs. "Don't speak about her like that." Vic leaves the room and Colin starts to run after him. Before he leaves me alone, he turns back with sadness in his eyes. "I'll make him see, V. He'll love you just as much as I do. You're not trash and I don't want you to leave."

"I won't," I hear myself squeak.

His eyes darken as he glares over at me. "Promise me?"

"I promise I won't leave you, Colin."

———

THAT WAS a promise I never intended to keep. The living room of Vic's old mansion fades and I feel Colin's love for me fade too. I never had a doubt in my mind that he loved me; I just got too scared to admit that he needed me as much as I needed him.

It's insane how much Oliver looks like Colin. Right down to his skinny nose and broad jawline, his tall and overbearing frame, and even the way he holds himself screams Colin Jackson. Maybe he learned it from him, I don't fucking know.

I think about my son and how I jumped in front of him when Casey shot that gun off.

After we fell, it was too hard to stay awake to make sure he was okay. I don't know where the bullet went or where Julie ended up, but Casey ran away with his damn tail between his legs like a coward.

He's nothing like his father.

As far as I'm concerned, he'll never know who that is.

———

"No," I whisper and shake my head as I look at the stick in my hands. The window has two lines inside of it and sets me into a frenzy of horror. "Shit, what am I gonna do?"

A few soft knocks on the door and it makes me drop the stick onto the ground. "Veronica? Are you okay in there?" Colin calls for me. "You've been in there all morning."

Frantically, I hide the stick between a few goldenrod bath towels and flush the toilet to make him believe I just have the stomach flu. He just let me back into his and Oliver's lives and this will ruin everything. He knocks again and jiggles the handle of the bathroom door. "V, open the door."

I quickly check myself out in the mirror and still look like a damn mess ran over three times on the side of the road, but I find the handle and unlock it, letting him come bursting inside to see me standing in the middle of the bathroom with worry on my face.

"What's going on in here?" His tall body hovers over me. I want to wrap myself around him and try to make this all go away, but that's not the life I live. He'll expect me to stay forever this time if I tell him I'm pregnant with his baby again. Shit, he expected me to stick around the first time, but

my own mind got the best of me and jerked my happy ending straight out from underneath me.

Yet he lets me keep coming back.

"Baby…" His warm hands slide up my arms. "What's wrong?"

I shake my head and quickly think of something to hold him off. "I'm just feeling a little sick, is all. I'm still getting rid of most of that shit in my system, you know?"

He cringes at my choice of language, but I don't know how to be anyone else for him anymore. "You know you can always tell me anything, right? I know you say that part of your life is over but…V, it doesn't just go away like that. Are you sure you won't let me pay for rehab? You could go somewhere nice like Arizona or Tahoe…you'd like that."

"I don't want to leave you again." I lower my eyes to the ground. "I want to be here with you and Oliver. That's what I want, Colin."

He smiles. "I know you want to believe that. You can stay here as long as you want, you know that. But, this is the last time, Veronica. If you leave this time, you're gone for good."

I have to stay.

"My mother wants me to visit her for a few months in July." I blink a few times to hold back the hot, lying tears about to fall down my face. "She damn near insisted."

His lips graze mine and I know I'm defenseless. I let him tip my chin up so our lips can meet and we click together like long-lost puzzle pieces at the bottom of a toy chest.

"That's over six months away." He laughs into my mouth. "I want to take this one day at a time. Oliver deserves that from me—he's only two, but he's already confused why you keep leaving and showing back up. Six months from now,

if you're still around…we'll cross that bridge with your mother."

I snort. *"You know she hates you."*

"I can't believe you don't hate her for leaving you at that inn to fend for yourself. My mother died in childbirth…or at least that's what my father told me. I know Marva's my real mother, but I'll never tell her that I know."

"Why not? She's the nicest woman I've ever met."

The sexy, half-cocked smile he's known for shines on his lips. "They didn't want me to know for a reason. It's their business to tell, not mine. When they're ready, they can tell their story."

All is right and good around Colin Jackson.

"V?" He notices my drifting daydreams. "I'm glad you're back. I've missed you terribly."

Ask him, Veronica.

"Why do you let me keep coming back? What's the benefit for you?" My lips move and I instantly regret my questions. He doesn't frown or get angry. Instead, he searches through answers inside his mind like he's got them all planned out and ready to pick one to run with.

"I get to be with you," he flatly says. "That's all I can ever want."

"When are you going to give up on me?" My mouth is dry, but I need to make sense of this. "I'm going to keep falling back into my stupid fucking ways, Colin. I'm never going to be the woman, mother, or wife you want me to be."

He swoops me into his arms and tucks me into his chest. "I just want you to be the woman I fell in love with at the cabin. I want you to be the pure and kind-hearted person you showed me you could be. You didn't care about my money or my material things, V. You wanted my heart and you wrapped yourself around it so tightly, it's hard to fucking let you go."

His voice turns into a growl. "I can't stop thinking about you. I'll never, ever stop wanting you. I think I'm just at a point now where it's not enough for me anymore. I need more from you, Veronica, and I'm hoping that this time you can give it to me or I'm going to have to let you go."

I nod. "Warning noted."

He laughs and it electrifies the bottom half of my torso. "No warning, baby—just communication."

"Call it what you want, but I don't have high hopes for myself."

"I'll always see you for who you are, Veronica. Always."

―――――

COLIN WASN'T LYING. He always saw me for who I truly was: a weak, poor excuse for a mother and lover. Why he kept trying to find the light inside of me I'll never understand, but I'm thankful for it, nonetheless. Somehow, it kept me going long enough to finally realize I'm tired of living that life.

It's way too fucking late.

Luckily, I'm not looking for redemption. I'm looking for peace in whatever amount of years I have left on this Earth...wait. I *was* looking for peace, and my years on Earth are all fucking done now. Oddly enough, I do feel like I'm floating on a cloud of serenity.

No more pain.

No more regrets.

―――――

The way Colin's chocolate eyes wrap around my soul washes every bad thing in my life away. He follows me around the bedroom as I unpack from my fake trip to see my mother in Tulsa. He wants to hear about my reunion with her and I've rehearsed everything that I'm gonna say, but he isn't giving me any damn space to breathe.

I turn to him and stop him from coming any closer with my extended arms. "I want to talk to you about this, but let me get settled, okay? I want to check in on Oliver—"

"He's asleep." *Colin blushes and turns away.* "My father is taking him to the country club tomorrow for Grandparents' Day."

I snort. "Vic is interested in being a grandfather now? I was only gone for three months."

"Three months too long," *Colin coos and takes my hand in his.* "I haven't spoken to you in a few weeks. You had me worried you weren't coming home."

"I told you I'd be back. I promised you…"

He laughs and quickly kisses my lips. "I know, I know. I'm sorry I assume the worst when you've shown me that things are really changing this time. So, how was the trip?" *He wastes no time in trying to catch me in a lie.* "Did you do anything exciting?"

I sigh and break free from his reach. "We did some horseback riding and she taught me how to make her famous spaghetti sauce, but other than that, not really. We talked a lot and I came to terms with a lot of questions in my life. I had questions and she had answers. That's all."

He notes that I don't want to talk about it anymore and my quick and bold answers will have to do for now. Colin's never one to push too hard, especially with someone as flighty as me.

Plus, I just gave birth to another son of his and left the baby on a firehouse doorstep.

He'll never forgive me for that.

"I'd like to take a shower and get some sleep...is that okay?"

"Of course it's okay; I'm sure you're tired. Tell you what —you take your shower and I'll let you unwind. We can talk more in the morning."

His trust is so suffocating that even the guilt mixed in is running scared. His lips press against my cheek and he bounces from the room, whistling the same fairy tale song he sings when he's extremely content and happy with things.

My heart sinks into my stomach.

It's not too late to get that baby back. Maybe Colin won't expect me to be a perfect mother this time.

The entire night, I lie next to Colin and stare into the darkness. There's something wrong with me to be giving up on all these children that are supposed to be a part of me. I'm supposed to protect them, not abandon them the first chance I get. Oliver didn't have it much better than the baby I just left, but at least he knew what it was like to have some sort of a mother for a little while.

That baby will never know me.

It's daylight and before I realize it, Colin's stirring next to me and wrapping his arms around me...I'm still a little sore from giving birth in the back of Mac's van, but I try not to show it to avoid raising any questions.

Colin yawns and stretches himself against me, making sure I can feel the hardness he's pressing into my backside. It makes me smile that after all this time and after all I've done that he still wants me like he does.

"Good morning, V." His hot breath tickles my ear. "I have

to get Oliver ready so Vic can take him to the club. I'm dying for some of your famous buttermilk pancakes." He pokes my side in a not-so-subtle hint. "The way they melt in your mouth is beyond orgasmic."

I want to kick and scream for him to stop treating me like his wife, but I love it too much to let it go.

Deep down I only want one thing:

I wanna chase that freedom.

Clearing my throat, I push his hands playfully back toward him. "You get Oliver ready and I'll make the pancakes. I want to take a quick shower first."

He kisses my forehead and pulls on sweatpants before leaving the room. He talks to Oliver in the distance, so I jump up and rummage through my things to find my stash of various utensils to get me through the day. I find what I'm looking for and rub the powder along my gum line and quickly put the small container back into my things before Colin comes back in. I didn't bring much into the house with me in fear that he would find it, so I have to limit myself to make it last.

I put the clear plastic bag into the false bottom of my designated bathroom drawer. As far as I know, he's hasn't found this spot yet. Not bothering to look at myself in the mirror—maybe because I'm scared of what's looking back at me—I find a clean pair of jeans and t-shirt and change my clothes. Colin is still getting Oliver ready when I head downstairs to start the pancakes, but something in the air changes my induced mood.

"When the hell did you come crawling back?" Vic's smoky, hate-filled voice finds me. "I thought I told my son to get rid of you for good this time."

My eyes scan the area and I see him sitting on the leather

sofa in the living room, tapping his fingers on the arm next to him and frowning. "I see he chose not to listen to me."

"Nice to see you too, Vic." I shake my head and start to head to the kitchen.

"Get back here," he demands, standing up. He's taller than Colin by a few inches, and that's even more intimidating. "I want to talk to you about where the hell you've been."

"I was at my mother's," I tell him in a robotic voice. "Not that it's any of your business."

He shoves his hands into the pockets of his expensive suit. "Who was the baby daddy, huh?"

"What are you talking about—"

His cold eyes burn into mine. "Don't fucking play dumb with me, you piece of unworthy trash. You're dumber than I thought if you think I didn't have you followed. Colin should've done it but, like always, he has a soft spot for you and your bullshit. If his mother were alive, she would've gotten rid of you by now."

"I still don't know what you're talking about." I start to stutter. "W-Why can't you j-just leave us be?"

"Because my son is blinded by you and it's going to eat him alive, that's why. You're not worthy enough for him, and I'm going to prove it to you. I'll pay you to stay away from him."

I scoff. "I'm not here for the money."

"Like hell you aren't." He laughs. "You're here for whatever you can get your grimy little hands on. I'm not a stupid man."

"So that's it? You're offering me money to leave?"

He holds up his index finger and presses it against his wicked grin. "That's right...what's the amount that will make you disappear?" He opens a black checkbook and waits for an answer. I silently admit to myself that I could take the money and run. Oliver and Colin are both better off without me; Colin is so consumed with making me into a better person that I don't want him to lose Oliver in the crossfire.

Something makes me back down.

"Suit yourself." He brings the checkbook back to his pocket. "But mark my words, I'm not letting this go. I didn't want to be a grandfather the first time, but that was a Jackson baby you threw away like the trash you are. Lucky for you, the investigator that tailed you called me to take care of it."

I gasp and cover my mouth. "If you just left it there, it would've been taken care of! What did you do?"

"Calm down, I found it a family so it wouldn't suffer."

Colin comes into the room with little Oliver in tow, his big and bright green eyes looking at me like I'm a complete stranger.

I have to try this time.

I have to really, really try.

I can't get Vic's black checkbook out of my mind.

But I'm going to try to hold on a little longer and be the person I want to be.

TWENTY-ONE
HEATHER

SACRIFICING all of the parts of my life that I've done so much work on wasn't a hard decision. I mean, not *really*, anyway. You just gotta know who and what you're sacrificing it for, and if it's worth the interruption in your soul to make room for something more.

That's what I did.

Brandon wiggles his nose as we start taping up the first box, looking at each other to see what we should pack first. After a long night of serious conversation, I decided that moving away together didn't seem so bad. After all, I won't be alone.

"Okay, so Nate has a few friends in L.A., so with their help I was able to narrow down our choices for lofts in the area. We're going to be living in Newton Beach, which isn't far from the city, so you can go to school, we can get jobs and do anything else we want to do, and it's all close by. Plus, Newton Beach is the cheapest place we can be without slumming it *too* badly." He catches his breath and looks over at the entertainment center. "I'm not sure how much room we have compared to this place, so maybe we should downsize a little just to be on the safe side?"

I stand up and move toward the coat closet next to the front door. "Okay, you start with the movies and video games and I'll start with the coat closet. Sounds pretty efficient, yeah?"

He nods. "Let's do it. Thanks for helping, Heather."

I push away his gratitude so I can make room for my growing pleasure. "I don't mind moving, honestly. There's really nothing left for us here except maybe Julie and Oliver." The first few coats I take out of the closet I throw into a pile off to the side to donate. "I tried calling her yesterday, but her phone keeps going straight to voicemail. I wanted them to know we were moving."

"Ah." He waves me off and already has his box halfway full. "They're probably just fucking in every room of that fancy new house he bought her. I'm sure everything is fine...he wouldn't let anything happen to her after what we all just went through."

Not that I *want* to think about Oliver and Julie having sex, but that's the picture that Brandon has painted inside of my mind and I'm sticking with it. I'm too tired to worry about other people anymore—except maybe for Brandon.

He's definitely my exception.

"Hey, it doesn't get all wintery in California like it does here, right? So, most of these heavy winter coats can be donated, and if we need them later on, we can figure something out. The less we move, the better off we'll be, I think. I'm going to start a space in the garage for donation stuff to be more organized." I flip my hair over my shoulder. "Unless you don't want me to be in charge of packing and moving since it's mostly your stuff."

He shrugs. "I don't care, babe. If you want to spearhead this expedition, go for it."

The laugh that escapes my throat startles me. "You gotta get used to me bossing you around if you want to move across the country with me."

Brandon's fingers find his forehead and he salutes me. "Noted."

For the next three hours, we joke and laugh about different things as we fill the cardboard moving boxes. As Brandon tapes the last one shut, we look around the living room and try to catch our breath. "We literally just emptied four rooms in three hours." He laughs and kicks his feet up onto the coffee table. "I like this; it's like we're cleansing our lives and we're at the beginning of an exciting new one."

I snicker and mix my legs with his. "We're about to break into a new exciting life, remember? I can't believe how much stuff you've accumulated over the years. Did you know you had like, three boxes of beer bottle caps?"

His eyes widen. "What did you do with those?"

"I put them in the trash pile in the garage."

Brandon leaps off of the sofa and throws things around in the garage. I wait for him to return with the three shoeboxes of bottle caps and they jingle as he sits them in front of me. As I prepare to turn up my nose at the apparent pile of junk he's brought to me, he taps the top of the first box and frowns.

"This is all I have left of my father."

I feel dizzy. "I thought you had—"

He shakes his head. "This is all that's left. He told me if I collected a thousand bottle caps before I turned nine, he would get me my first bike. I went around to everyone I knew, all the neighbors and even ran the streets looking for them. Nate even stood outside a liquor store with me one day, and we got over a hundred caps in one afternoon."

The faraway look on his face makes me sad. "I bet you miss Nate sometimes."

"Yeah, sometimes. He was the only real friend I had until I met Julie." He blushes and turns his gaze toward mine. "And now you."

He sits back down next to me and stretches his legs back to their original spot. I curl myself into his side, and his warm palm finds the thickness of my thigh and presses firmly against me.

"Let's eat whatever we can find in the fridge for dinner to get rid of some stuff." His voice is tired, but I'm already halfway asleep on his chest. "Then we can pack the rest of the house and not lose momentum."

I snuggle deeper against his heartbeat. "We don't have to leave for another week."

"True." He takes a deep breath in and holds it.

I don't know how long it took him to fall asleep as he held me on the sofa, but when my phone startles me awake, the house is dark and he's tucked me further into him as he sleeps soundly in the same position I last saw him in. The jingle of my ringtone in the other room echoes through the house, and I'm not quick enough to find it in the purple room before it stops.

Lucy.

Why is *she* calling me?

What could she possibly want at midnight?

I dial her back and listen to it ring a few times. When she picks up, I hear her sobbing and frantically talking to someone, but I can't make out who it is or what they're saying.

"Lucy?" I say loudly into the phone. "Are you okay?"

She doesn't hear me and keeps hurriedly speaking to someone on her end of the line. Before I know it, a loud bang fills my ear and I drop the phone onto the ground. I cry out in pain and Brandon races on his long legs into the room before he picks me up off the ground.

"What happened?" he asks, pushing the hair from my face. "Did you hurt yourself?"

I hold my ear and calm down. "I think that was a gunshot." The information sinks into my brain like molasses, but when it hits the center, my eyes widen and I start to panic. "That was a *gunshot*! Brandon, that was Lucy calling me and I didn't get to it in time…but when I called her right back, she was talking to someone and then…that sound…I think she got shot!"

He holds my shaking body on the floor of the purple room. "Baby, I think you were dreaming."

"*No*! Look at my phone!" I pick up the phone from the floor and show him the proof that she called me and I called her right back. I dial her number and put it on speakerphone, but now—even on the third time I try—it goes straight to voicemail.

"Dammit!" I slam it down on the carpet. "I know what I heard. What should we do?"

"I don't know." He shakes his head. "It's not like we can call the cops—we don't even know where she is or if that was actually a gunshot."

"But she could be in trouble…what if she dies or something and I could've saved her?"

He searches my eyes and figures out that I'm not going to give up. After he takes in a deep breath and sighs, he lets me loose from his grip. "I don't know why you're trying to be such a martyr lately, but okay, let's call the cops."

He stands up and goes into the living room to find his phone. When I find my bearings and call Lucy a few more times to make sure she doesn't answer, I find him speaking to someone on the phone in the living room in a hushed tone.

"Yeah, my girlfriend got a phone call from her and when she tried to call her back, Lucy answered but apparently there was a gunshot…No, we don't even know where Lucy is, that's the problem…Sure. I understand…Uh, I'm not sure, but I'll ask my girlfriend."

Brandon holds the phone from his ear and turns to me. "Do you know any of Lucy's other friends?"

I cross my arms over my chest. "Julie."

"Right." He clears his throat and continues talking to the person on the phone. "Yeah, I got it. I already gave her number to the first person I talked to. Yeah, thanks again." He hangs up the phone and looks over at me. "I gave them her number and they're going to try and call her, but there's nothing they can do without knowing where she is."

"I figured." My sadness finds my cheeks and flushes

them with heat. "Well, at least we tried. That's more than the old me would've done."

"Is that why you're doing this? Are you trying so hard to be someone else that you think you have to make perfect choices every time?"

I don't know what to say.

"I don't think I have to be perfect—I think I just have to be a different person," I answer him. "No one is perfect...that's something I have to remind myself daily."

He nods. "Okay, then. I just want you to be yourself, Heather. I love the real you, not whatever version you think you have to be to keep me interested."

The phone rings in my hand and Lucy's name flashes across the screen. Fear washes over me and Brandon takes it from my hand to answer it before the call ends.

"Lucy?" he says into the phone. "This is Brandon, Heather's boyfriend." His eyes widen at whatever she says; her voice is high-pitched enough that I can hear her, but I can't make the words out. *"What? Are they okay? Where are they? What the fuck happened?...* Okay, okay. We can meet you there—is she alive?"

Brandon's eyes narrow as he snarls, "I'm going to find him and fucking kill him...who got shot?" He glances at me and I want to claw his eyes out for making me wait. "...Okay, we'll be there soon, don't worry. We'll meet you in the ER entrance."

He hangs up the phone and looks me directly in the eye.

"Casey shot Oliver and tried to kidnap Julie."

I want to laugh. I really, *really* want to laugh. "That's not funny."

"I know it's not—I'm not joking. From what Lucy could coherently tell me...Casey tried to get Julie to come with him and he had a gun...Oliver tried to save her, and Casey shot him. They took Oliver, Julie, and Oliver's mom to the hospital."

I choke. "Why was his *mom* there?"

He shrugs. "I don't know, babe. But our friends need us right now, so this would be the time to saddle up and be that better person you want to be."

A smile tugs at my lips. "I just hope they're all okay."

I can't wait to be the one *they* all need and depend on.

Heather Michaels...the new unicorn in town.

TWENTY-TWO
JULIE

"JULIE?" Randy's voice echoes in the darkness. "Hey, Jules? Can you hear me?"

I can hear you!

My body starts to shake and sets into a panic. "What's wrong with her?" Randy screams. "*Help her!*"

"The sedative wore off too soon and she's going back into shock," a male voice says. "She took a nasty fall. I'm going to give her more sedative and let her body rest a little longer. How long has she had anxiety issues?"

Randy clears his throat. "I...uh, wasn't aware that she did."

"Oh, sorry. I thought you were her brother."

"I am. I just don't know the answer to your question."

They are silent for what seems like hours.

"Well..." the male voice says, and something smacks —I picture his hands clapping together. "She should sleep soundly for a while, and then when she starts to wake up again, we can just hope for the best."

"Thanks, doctor."

"No problem. Have the nurses call me if you need me."

I need you!

I need you to wake me back up!

The drugs start to kick in and I drift back off deep into the darkness.

———

"ALL RISE," the man in the sheriff's uniform shouts. "Let me introduce the Honorable Judge Vaughn." His arm moves like he's conducting a symphony toward a tall, thin woman stepping up in the middle of the long bench and gazing over the crowd seated in the courtroom.

"Be seated." She purses her lips and sits down in her black leather chair. "This is the matter of The State of California versus Bob and Dianne Remington. You're charged with nine counts of felony identity theft, sixteen counts of credit card fraud, and three counts of child endangerment and neglect. How do you plead?"

Bob and Dianne look at each other and then back at me. They're sitting at a table with a tired-looking older woman who asked me a lot of questions a few weeks ago. The woman doesn't bother looking back because she knows she's going to lose and probably doesn't even care.

"Not guilty," they say at the same time.

"It was our daughter, Your Honor," Bob pleads. "She was lying and stealing—she made all of those credit card applications and forged all of those signatures."

My jaw drops open. I didn't even want to be here, but my case worker said in order to move in with Randy's mom, Helen, I'd have to testify against my parents.

And now they're glaring at me like a stranger.

"Arrest her, she's the one who did it!" Dianne squeals and points to me.

The judge bangs her gavel. "Calm down! You two are disgusting! You come into my courtroom after being caught and blame everything on your own daughter? So, I suppose the keeping her locked in a dark room for weeks was of her asking?"

She stares at them, but they don't answer.

"And depriving her of basic needs like food and water? She wanted *to be starved? I'm surprised you let her out to use the restroom, but from the looks of you two, you didn't want to clean up the mess so you didn't let it get that far. Counselor, you may proceed with your introductions." The judge nods at the wired-up young attorney on the other side of the room who is itching to go crazy.*

The rest of the morning was slow and boring; all anyone talked about was the money that they stole and the people they deceived. They stole over half a million dollars from twenty-five people, and some have still yet to be uncovered. People stole glances at me the entire time, but I stayed silent and kept my eyes forward like I didn't notice.

I noticed.

"Next witness."

The wiry young man looks at me. "The State calls Julie Remington to the stand."

The entire room looks at me and time stands still. I know they all want me to burst out in tears and run to the stand to blame my parents for everything. I want to do that, but my legs won't move.

Randy nudges my side. "Hey, I didn't come all this way not to take you back with me." He winks and it makes me feel loved for the first time in my life.

"Okay," I whisper and stand up, walking slowly to the young attorney who waits for me next to the witness stand.

He swears me in and reads me everything he needs to read me before asking me questions. I tell him all about the credit card applications I found that lead us all here today. I tell him about the revolving door of people that come and go from my house with rolls of cash, about the time they asked me if I would sleep with an older man for money, and about all the times when they sent me out to do odd jobs and bring the money home to them.

I never tell them about the boy with the green eyes.

I never tell anyone about him.

"Miss Remington?" The man snaps his fingers and I come back into reality. "Is there anything else you know that you haven't already told us?"

"Objection!" the tired woman sitting next to my parents says. "We are basing this case on the lies of a confused teenager. She's not educated enough to be answering these questions."

"Yes, I am," I say and glare at her. "I know what happened to me and I know what they did and it sounds like you do too."

The crowd mutters and the woman looks shocked. The younger man that was questioning me looks pleased. "Miss Remington, if the opposing counsel has no further questions, you are free to go." He looks at the woman, who shakes her head. "You may step down from the witness *bench; you did an excellent job." He smiles at me and helps me out.*

Randy is concentrated and frustrated through the rest of the day, and when the twelve jury members come back into the room, he squeezes my hand so tightly that it might fall off. We wait for everyone to be seated and then stand again for the judge to enter the room. Once everything is back to the way it was before we left, Dianne turns to look at me with sadness in her eyes.

"I love you," she mouths.

I shake my head and she frowns and turns around. She doesn't get to say that now, not when we're here for crimes they committed. Randy lets go of my hand and pats my leg to comfort me. "Just a few more minutes and it'll all be over."

The main jury person stands up and addresses the judge, but I don't listen to what they say. I'm just waiting for the word, "guilty." The judge reads the paper that is passed to her and nods. "Madam Foreperson, in the matter of The State of California versus Bob and Dianne Remington, what say you?"

The woman clears her throat; she looks nervous. "On nine charges of identity theft, we find the defendants…guilty. On the charges of sixteen counts of credit card fraud…we find the defendants guilty. On the three counts of child neglect and endangerment…we find the defendants guilty."

The judge nods her head as Dianne cries. "Well, you two, I guess you're found guilty in my courtroom today. This holds the penalty and combined jail time of sixteen years each. Which, I find might not even be enough for what you've done to your daughter, let alone the other charges. I sentence you to sixteen years in California State Penitentiary with the possibility of parole after ten years." She bangs her gavel, and

Bob and Dianne don't even fight when they are taken into custody. Randy manages to scoop me up and out the doors before any reporters ask questions.

"We're meeting with Fern, your case worker, so I can take you home," he says and sits me down on a stone bench away from the courthouse. "Here she comes."

Fern walks to us and her wide smile comforts me. I've liked talking to her and it's going to be sad to leave her behind, but I want to go home with Randy so badly that it's hard to listen to anything she has to say just in case it's bad.

"Randy." She shakes his hand and her smile gets bigger when she looks at me. "Well, are you ready to board the plane?"

I swallow a hard lump in my throat. "I can go?"

She nods. "You can go. Your Aunt Helen will be taking care of you. A case worker in New York has already set you up and you're ready to live your new life."

My new life.

A life in New York.

I turn to Randy. "Does Aunt Helen live near you?"

He nods. "She lives three miles away. You can call me anytime you want, and trust me when I say this—she's nothing like Dianne."

I smile. "Do I call her Aunt Helen even though she's not my real aunt?"

They both laugh and Fern hugs me. "You can call her whatever you want: She's a nice woman. I've spoken to her on several occasions and I wouldn't be sending you somewhere you aren't wanted."

"She wants me?"

Randy nods. "She wants you, Julie. She knows how Bob is and wants to give you a better life."

A new life.

A better life.

I never liked my life unless I was with people who treated me like a human being.

"Since you're a little behind in school, you'll be starting in eighth grade, if that's okay." Randy smiles at Fern. "We'll make sure you don't get too far behind, and Mom and I will take you shopping when we get home and settled in for school clothes and anything else you need."

My eyes find the ground. "What about Marianna and Clyde? He's still really little…doesn't he need stuff too?"

Randy snorts. "He has what he needs; we're talking about you."

Fern squeezes my shoulder. "I have to get going, but I want you to know you can call me for anything, okay? Just because you're in a different state doesn't mean my job stops. I'm here for you, Julie, but your brother's going to take good care of you."

She leaves and Randy shakes her hand before she goes. "Thanks for everything."

When she's out of sight, he leans down and looks me in the eye. "Listen, don't worry about Clyde or Marianna. He's four, he's more excited about meeting you than anything else. I never apologized for how long it took me to come for you, Julie." A tear falls down his cheek. "Did they hurt you any more than what you said in court?"

"No."

"Are you sure? I want to get you into counseling if they touched you—"

I violently shake my head. "No one touched me. That one time they tried to offer me up but nothing happened. I promise."

He hugs me tightly and nearly squeezes my insides out of my body. "I just want you to have a good life now that you're free of them. By the time they get out, you'll be an adult and won't have to worry about being sent back to them, but it's still hurting me that it took so long to get you back."

I smile and my lips are so dry that they crack. "I know you tried."

He sniffles and wipes his tears away. "I promise that you'll never have to live that life again."

"You saved me, Randy." The words that he desperately wanted to hear make the light return to his eyes. "You're my savior. I owe you a lot."

"You owe me nothing." He stands up and takes my hand. "Let's go home."

Home.

My new life.

My better life.

Home.

———

MY EYES FEEL like glue but I manage to open them anyway. I don't know how long I've been out, but the bright lights above me burn into my eyes like fire and I have to look away. When I slightly turn my head to the right, Randy is softly snoring in a chair next to me. His hand is open like he was holding my hand and fell asleep; a blanket is draped over him like someone's been in here and tended to him while checking in on me.

"Hey, Aunt Julie," I hear Clyde whisper as he taps me on my other arm. His wild red hair is matted with sleep and sweat, and as he pushes it back out of his eyes, I see that he hasn't actually slept and his eyes are red with worry. "Are you okay?"

I cough and try to sit up a little, but I'm so groggy that I can't move. "Water," I manage to get out, and he bolts up to pour a glass of water and hand it to me. After I struggle to take a few sips, I wiggle my cold toes and notice that I'm still wearing my street clothes and not a hospital gown.

"What happened?" I hold my head and try to concentrate. "Where's Oliver?"

Clyde shrugs. "No one has told me anything yet. You've only been here for a few hours."

I gulp loudly. "*Hours*? Clyde, go get a nurse for me, please."

"Aunt Julie—"

I glare at him. "Find Oliver, Clyde, *please*."

He nods and leaves the room without arguing anymore. Randy stirs next to me and opens his eyes, surprised to see that I'm awake and he was asleep. "Where's Clyde?" He clears his throat and looks toward where his son sat just seconds before.

"He went to get information on Oliver," I say and look at my socks. "What's going on?"

He rubs his jawline and sits up in his chair. "That Casey guy, he had a gun and shot it off in the hallway as he tried to take you with him. Your friend Lucy managed to pull you into Oliver's apartment and shut the door before you got caught up in all of that, but you opened the door to check on Oliver and had a panic attack when you saw the blood."

I notice that I'm not wired up to any IVs or machines anymore. "So…I'm okay? I didn't get shot?"

He shakes his head. "You're fine, you just had some anxiety issues. Which…I didn't know about until today." Randy's eyes fill with sadness. "When did those start?"

I shrug. "I don't know…I've always been able to keep things bottled up. Just lately, my emotions are getting the best of me, and I can't control them unless I'm around Oliver."

Randy frowns. "I wish you'd let me help you when you started noticing the signs."

"I just want to see Oliver." I blink a few times at him and wait for him to argue. He doesn't; instead he stands up and smooths out his clothes.

"I'll see what I can find out."

"Who did Casey shoot?"

He turns back to me before leaving the room and can't make himself look me in the eye.

"Randy." My voice shakes. "*Who* did he shoot?"

"I don't know, Julie. I've been in here with you since the hospital called me."

Panic starts to shake my bones. "I need Oliver, I need to make sure he's okay."

Randy nods and leaves me alone.

Silence.

Oliver Jackson, you better be alive or I'm going to kill you myself.

TWENTY-THREE
OLIVER

"SO, is he going to be okay, then?" someone says at the other end of the room. I open my eyes and Randy is standing with a doctor, nodding his head. "What about his mother?"

Veronica.

"She's in pretty bad shape; the bullet ricocheted around and landed in her lung. We had to surgically remove it, but she lost a lot of blood and she can't breathe on her own for now."

"But, she'll pull through?"

The doctor shakes his head. "It's hard to say right now. But, if she hadn't pushed him aside and took the bullet herself, he definitely wouldn't be alive right now. The bullet would've pierced his heart judging from the way I was told it went down."

Don't say it, Doc.

"She saved his life."

Fuck.

Are you fucking serious?

Of course she would do something like that to make herself seem like the good guy.

"Where's Julie?" I demand, making the two men jump. "I want to see Julie right *now*."

Randy holds out his hands. "Okay, I'll take you to her, just take it easy, okay? You hit your head hard when you fell and it knocked you out."

"I heard."

He eyeballs me, telling me silently to stop being an asshole. "Oliver, listen to me. You're still fuzzy in the head, just take it easy. Julie is fine, she's down the hall in Room 311."

My legs have never carried me as fast as they do in the three seconds it takes me to run out of the room and down the hallway to get to Julie. Forget the fact that I thought I was dead—*again*—or that I had no fucking idea what Veronica did for me, but when I see her bright blue eyes as the door opens, nothing else fucking matters.

"Baby, are you okay?" I run to her and examine every inch of her body she lets me touch before swatting my hands away from her. "Are you hurt? I'm gonna fucking kill Casey."

"Join the club, I'm there too," Brandon says from behind me. He walks into the room with Heather. When he notices my reaction, he lowers his eyes. "Hey, uh— Heather and I will be outside the room, okay? When you're ready for visitors, we'll be right here. Let's give them some space." He looks down at Heather who doesn't want to, but she agrees and shuts the door behind them as they leave.

"What are *they* doing here?" Julie furrows her eyebrows. "Did you call them?"

I growl and shake my head. "I don't fucking care about them right now. Are you okay?"

"I'm okay." Her voice is small and I wrap her into my arms now that I know she isn't hurt. "Just a little groggy from the sedative, but I'm okay."

I snort and lie down next to her in the bed. "I think I need to buy stock in this place judging from the amount of time and money we've spent here in the last six months."

Julie laughs and snuggles into my side. "Let's get married on New Year's."

"New Year's? That's like less than two months away—"

Her giggle is warm like honey and I want to devour her mouth with mine. "Unless you're changing your mind and don't want to get married…then I guess we don't have to worry about picking a date."

"No fucking way." I tip her chin. "As far as I'm concerned, you're already my wife."

"One stipulation." She holds up her index finger. "I want Veronica to be there."

Shit. I didn't tell her about that.

"Oh, uh—Veronica is…well, we have to see about that." My fingers find my hair and they repeatedly run through the sweaty strands. Julie waits for a better answer, but all I can think about is how her heart is going to break knowing Veronica sacrificed herself for me. It may warm her heart, but for me it's just something she owed me.

Okay, maybe she didn't *owe* me her life.

Fuck, I'm starting to feel bad.

"Oliver?" Julie's wide, bright eyes glitter. "What is it?"

Just tell her already.

I bite the inside of my cheek. "It seems that Veronica pushed me out of the way and the bullet hit her side and ended up in her lung. She had emergency surgery and I'm not sure what else. That's all I heard before I ran here to you." I feel my cheeks flush; I'm embarrassed that she sees vulnerability in me when I try so hard to be strong. "I had to make sure you were alive."

She sighs and sits on the bed. "I'm alive. I'm always going to come out alive." Her smile invites me closer and pulls me down on the bed with her; the feeling of her love wrapping around me draws me into another reality for a few magical minutes until her hand meets mine and she squeezes for comfort.

I have to be that man for her.

"It's gonna be fine." I catch her head that falls on my chest. She sobs into my sweaty t-shirt but I don't fucking care. She can do whatever she wants to me and I'll follow her anywhere. "Hey…" I pull her chin up gently. "Let's go check on her, okay?"

I have to play like I want to know.

Julie deserves that much from me.

She sniffles and lifts her body away from mine. "Okay, that sounds like a good idea."

Her tired feet try their best to keep up with mine as she follows me out of the room and to the nurses' station. A few nurses zip through the station without looking at us, so I wave my hand in the air and catch the attention of a young male nurse as he tries to pass us by.

"Yes?" He blinks a few times trying to remember our names. "What can I do for you?"

I lick my lips and choose my words carefully. "We came here with my mother, Veronica Bennett." I nervously look down at Julie, who looks impressed that I care to use my mother's full name like I'm familiar with her like that. "She had a gunshot wound to her abdomen and had surgery—"

"You're her son?" His eyebrows rise. "And your name is?"

My chest puffs out and I'm not going to let some fucking idiot with a pair of hospital scrubs on get the best of me. "Oliver Jackson. She's my mother—I want information."

He looks like he's about to protest so I put my hands on the counter and lean in a little, hoping he'll get the hint.

"*Now.*"

We can see the lump in his throat as he swallows it down and backs off of me. "Let me see if she's allowed visitors."

"Don't bother because we're about to see her. What room?"

"Mr. Jackson—"

"What. Room?"

He checks the chart next to him and mutters something to himself that I choose to ignore. I know he feels the hole I'm burning into his fucking skull as he tries to stall so someone can save him from making a huge mistake. I don't even care about this guy at this point; I just want Julie to see that I can get shit done.

"She's in Room 415. Fourth floor. You're on the third floor," the nurse flatly says. "Don't let anyone know I told you or I can get fired, you hear me?"

I growl as he raises his index finger. "Threaten me or point that fucking finger at me one more time—" He lowers it quickly. "—and you're gonna wish you called in sick today."

"*Okay*!" Julie claps her hands and glares at me. "That's too far."

The nurse scoffs. "I'd listen to—"

The look I give him makes him back off, and I know I've gone too far without Julie even saying anything. She glares at me with knowing eyes; she's not stupid—she knows I'm trying and failing miserably at being a better person.

"That wasn't necessary," she says when we enter the elevator. "He would've told you what you wanted to know."

My eyes find the floor and I notice the dirt on her jeans. "Do you want to talk about what Casey did to you? I mean, do you want to wait until we're home and you've slept or are you ready to talk about it now?"

She giggles and wraps her arm around mine. "Oh, Oliver. I'm ready to check on your mother and figure out the rest of our shit later."

The elevator dings and we step onto the fourth floor. Brandon and Heather notice us as we start walking down the hall to find Room 415. I hold my arms in the air and reach out my hand so Brandon will shake it. He holds on tightly and nods when we let go; Heather extends her arms and wraps them around me in a friendly hug.

"We totally thought you guys were in trouble." Heather shakes her head. "Lucy called me and I heard a gunshot…it wasn't a fun few minutes to try and figure out." Her face turns green when she's realized what she's said. "*Oh*, I'm sorry! I didn't mean that what happened to me was worse than what happened to you! I haven't had any sleep since we've been packing and planning."

"Packing and planning?" Julie steps from beside me and returns Heather's hug halfway. "Are you guys moving somewhere?"

Brandon nods. "I've been blacklisted from the firms up here and Heather agreed to move to California with me to start fresh." He looks at Julie and smiles. "Newton Beach, of all places."

Julie blushes and it pisses me off. "Oh, that place is *beautiful*! I used to visit the little shops when I was younger and dream of owning one."

I pull her close and kiss her head. "Now you own a bar and restaurant, and if you want to own a little shop, you can do that too."

Heather groans. "It's going to be weird being so far away from here, but I guess I can get used to sandy beaches and more sunlight, right?"

A man in a white doctor's coat walks up to us and looks from me to Julie and back at me. "Are you Oliver Jackson?"

"Yes."

He opens a folder and motions for me to follow him. Julie latches onto my shirt and trails behind as we walk back toward the elevator and he stops. "I'm Dr. Samuels. I've been attending your mother since her surgery. She took the bullet in her left side and it traveled through and exploded in her lung. They got all the pieces out, but she's not breathing on her own right now. Her lung isn't strong enough yet."

Julie holds my hand and squeezes. "Will she be okay?"

He looks confused. "Didn't your brother find you and tell you any of this?" I don't know what the fuck he's talking about; he looks confused and shakes his head. "She isn't getting any stronger, and without *both* her lungs, she won't survive. There isn't any easy way to say this, but...if it comes to it, you might have to make a hard decision to take her off her support. But that won't be today. Do you have any questions right now?"

I shake my head. "I got it. Thanks."

He nods and leaves us alone; Julie steps in front of me and puts her hands on my face. "What do you want to do?"

"What do you mean?" I slide my hands over hers. "He said I didn't have to decide today."

"You're going to wait, though, right? I mean, you're not going to just take her off support tomorrow?" The fear in her voice saddens me.

My voice cracks. "Is *that* what you think of me?"

"No, I just—please don't be mad, I needed to make sure you're going to give her a chance."

I take a deep breath in and watch her honey blonde hair move when I blow it back out. "I'm going to wait, Julie, she's my mother. Even if it *weren't* my mother, I would wait. Maybe all the drugs she's done haven't torn her insides to fucking shreds and she has a fighting chance."

Her eyes narrow and she smiles. "You care about her."

"I don't."

Her fingers find my hair and she lightly runs her nails over my scalp. "You do, and I can see it. I love that you're worried about her, and I would also understand if you weren't. The man you are today isn't because of anyone but you, and I think your dad would be proud of how far you've come with her."

I close my eyes and pretend she didn't just say that.

"You didn't know him, Julie—don't say things like that."

Her arms fall to her side and she blushes. "I'm sorry, I was trying to make you feel better."

I wipe the tear falling from her eye. "I know, it's my fault. I'm too sensitive about that subject, I'm sorry. I love that you want to help me and trust me...I need you more than you'll ever fucking know."

The sweet smile returns to her lips and I kiss her gently, hardly remembering—or caring—that Brandon and Heather are just feet from us down the hall.

"You're crazy," she whispers and kisses my lips with such fucking passion that I have to hold myself steady. I grip the back of her head and catch her lips with each move they make against mine; her soft hair gets tangled between my fingers.

"You *make* me crazy." My lips find her ear. "Let's get rid of them and go home."

"None of this changes the fact that you brought

Lucy home." A light burns in her eyes because she's just remembered why she was out walking on the street in the first place. "Why didn't you come after me? Why did you call *Lucy*?"

I take her hand in mine and kiss her fingers. "We can spend the next fifty years talking about all of this... anything you ever want. I will be honest with you and tell you everything you want to know, but right now let's just settle down."

She snorts. "*Settle down*? Our lives are always chaos."

A smirk finds the corner of my mouth and I can't escape it. "I have a feeling that breaking all of these fucking rules are going to pay off for us soon." She breathes in deep and her face pales. "I know you don't like rules and I know we agreed to not having any more of them, and we won't. But Julie, don't you see? It's breaking those rules that brought us together even before we realized."

"Hey, guys?" Brandon interrupts us. "We're going to take off—is there anything we can do for you?"

I shake my head and look at him. "I think we're headed out too. I promise I'll make sure she has everything she needs, okay?" My eyes go back to Julie. "Veronica will be fine."

She nods and lets me put my arm around her and we lead everyone to the elevator. It's been a long fucking six months, and I just want to tuck Julie into my body and sleep with her forever. She leans her head on my shoulder as the elevator goes down and Heather turns to us with fear in her eyes.

"What about Casey?" She gulps. "Isn't he still out there?"

Fuck.

"Shit, she's right." My body vibrates with rage. "If he knows what's good for him, he'll fucking stay away. It's better if we don't go back to the apartment tonight."

Heather nudges Brandon. "You could stay with us."

"We'll stay at Randy's." I make a weird face on accident. "I'll text him and let him know we'll wait for him down in the lobby." Quickly realizing that Julie and I left our rooms without our things, I pat myself down one more time to make sure I don't have my phone or wallet.

Brandon notices that I'm struggling and pulls me aside. "I'll keep an eye on her while you run back for your shit." He smiles and pats my shoulder. "I'm glad you guys are okay."

My eyebrows furrow, but I don't have the time to ask questions.

The elevator takes forever to get to the third floor where I left Randy, but finally the doors open and I almost run into someone as I step outside.

"Oliver."

I look into his cold eyes and freeze.

Casey.

TWENTY-FOUR
CASEY

WHAT THE FUCK WAS THAT? I thought the gun that my father hid in his desk *wasn't* loaded—at least that's what he always told us when we asked.

I'm so fucking stupid.

What is *wrong* with me?

Forget about Julie, something inside of me clicked when she fought as hard as she did to get away from me. What was I thinking? Did I really think I could have her like that? I went about this all wrong, and now I'm going to be running from what I've done forever.

I try to catch my breath as I run down the flights of stairs to the parking garage of Oliver's apartment. The last fifteen minutes replay like a movie in my mind as I find my car and slam the door shut behind me.

I have no one now. *Literally* no one. I've fucked all of my relationships up over…lust and greed.

Maybe I *am* just like my mother.

It's getting hard to see through the sea of tears that fall from my eyes. There's no going back from this.

Oliver is going to see to it that I'm put away for fucking life for this.

The gun went off.

Did I shoot anyone?

I think really hard as I squeal the tires onto the main road and make my way to my parents' house. By now, someone would've called the cops and I wait for them to pass me, but I safely get into the driveway and inside the house before I see any. I stash the gun back where I found it and seriously think about driving back to Oliver's apartment to make sure Julie is okay and I didn't kill her.

My knees get weak, and if I don't get moving soon, I never will. My fingers shake when I open the safe in my father's office and pull out a few bundles of cash and stash them in a small messenger bag I find on his leather sofa. I'm making so much noise that the foyer light comes on; I'm able to quickly close the safe and hide the bag before my father comes into the room.

"What are you doing here so late?" He yawns and scratches his head. "Why didn't you call? I would've gotten up for a nightcap with you."

This may be the last time I see him.

"Dad…" I shake my head and can't contain my grief. "I…d-did something."

He looks concerned and sits on his sofa. "What did you do?"

There's really no other way to say it other than…just saying it.

"I stole your gun and I think I shot someone."

He stands up immediately and goes to his desk

where he finds the gun back in its place. "I'm confused, my gun is right here. Are you playing a joke?"

"No, I'm not." I turn and face him; the look in my eyes startles him and he knows I'm not lying. "Something is *wrong* with me, Dad. For the past six months I've become this jealous person and it's consumed me so much that I tried to force Julie to be with me."

He cocks his head. "Julie Remington? Oliver's girlfriend?"

I grit my teeth. "Yes, her. I love her, Dad."

"Does she love you?"

That's a loaded question. Julie *does* love me…just not in the way I want her to.

"No, not like that."

He licks his lips and tries to take in all this information without his brain exploding. "So, you stole my gun and shot her?"

"*No!* I had it for protection against Oliver because he already wanted to kill me for letting Julie get kidnapped."

His eyes bulge from his head. "*Kidnapped*? Julie was *kidnapped*?"

As I quickly run through the whole story, his interest is really piqued when I speak about Veronica. "She tried to talk me out of it, but everything was red and I felt so backed into a corner. When Oliver challenged me and told me to shoot him…I just…did. I shot at him."

My father closes his eyes. "Did you kill him?"

"I don't know, Veronica jumped in front of him, but I don't know if I clipped her or got him. I don't know if anyone was hit…I just ran."

"Oh, Casey…"

I put the messenger bag around my shoulders. "I know I fucked up, you don't have to tell me. I've *been* fucking up and now I have to leave." I start to walk away from him, but he calls me back with fear in his voice.

"Where are you going? If you stay here, we can get you a lawyer and help you."

Before I clear the doorway, I turn and look at the man who looks nothing like me. "I don't want any help. I did this, and I have to figure it out. Can you call the hospital and check on Oliver and Julie if they're there, though? Especially Julie—if I hurt her, I can't bear it."

He looks at me like a stranger. "Casey, don't do this. Don't do this to yourself, to me, or your mother. If you love Julie like you say you do, don't do this to her, either. We don't want to lose you, son."

My stomach sizzles from the words coming into my mouth. "You can't lose someone that was never actually yours to begin with." He wipes a tear from his eye as I leave him and run back to the car. It's hard to catch my breath through my flowing tears, but I manage to start punching the steering wheel anyway and scream at the top of my lungs.

I fucking *hate* this.

Why did I let it get this far?

The streets are deserted as I pass two ambulances with their sirens blaring. They're headed toward the hospital from Oliver's, and my heart starts to fucking burn.

I killed someone.

I can't run from this, I really fucking can't.

Am I going to live a life on the run forever?

No, I have to turn myself in.

I can't go back to my parents' house or the cops will try to involve them in this. This was all my fault, and I just want to see Julie one more time before I turn myself in. I need to see her face when I tell her I didn't mean to force her to be with me, but it was my only option to make her see how much of a better choice I am than Oliver.

Am I, though?

I've hurt her just as much as he has.

"Shit," I hiss and turn the car to head toward the hospital. There's no way I can confirm it was either of them in the back of those ambulances, but I have to try. I pull into a faraway parking lot and wait for a few paramedics to exit the open ambulance bay doors before I slip inside and try to find my way around. I find a door that leads to a long hallway and a lonely nurses' station with an older woman sitting behind the desk. I smile at her, but she doesn't smile back.

"What do you need?" she snarls at me, rubbing her eyes. "Better have a good reason for waking me up from my nap."

I snort. "I need to know what room Julie Remington is in, please."

She doesn't move. "Are you family?"

"I'm her brother," I lie and cringe at the thought. "She came in not long ago."

Hoping that Julie actually is here, I wait for the old woman to type something on her keyboard and take her sweet time giving me the information I fucking want. Before she says anything, a pair of double doors bursts open and several people in scrubs and doctor coats rush through with someone on a gurney. Blood spills over the sides of the bed as they rush past me and scream orders at each other.

I get a glimpse of the woman on the gurney and freeze.

Veronica.

That's who I shot.

She jumped in front of Oliver when he challenged me and she took the bullet.

I killed my own mother.

"That's my mother." I point to the doors they take her through. "I want to follow her."

The nurse shakes her head. "Your mother *and* your sister?" After rolling her eyes, she gives in. "You can't just follow them, you have to wait in the waiting room for any answers you're looking for. Go straight through there." She points her sausage fingers toward a narrow doorway next to the double doors they took Veronica through. "And you're going to take your first left into the emergency surgery waiting room, okay?"

Her smile doesn't warm my insides.

"Fine. And what room is Julie in?"

She looks on her computer again and frowns. "311."

I tap my fingers on the desk and nod down at her. "Thanks for your help." After pushing through the door she directed me to, I flag down a doctor in a white coat.

"I'm here for Veronica." I pause, realizing that I don't know her last fucking name. "She's my mother and she just came in here with a gunshot wound."

He places his hand on my shoulder. "We're doing all we can—she's in surgery now. I think the police have some questions, if you don't mind while you wait." He nods and looks down the hallway, where a pair of cops stands outside the surgery room doors. They finish talking to a nurse before she disappears beyond the doors and the taller one makes eye contact with me.

"This is Veronica Bennett's son." He motions down at them and turns back to me. "I'm sorry, I really must get ready for her post-surgery needs. My name is Dr. Samuels and you can find me when you're done with your questions." He leaves me and the two male cops close in on me.

Don't run, they'll chase you and find you out.

I wanted to see Julie one more time before I turned myself in.

"Hey…" I nervously wave my hand in the air. "I'm Oliver Jackson; I'm Veronica's son."

The shorter one takes out a notepad and pen, writing something down. "How did her gunshot wound happen, Oliver?"

I shrug. "I'm not sure. I went to visit her, and her neighbor told me about this so I came down as soon as I found out. I don't know anything, I'm sorry." The clueless look I've painted on my face better be enough to buy me more time to say goodbye to Julie. I have to apologize to her for everything I've done; I have to make her see that this isn't the fucking person I wanted to be. I didn't want to let jealousy overrun my body to the point of no return.

The cop with the notepad looks between me and his notes several times. "So, you just happened to be visiting your mother at this time of night? A little late, isn't it?"

I act annoyed. "I wasn't aware I'm only allowed to

visit my own mother between certain times of the day. I happen to work the late shift and was on my way home from that plant down past the highway."

The taller one looks me up and down. "You don't look like a plant worker."

"I'm management."

"Manager of the entire plant?"

I scoff. "No, manager of production. Anything else? I'd like to head home and shower before my mother gets out of surgery."

They look at each other and shrug. "What's your phone number so we can reach you?"

I motion for the pad and pen, scribbling a fake number on it before handing it back. "Can I go?"

"You can go," the taller one says. "Don't leave town."

I wave at them before going back through the smaller door, past the older woman at the desk—who is now sleeping and snoring—into the main lobby and quickly press the button to the elevator. I try to hide my face without being too obvious, and when the elevator dings and the people exiting are out of the way, I dart inside and press the third floor button frantically. Before the doors close, two people make their way to the elevators and my heart jumps.

Heather and Brandon.

Why are they fucking here?

I push the close door button as fast as I can and take a deep breath when the elevator starts moving. I have to see Julie one more time before I turn myself in…that's my goal.

Ding.

First floor.

Ding.

Second floor.

I gasp for air because I haven't been breathing.

Ding.

Third floor.

The doors take forever to open; I edge my body out slowly so I can look and see who's around. I find her room and take a deep breath, but the door starts to open so I slip onto a bench and cross my leg, hoping to look like I'm waiting for someone inside another room.

"So, she's just having really bad panic attacks?" I hear a man ask.

"Yes, her body has adapted to the terror of something traumatic, maybe even without her realizing it. Some could argue that she has PTSD as well, but I'm not a psychiatrist. It might benefit her to see someone to sort all of that out."

"Can I take her home?"

"You can take her home."

"And Oliver Jackson?"

"He's suffered a light blow to the head from falling. He'll be fine to leave if he's feeling up to it as well."

"What about Veronica Bennett?"

The other man laughs. "How many patients do you *know* in our hospital?"

"Veronica Bennett?"

The man clears his throat. "She's in surgery now. The bullet she took ruptured her lung and she isn't breathing on her own."

Fuck.

I really *did* kill her.

She's not dead yet, but she will be.

"Thanks, doctor. I'm going to find my son downstairs and then I'll be right back up."

I hear the two of them shuffle away and the elevator dings. When I'm brave enough to look up almost five minutes later, the hallway is empty and I'm free to slip into Julie's room to talk to her.

The doorknob squeaks when I open it and gently push it closed behind me. It's dark, but I don't turn on the light to make sure I don't draw attention. This moment is going to be the worst moment of my life. I know she's not going to fucking forgive me; it's going to be a long damn time before I even forgive myself. I wanted her so badly that I was willing to do anything to get her and I don't even know why.

I need help.

When I reach the bed, my fingers find the hospital blankets and I feel around for her, but no one is there. Finally reaching the light, I flip it on and the room is empty. The nurse must've told me the wrong room… but why were those men coming out of her room talking about her?

Confused, I open the door and sneak back into the hallway. I push the elevator button and it opens quicker than before. Someone steps outside and bumps into me, and I realize who it is after taking a step backward.

"Oliver." I find my courage deep down inside of me.

He looks like he's about to pound me into the floor.

I never got to see Julie before everything ended.

TWENTY-FIVE
OLIVER

"I'M GONNA FUCKING KILL YOU!" I scream and pounce on Casey. We fall to the floor and my fists find his face. I keep smashing them into his nose and eyes as hard as I can. He pleads with me underneath my rage and weight, but I don't fucking care. "You tried to fucking take her from me! *You!* I thought you loved her? Why would do fucking do this?" My voice rises so much that several nurses come running down the hallway to check on the commotion. When they realize they can't do anything to help, one of them runs off to call security.

"Call the cops!" I scream at them. "He's wanted for attempted murder!"

They squeal and scatter like frightened mice. Casey starts to find the strength to fight back and he pushes me off of him, scrambling onto his feet.

"You don't deserve her," he growls, wiping the blood from his mouth. "She's too good for you and she'll see that someday."

"So you threaten her and try to take her away?" My chest heaves so badly that it's hard to stand. "What the actual fuck is *wrong* with you? All I've ever done is be your friend!"

He laughs loudly and it echoes in the hall. "*Friend*? You're fucking kidding me, right? You've always been looking out for Oliver Jackson and no one else. The rest of us peasants you could give a fuck less about, yeah? Except *Julie*—she stole your heart and made you a better man, and you didn't deserve someone to fix you like that. You deserved to be broken."

"You slept with Heather and now you tried to take Julie." I shake my head. "Why are you always taking what I have? Jealous, much?"

He moves his hands and I flinch but don't see the gun. "I want what you have because I *deserve* what you have. I'm your brother—your full-blooded brother—and what's yours should be mine too."

No. He's fucking lying.

"My dad was just fucking that—my dad. Not yours. You have a dad and I bet he's going to love hearing about all of this."

He throws his hands into the air. "Why do you even care? You fired him and left him without a job. You don't give a shit about him."

"He *stole money* from me."

"It doesn't matter!" he screams, and the nurses peek their heads from behind the corner to see what's going on. Several pairs of feet run down the hallway and come to a halt when they notice what's happening before them. "You don't appreciate what you have, Oliver—you never have. Your life should've been *my*

253

life. I would appreciate it a hundred times more than you."

"Casey?" Julie's voice wafts through the crowd. "What are you doing here?"

He turns to face her, but I step in between them. "Don't you even *dare* fucking talk to her. Don't say one fucking word. You want my life? You almost took it from me. Don't look at her!" The vibration from my anger pulsates in my chest. "Don't even *look* at her. You're *nothing* to her...you mean nothing to anyone anymore. Veronica is *my* mother, not yours. Colin was *my* father, not yours. You didn't even know them... you're a fucking stranger to my parents."

Julie clutches the back of my shirt. She's hiding from Casey, and that's completely fucking fine because I'm not letting him get anywhere fucking near her, she can count on that. If I have to jump in front of another bullet for her, I won't even think twice.

"Hey, guys, arrest him. He's the one that shot Veronica Bennet," Randy says, pointing to Casey. The two officers look puzzled and then angry when they figure out what's going on.

"I thought you said your name was Oliver Jackson?" One of the cops smirks. "What's your name, kid? Tell the truth this time."

Casey points to me. "He's Oliver Jackson and I'm Casey Anderson. You can take me away now." He hangs his head and puts his wrists out. "I shot her, he's right. I didn't mean to, but it happened." When one of the cops reaches out to handcuff him, as he turns Casey around, he looks at Julie and frowns. "I just wanted to show you what you deserve, Julie. I'm sorry that I hurt you—I *never* meant to hurt you. Please don't hate me."

"I told you not to talk to her!" I reach out, but Randy grabs me and holds my arms at my side. Julie gets pushed closer to Casey, which pisses me off even more. He doesn't reach out for her because he can't, which I'm thankful for because if he even grazes her skin—even a little fucking bit—I'm going to go ballistic to the point where I'm not going to be able to stop.

"I *do* hate you, Casey," Julie says from my side. "I can't even stand to look at you right now."

He shakes his head. "Don't say that."

The cop holding him tugs on his handcuffs and starts to pull him away. "Come on, let's go."

"Hold on, please," Julie calls after them. They stop long enough for her to collect herself and figure out her next move. I've never seen darkness in her eyes like right now. She purses her lips and steps out in front of me, crosses her arms over her chest, and looks directly into his eyes.

The air gets cold and we can all feel it. "You're never to contact me again. For as long as I live, you're never to see me. Don't visit, don't call, and don't write. Oliver is right; you're *nothing* to me. I let you in and told you things that I hadn't told anyone else, and you took advantage of my weakness when Oliver was in the hospital. I don't know what you think I've done to lead you to believe I want anything more from you than friendship, but I'm sorry. I really am. You were a good person, Casey, and you were my friend. Now you're nothing more than a stranger who's hurt me so badly that we can never go back to anything more than predator and prey." She nods at the police officers. "You can take him now, thank you." Even though Casey protests, struggles, and calls out her name…

She walks straight toward me with her head held high and tears in her eyes.

She's letting him go.

Randy lets my arms free and I catch her before she starts to sob into my chest. The cops take Casey away and Randy pats me on the shoulder as he starts to follow them. The nurses have dispersed to tend to the patients we've woken up in the process of this, and as Randy passes Brandon and Heather, he pats Brandon on the shoulder too and secures a ride home for us.

I wrap my arms around her so tightly that it's nothing to pick her up and carry her into the elevator with Brandon and Heather in tow. Brandon helps me get her gently into the backseat of his car and she lays her head in my lap as I climb in next to her. I stroke her hair as Brandon drives us back to our apartment; now that Casey isn't running around anymore, we can go home.

When he pulls up outside, Julie climbs out and gives Heather a hug. I thank Brandon for the ride and promise Heather that we will get together before they move out of state. But I don't even think twice about them after we wave goodbye and go back into the building. The hallway in front of our door is daunting and there's a blood stain on the floor where Veronica lay after she saved me. Julie rushes me inside so we don't have to look at it, and once the door closes behind the two of us, we both take deep breaths and let go of everything that's happened.

"We have a lot of shit to talk about." I lower my head. "Starting with Lucy, right?"

"Right, I'll get the beer." She nods and motions toward the living room. "You have a seat and we can get through all of it tonight."

I do what she asks and she brings four bottles of beer into the living room, handing me one and putting two of them on the coffee table for later. Once the air between us settles, I find a few seconds to really look at her.

She's so small compared to me.

Her radiating goodness hasn't dulled from all the pain we've put her through.

When her lips touch the beer bottle, my insides explode.

I clear my throat and decide that I'll start. "I met Lucy at The Tavern. I thought we'd broken up and you'd said goodbye to me. I thought I lost you, Julie, so I met Harley there and we drank and I obviously got drunk. I called Lucy over here tonight before I came to find you, and she can tell you herself that nothing happened—that's why she was here. I wanted her to tell her side. Anyway, she kissed me, but I didn't touch her and then Mac and Veronica showed up and scared her, so she didn't want to leave until daylight. She slept in the bedroom and I slept on the sofa."

Julie frowns. "But I was trying to get ahold of you about the baby situation and you were here with someone else."

I nod. "I know that. Fuck, I know that. Julie, I never want anyone but you. It was just my tactic to drown you out since I'd thought you'd left."

"I didn't leave," she tells me. "You just didn't understand that I needed space."

"And my life will never be the same because of it. I'll never forgive myself for what I've done to you, and I'll spend my fucking life trying to make it up to you."

She giggles and sips the beer in her hands. "You're a mess."

"A huge mess." I laugh and relax into the sofa. "I'm going to be better, I promise."

She turns to face me, her blue eyes burning into mine. "You have to let all that negativity go, Oliver. There's nothing wrong with you—you're normal just like the rest of us...Well, most of us, anyway. In your own overbearing way, I know you always try to do the right thing."

"So, you're not pissed about Lucy?"

She shakes her head. "You said nothing happened and I believe you. I just wish I would've known before I became friends with her. Did Casey know about that when they were dating?"

I shrug. "It happened before Casey met her. When he asked us to come to the bar to meet his new girlfriend, me and Lucy were shocked. We sort of silently made a vow not to say anything...that's when I knew she was embarrassed and wasn't trying to tell anyone."

"I'm sure he knew afterward though, right?"

"He tried to threaten me into telling you. He thought that maybe it would win you over to his side or something, I don't know."

"I hate him." Her voice is small. "I don't want to see him ever again."

I lean forward and put the beer bottle on the coffee

table so I can pull her into my lap. "I know, baby." I stroke her hair while she snuggles and breathes me in deeply. "I promise you that no one is ever going to fucking hurt you again."

She snorts through her tears. "You can't promise that. You can't predict the future."

"Julie…" I pull her away so I can look directly into her eyes. "How many times do I have to tell you? No one will hurt you as long as I'm alive and with you. No one. I've let too many bad things happen to you and I'm done with that."

"You didn't do anything—"

I wipe the tears from her cheeks. "I'm supposed to protect you. That's my job."

She cuddles back into my chest and I hold her there as long as she wants me to. "What about our other loose ends? The new house and now the wedding?"

"Wedding? You still want to get married on New Year's Day?" My heart skips a beat because I really, *really* want to fucking marry her. The moment I see her walking down that aisle toward me is going to be the best moment of my damn life. I'm not sure how goofy my smile is, but she laughs when she notices the look I'm giving her.

I honestly thought she would leave me after finding out about Lucy, but I hold onto the hope that someday we can look back on it and say it was another stepping stone to finding our happiness. I have to start making better decisions when it comes to her, or she'll never go through with the wedding and our own happily ever after.

She nods. "Do you think that's too soon?"

"Hell no, it's not!" Excitement floods into my voice and I tip her chin up to kiss her. She wraps her lips around mine and together we melt into one. The room disappears, the apartment disappears. Every weird and bad thing that's happened to us in the past six months disappears and all we can see are the endless possibilities with each other and our future.

"I can't wait to marry you," I whisper, watching her blush. "You know I've been waiting for this for a long time."

She laughs and rolls her eyes. "A few weeks isn't a long time."

"No, I've wanted you to be mine since I first met you on the rainy street underneath the streetlight. I've dreamt about you and yearned for you in ways I never understood, and now that you're here and you're real... I feel like my life is finally complete. Like nothing is going to stop me from achieving my dreams or something, I don't know. You make me feel powerful and worthy."

"You *are* worthy."

I shake my head. "Because of you. If I don't have you, nothing else matters."

"I feel the same way." Her fingers twirl around in my thick, dirty hair. "You drive me crazy in more ways than one, and I wouldn't have it any other way. I keep coming back to you and at first, I didn't understand why, but now...I keep coming back to you because you're the one for me."

My smile broadens. "Likewise, baby."

She finishes her first beer and cracks open the second one. "So, we've settled the Lucy issue—"

"Have we? Lucy is still your friend, isn't she? Does this change anything between you?"

When she swallows the mouthful of beer she's just taken in, I notice that she's thinking hard about my question. "That's a really hard question. How can I forgive you but not her? She didn't know me at the time, and I can tell she really regrets it. Plus, I know how much it stings when Oliver Jackson rejects you… it's not a good feeling," she jokes and winks at me. "Besides, we're not all innocent in this family of ours, either. I hate to admit it, but I may have led Casey on at some point."

Heat flushes down my cheeks and onto my neck. "Okay…explain."

She hands me my second beer and finishes hers, and for the first time since we've met, I see a raw and real side to her. Julie's legs aren't as long as mine, but she relaxes onto the sofa and tries to put them onto the coffee table just the same. It's cute how she tries to stretch her body to match mine, but she knows it's a lost cause so she grunts and plants her feet on the floor.

"I don't know, maybe. When you were in the hospital, we had a few moments where we connected, and I guess I let them go a little too far…you know, judging what happened."

I snort and down the second beer before putting it on the table. "You did nothing wrong."

"I'm not a saint, Oliver. I do the wrong things sometimes."

I shake my head and swallow the liquid. "No, baby, trust me, you did nothing wrong. Casey has always been jealous of me and my life, although I'm not sure why. I haven't had it as easy as people like to think I have. I had a rough start in my childhood and—even though yours was much worse—there was nothing to be jealous of. But, at least we knew where we came from and knew our parents no matter what kind of animals they turned out to be."

She understands my point. "I wish Casey hadn't turned out like that. He was a good friend to me."

I pat her leg and she swings them onto mine. "He loves you, I know he does. I think he's just too screwed up to process what that means to him. If he really loved you like I do, he wouldn't ever put you in that kind of danger like bringing a gun and shooting someone. You know that, right? You know that you did nothing wrong?"

She slowly nods. "It's going to take some time to really feel that, but I believe you."

I lower my forehead to hers and smile. "Smart girl."

"So, we've talked about Lucy and Casey and the wedding…" She bites the inside of her cheek and I want her so fucking bad right now my pants are suffocating the part that wants to reach out to her. "Anymore loose ends we need to tie up?"

I yawn so big that she giggles. "Moving into the new house?"

"I thought we could do that after the wedding; maybe we can move in but stay our first real night there the night of our wedding?"

I pull her body onto mine and she snuggles into my chest. This is my favorite thing that she does because I know she does it to feel safe and secure and that's all I ever want to fucking give her. She can have everything of mine: my money, my heart, my soul, and my body. Everything.

"That's a perfect idea. Where do you want to go on our honeymoon? I was thinking somewhere tropical with beaches and sun and private rooms right off the ocean." I stroke her head and can feel her relax into me to start drifting off to sleep. I love how no matter what happens, she always bounces back and rolls with the punches.

Falling in love with a rule-hungry man.

Breaking all the rules just to be with him.

Following his rules to make him happy.

Having her heart broken several times by that man.

I start to drift off not long after she does because I know none of that matters to her.

I matter.

We matter.

Love matters.

There's nowhere else I'd rather be than right her with her, falling asleep on the sofa and listening to the silence of a dark Rockford night.

Dreams *do* come true.

TWENTY-SIX
VERONICA

JESUS, everything hurts.

I can't even breathe without searing pain shooting like rockets through my body. I want to scream my fucking lungs out, but the bright light that's burning my eyes as I open them distracts me for a few seconds until I get used to it.

Someone's snoring and it takes a few seconds to focus on everything around me. Machines surround me as I lie in an oversized bed with things stuck to me and sticking out of me. Across the room, another bed has been set up and Oliver sleeps soundly in it, wrapped in a blanket. His feet are poking out of the end of the blanket because his legs are too long for it, and it makes me smile.

I find the remote on the bed and slowly put myself into a sitting position. It hurts to do anything, but I get through the pain and breathe as shallowly as I can. The door to the room opens and Julie tiptoes inside with a few bags in her hands. She puts them down on the floor beside Oliver's bed and bends over to brush the hair from his face and kiss his forehead.

She turns to check on me and gasps. "You're awake!" she whispers, careful not to wake Oliver in a panic. "How long have you been awake?"

"A few minutes," I croak. "What are you two doing here?"

She sits on the edge of my bed and frowns. "We come and go, we visit whenever we can. How are you feeling?"

I'm so fucking confused as to why my son—who hates me—and his girlfriend—who I kidnapped for ransom—would be sitting in my hospital room fretting over when I'm going to wake up or if I'm going to be okay. None of this makes sense.

"Everything fucking hurts," I tell her, and she laughs.

"Well, you did get shot and had to wait almost a month to wake up, so I'd assume you'd be in a little bit of pain there." She laughs harder and snorts. "I'm sorry, I'm really tired."

"Why aren't you sleeping with him?" I nod over to Oliver.

She shrugs. "I can't sleep here, it's just something about this place that makes it too cold and creepy to sleep. He's been here every night for the past week, though."

"Why?" I sip through the straw of the cup she's holding out and the lukewarm water feels fucking amazing in my throat. "I'm supposed to be out of town by now...why would he come and visit me?"

"You saved his life. We both owe you, and

besides…" She puts the cup back down on the bedside table. "No matter how screwed up everything is, he knows you're still his mother. What you did for him doesn't erase everything, but it helps. Do you want me to wake him?"

I grunt and shift my weight. "No, let him sleep. I'd like to sit here and talk to you for a while, if that's okay."

She pulls up a chair to my bedside and plants herself in it. "Sure. What do you want to talk about? I really should tell a nurse that you're awake."

"Can you tell me what happened? I'm still a little fucking foggy and all I can remember is Casey shot a gun, and I stepped out in front of it so it wouldn't hit Oliver."

She nods. "Yes, and you had surgery because your lung was collapsed and it's taken a little over a month to be able to breathe on your own. Oliver took care of everything—the surgery and this room—and it's a week until Christmas now."

"Holy shit, I've been out for a month and a half?" I panic and it hurts me inside. "And you've been coming here all this time?"

"For the past few weeks, yes, we have. We just wanted to make sure you were okay."

For the first time in a long fucking time, I feel my cheeks flush and it travels all the way down my neck. I never in a million damn years thought this would happen; I especially never thought I would make it out of being shot alive.

"Oliver's seen to it that you had the best doctors and everything you needed."

I don't know what she wants me to say.

"He's been here day and night for the past three days…"

My lungs are already spent and I start to cough; it feels like zillions of needles are inside my body fighting over space and who gets to cut me the worst. "I don't deserve any of that. You two should go home and not worry about me."

Julie looks confused. "We wanted to help you after you sacrificed yourself—"

"—Well it's the least I could've done, ain't it?" I growl, and she looks startled. The sooner these two get far away from me, the better. I should've just hopped on a plane and been out of town before any of this happened.

Oliver stirs in his bed and the snoring stops. Julie glances nervously over at him and then back at me, warning me not to stir up shit and be grateful.

That's the fucking problem.

I *am* grateful.

I'm also embarrassed and pissed off that my son had to save me.

"Julie?" Oliver says, stretching his long body. It takes him a few seconds to wake up and realize she's across the room talking to me. He leaps up and rubs his eyes to make sure he's not dreaming. "You're awake? Did you call a nurse? How do you feel? Can you breathe? Are you in a lot of pain?" He reaches me and frets but doesn't take my hand or hug me.

I'll take what I can get.

Julie looks at me and clears her throat; the horror in her eyes is going to tip him off. "I'll go grab a nurse; I think they already changed shifts this morning."

Oliver nods to her and she leaves the room. "Do you need anything?"

"Yeah, I need you to take Julie and go home. You don't have to be here." I try to look him in the eyes, but I can't. "I don't need you here taking care of me and I sure don't deserve it."

He pulls up a chair to sit next to me and crosses his arms over his chest. "Hold on, let's just pretend you didn't fucking say that to me. I get it, you don't think you deserve my help, but for this...you do. You saved me and I have to repay you."

"Julie is forcing you to help me, you mean."

He laughs and rubs his jawline. For a split second it feels like I'm sitting here with his father because of how similar they are. "Let's just get one thing straight: Julie doesn't *force* me to do anything. She isn't going to let me leave you alone in here, either, so get over it. We're here and we're going to be here until you're better enough to leave."

"I don't want you here."

He growls and takes a deep breath. "Way to be inconsiderate. Julie isn't going to leave until you're better, and even then she's going to want to tend to you, so just suck it up. You obviously wanted to be part of our lives or you wouldn't have jumped in front of that bullet. Which, thanks for that, by the way."

The way he says thank you makes us both uncomfortable. "You're my son, of course I'm not going to let someone fucking shoot you." I scoff. "Not even your ungrateful brother."

He leans back in his chair and relaxes. "Yeah, let's talk about that. Who is Casey's father?"

"You share a father too," I blurt out, because there's no use in pretending anymore. Keeping this secret and following the rules didn't get me very far, so what else is there now than to tell the truth? "When you were two, your father and I were together again and I never told him about Casey. I told him I was visiting my mother when I gave birth to him, and then Mac and I dropped him off on a firehouse doorstep. I was never really sure where he ended up after that."

He clicks his tongue. "So, we share a father now too. Does he know that?"

I'm a little taken aback that he isn't judging me on my decisions back then. Normally when people hear about the choices I make, they pity me and look at me like trash. But Oliver just keeps the conversation moving on like it doesn't faze him at all…just like his father.

"He knows…I'm sure he knows."

Julie comes back into the room with a nurse and looks at both of us to make sure we aren't arguing before she subjects an innocent outsider to it. The nurse hurries toward me and starts checking all of the machines while Oliver pulls Julie aside and starts whispering. The conversation gets intense before the nurse is done and speaks to them in private before leaving the room.

"She said your vitals look good. You've been breathing on your own for a week or so, but they've kept you in a coma so you can get stronger." Oliver shoves his hands into his jeans pockets as they walk back next to me. "She even thinks you'll be released in time for the wedding."

Julie squeals and tucks herself beneath his awaiting arm. I can't help but smile, and for once it doesn't feel wrong to be proud of something my son is doing. I know I have a long fucking road before I deserve any of this, but I'm taking what I can get—when I can get it.

"*Wedding*? You two are getting married?" My eyes dart between them. "When?"

"New Year's Day," Julie says. "In the garden of our new house."

I hum a little and let the information seep in. I'm trying my fucking hardest to be motherly and give him what he obviously desperately wants. "You don't have to wait for me to be outta here to get married—you live your lives how you want."

Oliver swallows loudly. "Listen, why don't we wait until you're better to talk about this, hmm? We have a long time before I can fully trust you, but I'm willing to try if you are."

"I want that." My mouth moves uncontrollably. "I'm ready for that."

"But there are rules."

Julie looks sickened but stands her ground. "We have rules and conditions if you want to be part of our lives. If you accept them, we will be holding you to a high standard. If you mess up once, we're done. We're only going to try once."

I hang my head no matter how much it fucking hurts. "Honey, I tried to kidnap you. How can you forgive me for somethin' like that?"

"I *haven't* forgiven you for that." Her eyes find mine.

"But Oliver and I have agreed that we're cutting off the past and creating a new future. Do you want to be a part of that?"

I nod. "I've wanted that for a long time."

"Then act like it," Oliver chimes back in. "Are you sure you're up to talking about this now?"

"I want to know everything."

He nods and sits down in the chair while Julie rests on the arm next to him. "Okay, so obviously you can't ever fucking talk to or see Mac again in your life." He rubs his jaw and turns to me. I shiver underneath his fierce gaze just like I did when Colin gave me that pene-trating look. "And no drugs. Ever. Period. Not even weed, not even anything. Got it?"

"Got it. Anything else?"

"I'm going to hire you as a waitress at the bar I'm opening, can you handle that? You need a job once you're better and able to move around enough."

I crinkle my nose. "I thought you wanted me to move away and never come back? What happened to that?"

"That was before you saved my life in front of Julie. Make no mistake, if it wasn't for her...we wouldn't be having this conversation. I can't let her down and be the man I was before, so I'm being the man I want to be when I'm with her. And I want to help you."

A tear forms in Julie's eye and she looks away to the wall. It's charming when you see them together, how they interact like a ballet. When he moves, she moves. He looks at her with hungry eyes and doesn't care that the world can plainly see his love for her.

"I'll try my best." I want to promise him but I know

271

I have a lot of changing to do if I wanna make this work. "I can't promise you anything, but I can try."

He nods. "Fair enough. Is there anything you need before we leave? Now that you're awake and every-thing...the room's going to be full with doctors any minute, and we'll just be in the way. Do you want us to bring you anything?"

I don't know how to ask for anything and I'm embarrassed to even try. Julie notes my reservation and tugs on his t-shirt to get his attention focused back on her. "I can put together a bag for her. I'm sure she'd like to attempt to shower sometime soon and wash her hair. That always feels nice and puts me in a good mood." Her smile is bright and cheery. "And maybe some magazines and trashy romance novels to help pass the time until you break free?"

I cringe and think about my sprained ankle from the prison fight. My left foot is wrapped up in bandages like they scoured my body for other ailments while they were fixing the real problem.

Oliver accepts her answer and stands up to gather his things. He puts his leather jacket on and nods to Julie before leaving her alone with me in the room.

"Are you sure you're okay with following those rules? He's big on those." She laughs nervously like the rules make her uneasy. "He means well, though. Is there anything you want that you were afraid to ask for when Oliver was here?" She stands and finds a pillow to add behind my head.

"I like you." My head rests on the extra padding and I'm instantly drained. "I can't wait to see Oliver make a good choice and marry you."

She giggles. "I think he gets his charm from you a little bit. I haven't forgotten about what you've done to me—or to Oliver—but I can try to get past it if you'll let me."

"Thank you, Julie." I reach out for her, but she doesn't take my hand.

"I'd better go—Oliver is waiting." She quickly smiles and walks for the door. She turns around as she opens it and her braided hair falls to the side of her body. "I hope this is a good start to a fresh beginning for everyone. I'd hate to waste the last bit of hope for you I have and find out I was destined to be wrong all along."

Before I can answer her, she's gone.

I won't let you down.

Not this time.

TWENTY-SEVEN
JULIE

I'VE CHANGED SO MUCH in the past eight months that I hardly recognize myself in the mirror anymore. It's not a bad thing. It's just a weird thing. When life becomes too much work, we sort of lose ourselves in the chaos and most of us never make it back to a good place.

I found my place.

"I'm afraid I'm not much help," Veronica says from inside the walk-in closet in the new house. "Everything that tart Staci brought over is either too short or too low-cut."

I smile in the mirror. Veronica's come around since her recovery and she's taking life one day at a time—which is more than most of us can say. Oliver paid for another year lease on his apartment and once we moved out, he let her move in so she could live a year rent-free and save some money of her own. He's never asked her about the money he'd given her to disappear, and I'm willing to bet anything that he never will.

The deep red lipstick that covers my mouth makes my lips look sexier and wider. I like the way Veronica has done my hair too; she's curled the ends and pinned up the top half so the curls would fall around my head.

"It's just a rehearsal dinner, right?" she calls from the closet.

"A rehearsal dinner and New Year's Eve party." I snort. "He's gone all out and has spent the last week preparing for this party in the backyard."

She pops her head out and I turn to look at her. Since her recovery, her hair is growing back thicker and her skin isn't looking as gray and clammy. I notice her in Oliver more and more each day, and even though he's kept her at arm's length and left it to me to handle her, it's been worth it getting to know the story of why she is…the way she is.

"He loves you," she coos and goes back into the closet. "And I know you love him. Watching you two together these past few weeks, it's been like watching a movie."

I laugh and walk toward the closet. "Yeah, a horror film maybe."

She shakes her head and smiles. "You know what I mean, don't play dumb. Look at this one." She holds up a cream and royal blue dress with nude lace that would hit me at the knees. The bottom of the dress fans out and it looks like a dress for a princess. "I think this one will complement your eyes nicely."

I sift through the rack she's been looking at. "That's the only one that's decent, you mean."

"Put it on and let's see." She steps out of the room so I can slip into the dress. Once it's on, it fits me like it's specially made for my body. I smooth out the stomach part and twirl around in the mirror for a minute before stepping back out to show her. She whistles and claps her hands as I turn once again to show her the whole dress. Someone clears their throat from the doorway and I stop twirling. I feel his eyes on me before I can blink.

"Oh, don't stop on my account." Oliver's smooth voice excites me. "Is that the dress you're wearing to the rehearsal dinner?" He narrows his eyes at Veronica, who excuses herself from the room and shuts the door behind her. I take a step backward and put my hands on my hips.

He's already in his dress slacks and white dress shirt; he looks like an expensively dressed Ken doll with every wave of his muscles tightened as his shirt covers them. His black tie is hanging halfway tied around his neck so I reach up to tighten it, but he stops me mid-air.

"That dress makes me wanna do bad fucking things to you, baby. Are you sure you want to wear that?" His arms catch me and he grazes his warm lips over my ear as he pulls me close.

"When are you going to learn that I do what I want?" I tease and his rough hands slide up the sides of the skirt. His palms find the bottom of my ass where the lace panties stop and he grips the flesh.

"Trust me, I know that already." He laughs into my hair. "That's what I love most about you." Once he has a good enough grip on me, he picks me up and wraps my legs around his torso. One arm releases its grip around me and he unzips his pants swiftly before pushing my lace panties aside in a matter of seconds. I lick my lips when the tip of his hard-on reaches the sensitive part between my open legs. He laughs into my neck as he teases me and moves a few feet over to a nearby chair.

His eyes lock onto mine. "You're gonna be my wife tomorrow."

"I know, it's still crazy to think about." He trails kisses down my neck. "I can't believe this is our life."

He chuckles. "I can't believe this is *my* life." My arms wrap around his neck as he prepares to sit down into the chair behind him. "You are the most perfectly imperfect person I've ever fucking met, and there's no room in my life for anyone else but you. Have you written your vows yet?"

I blush. "I've started them."

"I've had mine done before I even asked you." He blushes too. "That's how fucking badly I wanted you to say yes and be mine."

I hungrily kiss his lips and press myself against him. "I've always *been* yours."

Oliver slowly sits down in the chair and eases into me with passion; my dress flows around us as I tighten my legs around his body. I moan into the air and tip my head back while his fingers find the straps of the dress and push them down. He massages my breasts and kisses them lightly while moving up and down with the strides of my body pushing against him. I lean in and he buries his face in between them; he moans into my flesh and it vibrates every last nerve in my body that hasn't already joined in the frenzy.

My hands hook behind his neck and he finds my

lips with his. "You were made for me," he whispers and brushes hair from my face. "I'm going to give you everything you've ever wanted."

"And more." I catch my breath and his hips quicken. "So much fucking more."

We didn't realize how long we'd been in the room until we hear someone slightly knocking and jiggling the door handle. "Uh, hello? We have a rehearsal dinner to get to?" Staci's voice is muffled from the other side. I silently thank Veronica for locking the door on her way out, and as romantic as we both wanted it to be...we have to hurry and finish before Staci knocks the door down.

Oliver holds his hand over my mouth when I finish because he knows I'm uncontrollably loud sometimes. This time is no different; he kisses my forehead when everything comes back into focus and laughs. "I love you." His chest heaves up and down. "I literally love my fucking life."

I smile and peck his lips. "I'm glad to hear that."

His left eyebrow rises in humor. "So elusive, Miss Remington. Better watch out, because less than twenty-four hours from now you're going to be Mrs. Julie Jackson." The smile widens on his lips and it's hard to lift my body off of his because I don't want to go to the dinner. I just want to stay here with him and wait for tomorrow.

He stands up and shakes his dick back into his pants, zipping them back up. I adjust my panties back to their original state and he helps me re-strap my dress and fix my hair so it doesn't look like we were having sex. He snorts and kisses me on the nose when he sees my frown. "Oh, baby. It's not that bad and these are people who love us. We deserve this. *You* deserve this." He kisses my fingers and walks me over to the door. After he unlocks it, Staci bursts in with a scowl on her face.

"I did not plan this entire thing—and your entire wedding—to be booted out the night before it all goes down. What is happening in here?"

Oliver laughs and puts his arms over both our shoulders. "Oh, Staci. Let's just get downstairs, okay? You have plenty of time to yell at us after the wedding."

Staci looks surprised and honestly, so am I. She doesn't say anything to ruin the moment and we let him lead us downstairs.

"Here we go." He squeezes my side and lets Staci walk to Randy. Everyone I love and care about is scattered around the backyard with smiles on their faces. Mrs. Atchley holds her champagne glass in the air and everyone follows suit.

"To Oliver and Julie," she calls out. "May your forever start now and never end."

Everyone toasts and starts chatting amongst themselves as Oliver and I split apart and each take half of the backyard to mingle. Harley and his brother Victor sit at a table with two very dolled up younger girls who look like they're at a celebrity event. Their wide eyes sparkle when I approach them and the more I speak to them, the more uneasy it makes me to feel like someone they look up to.

I'm average.

Ordinary.

"Hey, I'm glad you guys made it back for this!" I

hear Oliver say behind me, and when I look to see who he's talking about, Heather runs to me and scoops me into a hug. Oliver and Brandon shake hands and talk about California while Heather breaks free from me and hands me a small package wrapped in lilac-colored paper.

"For you." She catches her breath. "We just now made it back, sorry we're late."

I wave her off. "No worries, what's this for?"

"Open it!" she squeals and her body shakes. "It's a surprise!"

I open the small package and there's a box inside. I take the lid off and Brandon and Oliver join us to catch my reaction to whatever's inside.

There's a charm inside shaped like a baby's foot.

"You're pregnant?" Oliver gasps and looks at Heather. "I thought you couldn't have kids?"

I hold the box for everyone to see and the crowd gets excited. "I thought so too, but here we are." She laughs and Brandon moves to be next to her. "I wanted you to be the first to know, Julie."

"Why?" My mouth moves before my brain. "I mean, it's an honor, but why me?"

"You brought us together. You may not know it, but all of this—" Brandon waves his hand around the backyard. "—This is because of you and your inability to give up on people. You didn't give up on me and I tried to get you back because of it. I wouldn't have met Heather if it wasn't for you, and I wouldn't have every-thing I've ever wanted if it wasn't for you. You're magic, Jules." He smiles and Oliver slides his arm around my waist.

He looks down at me with a tear in his eye. "It's true what he's saying, you know."

I bite the inside of my cheek. "Well, congratulations, I'm really happy for you." I reach out and hug Heather, but I don't feel like I did anything to help them with this.

I'm not a unicorn.

I'm not magic.

"Baby, *smile*. I know you don't believe us when we tell you stuff like that, but why would everyone around you lie about the same thing?" Oliver whispers in my ear.

I don't answer him and continue making my way around the backyard, talking to people and nibbling on snacks before it's nightfall and people start saying their goodbyes and telling us they will see us tomorrow. Oliver decided not to stay somewhere else for the night, but he promised that he'd stay downstairs and stay true to the tradition of not seeing each other until we walk down the aisle.

I didn't get a chance to talk to Randy about any of this, but he and Clyde have already made it known where they stand. They have fallen for Oliver just like I have, and they've accepted him as part of the family. Veronica and Mrs. Atchley talk for most of the night and Lucy even pops her head in for a few minutes after her shift at work.

Everyone that matters.

Everyone that deserves to be here, is here.

Oliver winks at me from across the lawn, and I know he's not going to get through the night without trying to sneak into the bedroom. The way he walks toward me sends chills down my spine and I cross my legs without knowing it.

"Are you glad we broke the rules?" he asks.

The wicked smile that spreads across my face makes him lick his lips and nervously look around.

"Fuck the rules."

His eyes darken and he steps closer to me, making me nervous because I know he doesn't care who's around and he'll take what he wants.

Fuck the rules.

TWENTY-EIGHT
OLIVER

I DIDN'T FUCKING sleep at all last night. Not only did my wonderful future wife lock me out of my own bedroom, the fucking sofa that she insisted on putting in the living room is uncomfortable as hell. I smile anyway regardless of what lack of sleep I got because in just a few short hours, she's going to be my wife.

I zip into the kitchen and start the coffee; I check the fridge for anything edible and find some eggs and milk so I take them out and shut the door. Julie is flittering around upstairs and she opens a door to call out, "There's pancake mix in the second cabinet!" She shuts the door again and I have no trouble finding what I need.

When I've made a large stack of pancakes and fluffy scrambled eggs, I make a quick plate for her and dash outside in the backyard to steal a flower from one of the vendors already setting up. Actually, they've all been coming and going since dawn, but I'm sure Julie was up way before that. The guy bringing in the white roses looks at me like I'm crazy, but I don't fucking care. After darting back inside and putting the flower on the tray, I pour a cup of coffee in her favorite mug that says, "Best Aunt Ever" and add a few spoonfuls of sugar. Stepping back to examine my masterpiece, I frown.

It needs something else.

I click my fingers together and rummage around for a piece of paper and a pen. When I find what I need, I can't think of anything to say that I haven't already said in my vows. I don't want to spoil the surprise for later, but I have to think of something quick.

SUNSHINE,
FUCK THE RULES.
I LOVE YOU.
LOVE,
OLIVER

I smile down at the vulgar words that no one's going to get but the two of us. I like that about our relationship—we have little inside conversations that no one else knows. I don't like to share her, but I know it's necessary because of the kind of person she is.

Sticking the note on the tray, I hurry up the stairs and place it on the floor in front of the closed—and probably still locked—bedroom door. I knock a few times and she walks up to the door but doesn't open it.

"You know I'm not opening this door," she says. "What do you need?"

I laugh and take a few steps backward. "I made breakfast; it's outside the door and I'm walking away." I do what I say and go back downstairs to answer the ringing doorbell. When I reach it, Staci is chomping at the bit to be let in like a stray dog.

"Where is she?"

I point to the ceiling. "Upstairs."

She doesn't say anything else to me as she brushes past me with a dress bag and it dawns on me that if I intercept her, then I can see Julie's wedding dress early. Staci hightails it up the stairs like she knows my plan and it disappears quicker than I thought of it.

"Hey, man," Harley says as he opens the front door and lets himself in. "It's a zoo out there. Your mom is out there dictating everything and growing horns." He laughs and pats me on the shoulder. "So, is it time to drink yet?"

I snort. "It's barely eight a.m. I'm not trying to be sloshed at my own wedding."

"Just afterward, right?" He chuckles. "Come on outside, I have a surprise for you. Call it my wedding gift to you guys if you want." He pulls me outside and he forgets that it's fucking January and cold as hell out there for a guy in pajamas. His arms wave around like a magic wand and I follow his gaze to a Jeep with a big red bow over it.

Wait.

That's *my* Jeep.

"Is that—"

He jumps up and down like an excited schoolboy. "That's almost seventy percent your original Jeep, man! I salvaged and repaired enough to make it count…do you like it?"

I run down the driveway and slide my hand over

the new hunter green paint. "It looks just like the original one! How is this even possible?"

Harley shrugs his shoulders. "You're one of my best friends; I had to try. I'm glad you like it and it doesn't bring back fucked-up memories for you."

I shake my head. "No fucking way. Thanks man, I love this. Can you call Julie and tell her to look out the window?"

He does what I ask and I try my hardest not to turn around. I hear her squealing on the phone and after a few minutes of his eardrums being blown out, Harley says goodbye quickly and hangs up. He's probably waiting for me to be pissed at him for hanging up on her, but I understand completely and feel bad that I made him do that.

"She likes it." He chuckles and shoves his phone into his pocket. "She already knew I was doing this, honestly, and it's even registered in her name."

I start to turn around and look up at her, but I dig my heels into the ground. "This is the best present I've ever gotten. Thanks, Harley." I slap him on the back and grin. "You're a real friend and a really good guy."

He blushes and rubs the back of his neck. "Ah, I was just being nice. Look, I owed you one anyway for not warning you about Casey. There was something about him that put me off and I should've acted on that. I just wanted to make it up to you."

"None of this was your fault." I laugh and shift my weight from my injured knee. It's not fully healed yet and all the stress I've been putting it through isn't making that problem any better. "All of this is on Casey.

286

He's fucked up in the head and he's getting the help he needs."

Harley nods. "Yeah, I heard you suggested he get admitted to a psych place instead of prison. That was awfully big of you considering everything he's done."

I take a deep breath and remind myself that I have to start trusting people again. "That was all Julie, honestly. I wanted him to go to Brownsville and be someone's little bitch." Harley laughs and shoves his hands into his pockets; the mood has lightened now that I'm openly speaking the truth about how I feel. "She attended his hearing and suggested that, but I fucking said nothing. I can't see his face ever again or I won't be able to stop myself, ya know?"

"Yeah, I feel ya, man. You've been pretty calm through it all, I'm impressed."

I clap my hands together. "Okay, enough of this. Let's get the fuck back inside and get that drink."

He laughs but follows me back into the house. "I thought you weren't getting pissed before your own wedding?"

I open two beers from the fridge and hand one to him. "A few beers aren't going to get me pissed drunk, I can handle my shit."

As we clink the bottles together, someone scoffs behind us. Staci shakes her head and frowns. "Hours before your wedding and you're drinking." Making sure we're alone, she steps farther into the kitchen and holds out her hand toward me. "The least you can do is share."

Harley and I look at each other and laugh. I hand her my beer and take another from the fridge. Staci compliments Harley on the Jeep and they engage in a conversation, but all I can think about is slipping away and seeing Julie. Staci watches me like a hawk so I know that's impossible and I'm going to have to wait until later.

"Julie told me to tell you she loved your note." Staci rolls her eyes. "Something about fucking and rules or something, I don't know."

I smile. "Don't worry about it, I know what she means."

"Gross." Staci sticks out her tongue. "Okay, I'm headed back up. Can you send your mom up when she gets in here?"

Downing the rest of the beer, I nod and say nothing. I don't want to talk about Veronica and I really don't even want her here. What kind of person would I be if I just forgave her for everything she's done to me and Julie?

Harley sees a few women outside he wants to chat with, so he excuses himself and I'm left alone in the kitchen. I don't have to do anything for a few hours, so I decide to test my strength and work out in the makeshift gym I created in the basement. Julie wanted a treadmill so I put that in the corner and the rest of my equipment on the other side of the room. I carried a mini fridge down here too and stocked it with small water bottles next to a pile of white towels.

Two hours into my workout, I have to stop. Not only am I spent, I need to shower before the salt from the sweat burns my eyeballs. I grab a bottle of water and a towel to wipe my eyes before heading back upstairs. Veronica is in the kitchen as I go in to throw the bottle in the recycle bin; she's still learning how to work her new phone and sits at the kitchen table with her eyebrows furrowed.

"What's the matter?" I breathe heavily when I walk into the room. "Can't find the kind of porn you want to watch?"

She shakes her head. "Oh, I was checking an email. My mother died, it seems."

I look at her with pity and she knows it. "And you found that out through an email?"

"Looks like it."

"When is the funeral?"

She checks the email again and puts the phone down. "Next Saturday in Alabama."

"Alabama?" I snort. "You're from Alabama?"

"No, I'm from Lake Reed; that's where I was born. I guess she ended up in Alabama."

I throw a piece of a pancake into my mouth. "Do you want to go to the funeral?"

She thinks for a few minutes and then puts her phone down on the table. "No, I don't. She left me to raise myself, and if it weren't for Madrie and Paul, I never would've made it. I have no desire to waste my time traveling down there for a woman who never wanted me."

Funny, I could say almost the same thing...

"Madrie and Paul from Lake Reed? They raised you?"

She nods. "They raised me. They wouldn't recognize me now and they didn't the last time I was up there. I'd like to spend some time with them if I could, but I have no desire to go to my mother's funeral."

"Well, if you want to go, I can arrange that. If you change your mind, that is."

Veronica smiles and stands up from the table. "We have much bigger and better things to worry about today. Like how my oldest son is getting married and how grateful I am to be here to see it."

I snort. "Consider yourself lucky."

"I do." She pats my shoulder and leaves me alone in the kitchen. Veronica has completely changed these past few weeks, and it's hard to believe it's all real. She's trying so hard to be the mother she thinks I want her to be, but honestly, I just want her to be a decent human being. She's kept away from Mac and the drugs and I don't know how well she's doing, but she's even attending NA meetings and talks nonstop about her pending job at the bar when it opens.

For the first time, Veronica Bennett has hope.

And I gave some of that to her.

After fucking around for an hour in the kitchen on my laptop, I put the finishing touches on the surprise I have for Julie and some other things. Paul and Madrie are fixing up the lake house for a romantic honeymoon week because I thought taking her there would be a spectacular end to a fucking amazing beginning. I can take her anywhere, but that's the only place that holds true meaning for us. People run in and out of the kitchen, but it's not until Harley finds me with his face red and out of breath that anyone bothers talking to me.

"Those caterers are horny as fuck." He laughs and smooths out his hair. "Whatcha doing in here all alone? Having second thoughts?"

I know he's joking, but I don't find it funny at all.

"Of course not. I was about to head up and shower to start getting ready. Don't you and Victor have tuxes to get into? Where the fuck is he?"

Harley chuckles. "Balls deep in his new girlfriend, I guess. I saw them pull up an hour ago, but I think he's been fucking her in the backseat of her car."

I close my eyes and shake my head.

I can't fucking wait to get out of these high school games.

Harley looks awkward. "I'll go get him."

Not bothering to follow him, I head upstairs to take a shower in the second bathroom because I know Julie won't let me into the master bathroom even if I begged. They've probably got hair products and makeup strung around the room anyway.

This is fucking killing me.

I want to see her.

My body strays from the closed master bedroom door, and I force myself to turn on the shower of the other bathroom and lock the door behind me. There's too many fucking people in this house to keep that door unlocked. I think about texting Julie and casually letting her know I'm in the shower, but if she's already got her hair and makeup done…there's no fucking chance she cares.

Once I'm showered and clean enough to meet Julie's standards, I groom every inch of my body because I plan on being naked ninety percent of the time that we're at the cabin. There's so much of Julie I haven't explored and this week is *all* about exploration.

And love.

And trust.

And no fucking rules.

The next few hours fly by so fast that once Harley and Victor come into the guest bedroom we're sharing to get ready, we fuck around and laugh as we dress each other. Once Harley ties my tie, he hands me a small black box.

"Your mom said these were your dad's; she said don't ask her how she got them. But she wanted you to have them for your wedding."

I open the box and find a set of gold cufflinks with a J engraved on each of them. Harley helps me put them on my cuffs and pats me on the back. "Well, it's damn near time...are you ready?"

The smile that appears on my lips hurts because it's so big. "I've been ready since the day I met her."

"Good answer." He laughs and the three of us look once more in the mirror before heading downstairs. People have started to arrive and the backyard is full of family and friends and whoever Staci has taken it upon herself to invite. When we walk up the aisle and I shake the hands of the people who have them out for me, I notice that it seems like half of Rockford is here. Even Brandon and Heather wave at me, excited and ready.

Except Casey.

He's exactly where he belongs.

And I'm exactly where *I* belong.

The air is perfect and Staci and Veronica did a fantastic job planning everything and getting it all sorted out. Randy and Clyde sit in the front row, and Randy waits to be called on to give Julie away to me. Mrs. Atchley sits across from them with an empty seat for Veronica next to her, and each person I glance over has the same look of amazement on their face. Randy takes his leave and my heart skips a few beats because it's finally time.

The pianist starts playing and everyone looks down the aisle where the doors to the house open. When I see her, I nearly fucking faint.

She's the most beautiful creature I've ever seen.

Her eyes cut into mine as Randy leads her down the aisle and her long, white, and silky wedding gown trails behind her as she floats toward me. The smile that spreads across her lips shakes me to my core and I just want to reach out and make sure she's real.

Veronica takes her seat next to Mrs. Atchley and hands the old woman a tissue. I hardly notice them out of the corner of my eye because every ounce of focus I have is on the woman floating down the aisle to become one with me.

Randy guides her to the end of the aisle and he sheepishly looks at me. Once he places her hand in mine, he steps to the side and up to where the officiant should be. "Surprise. I'm the one marrying you two today." He winks at his sister and smiles. "I got ordained last week."

Julie laughs and shakes her head. "Let's do this."

I clutch onto her hands and focus on her lips.

Fuck the hundreds of people staring at us.

Fuck listening to Randy drone on.

Fuck the rules.

I turn to him and frown. "Can we just skip to the 'I do' part?"

He laughs and pats me on the shoulder. "Don't you want to say your vows?"

Shit, I forgot about the damn vows.

The piece of paper is shoved into my pocket, so I take it out and start reading from it. "Julie, from the moment I met you, I was mesmerized by everything good that you radiated into the world. No one could compare to you, and no one has ever loved me like you do. You completely get me in every single way, and I can't ask for anyone better to share the rest of my life with. I would give you the last breath in my lungs and the last penny in my pocket if it meant that you were happy and content. I promise to do everything in my power to help make the rest of your life amazing because every minute I know you're standing next to me…that's what my life is: amazing."

A tear rolls down her cheek and I wipe it away. "There isn't a day that goes by that I don't dream about you even though you're right next to me. I dream of what our future can be and what it's going to be. I dream about the life we're going to have and how we'll add to it as time goes on. I'm the luckiest person in existence because you chose me, because you said yes to me. I owe you so much, Julie, and I'm going to spend every day of the rest of my life repaying you for it. I love you."

She wants to kiss me—I can see it when she licks her lips.

"And Jules?" Randy looks over at her, and a wicked smile paints her face.

Her eyes burn into mine.

"Fuck the rules," she whispers so only Randy and I can hear her.

That's all it takes for me to scoop her up and devour her lips with mine.

Randy throws his hands into the air and laughs. "By the power vested in me by this great state of New York, I now pronounce you man and wife! You can kiss—*ah, hell*! Mr. and Mrs. Oliver Jackson everyone!" He laughs louder and the crowd stands up to cheer us on as we devour each other in front of them.

Once we make it back down the aisle fifteen minutes later, she turns to me and smiles.

"Are you ready for what's to come, Mr. Jackson?"

I twirl her around and dip her low, grazing my lips against her neck.

I'm ready.

BEFORE YOU GO...

If you enjoyed my book please take a second to leave a short review. These reviews help me as an author be found by other amazing readers like you.

THANK YOU SO MUCH! :)

ABOUT THE AUTHOR

I live in Kansas City with my husband and our son, Ryker. I have been writing for over a decade, I started out writing songs and music and then realized that those stories were too short for the tales I wanted to tell, so I switched to writing books and articles, which then blossomed into writing contemporary romance and fantasy novels. I am in indecisive person at heart, I love coffee more than a Gilmore girl and my most favorite time to write and create is during a rainstorm (with coffee!).

I love hearing from those who read my stories, I love to hear how much people relate to each character and how they are rooting for their favorites to succeed! I don't only create stories, I create entirely new worlds and people that come to life!

Wattpad
https://www.wattpad.com/user/NBenson

www.ingramcontent.com/pod-product-compliance
Lightning Source LLC
Chambersburg PA
CBHW052024240626
47153CB00006B/1945